BRIA AND THE TIGER

THE SHIFTERS SERIES
BOOK FIVE

ELIZABETH KELLY

EK PUBLISHING INC.

Edited by
L. Nunn Editing

Cover art by
The Final Wrap

BRIA AND THE TIGER

THE SHIFTERS SERIES BOOK FIVE

When the heat rises, someone is bound to get burned.

For tiger shifter, Bria Norsen, her life isn't turning out the way she thought it would. Unemployed and single for the first time in years, she's on a mission to change her life for the better.

Too bad her pesky heat cycle is making her crazy. Going home with a total stranger and screwing him six ways to Sunday isn't her normal behaviour. Neither is sneaking out of the sexy tiger shifter's bed the next morning.

Jace Shepherd might be an expert at helping cat shifters through their heats, but he didn't expect to be helping a complete stranger that night in the club. The tiny tiger shifter's response to his touch sets off every mating instinct in his body, and he's more than happy to satisfy her every need. It's a damn shame when he wakes up to nothing but her lingering scent on his sheets.

Bria is mortified when her potential new boss turns out to be the very shifter who made her purr with pleasure. To her shock, Jace hires her on the spot. Seeing him every day sends her lust skyrocketing, but Jace makes it clear he's not looking for a relationship. He'll help her through her monthly heat cycle but nothing more.

As Bria and Jace grow closer, Jace begins to understand that love doesn't always have a price. But will a terrible tragedy from his past tear them apart and doom him to the same fate?

CHAPTER 1

"You look like shit, Bria."

"Are you always this sweet to your customers, Porter?" Bria asked as she slid onto the bar stool.

Porter winked at her. "Only the lucky ones. What can I get you to drink?"

"Whiskey."

Bria ignored the wolf shifter's look of surprise. When he brought her the glass of amber liquid, she drank it all in one gulp.

"Hoo…that burns," she muttered. "Give me another one."

Porter studied her for a moment before pouring her another. "Drink this one slower."

"Yes, Sir." Her voice was heavy on the sarcasm, but she sipped at the drink. Porter leaned on the bar and crossed his arms.

"So, you going to tell me what's wrong or just drink all the whiskey in the bar?"

"Is the bar officially yours yet?" Bria asked.

Porter nodded. "Yeah, as of two days ago. Bud's wife was good about getting all the paperwork sorted out after his death. But, because it was a homicide and they never found the bank draft I gave Bud, it was complicated."

A brief flicker of pain crossed Porter's face, and Bria gave him a sympathetic look. She knew Porter felt guilty over the death of the former owner of the bar. "It wasn't your fault."

"Yeah, I know," Porter said. "It's just…difficult."

"You didn't know that Vaughn would kill Bud just to frame you for the murder. Vaughn was a cop, for God's sake. He was supposed to uphold the law, not break it."

"I should have," Porter said. "I knew Vaughn would do anything to get Maggie, but I didn't think… Bud died because I didn't understand just how dangerous Vaughn was."

"From what Kat told me, no one did. Besides, all that matters is that Maggie is safe, right?"

"Yes," Porter said immediately. "My mate is safe."

"When is the wedding?" Bria asked. In shifter terms, Porter and Maggie were already married. Wolf shifters bit their mates to claim them. Kat had told her that after Vaughn kidnapped Maggie and Porter saved her, he had claimed Maggie later that same night. But Maggie was human, and Bria assumed she would want the traditional human wedding ceremony.

Porter shrugged. "Not sure yet. Maggie wants to go back to school to get her accounting degree. She can finish this semester by taking a few extra math courses online. It would be tough for her to do her classes and plan a wedding."

"Does that bother you?" Bria sipped at her whiskey.

"Nah, it bothers my mom and grandpa, but I'm fine. Maggie is my mate. I love her, and I don't need a ring or a piece of paper to know she loves me too."

Porter's face was nearly glowing with happiness, and Bria felt a pang of jealousy. Had Kyle or Raden ever looked at her that way? She couldn't remember about Kyle, but she knew for certain that Raden hadn't. More jealousy mixed with guilt and regret coursed through her, and she finished the rest of her whiskey.

"Another, please, Porter."

"You sure?" Porter asked.

"Yes."

He poured her a third one. "Is your guy joining you?"

Bria shook her head and took a sip of whiskey, wincing as it burned its way down her throat.

"What's his name again?"

"Raden."

"Right. So, he's not joining you?"

"We broke up."

"Sorry," he said. "When?"

"Forty-two days ago."

"You break up with him?" Porter asked bluntly.

"Nope," Bria said.

"Well, he's an idiot. Also, his man bun looked ridiculous."

She laughed despite her embarrassment, and Porter grinned at her before punching her lightly on the arm. "Most of us were surprised you were with a lion shifter anyway. They're all a bunch of kinky sex addicts who hate to commit to one woman."

"Raden wasn't. He couldn't even fully satisfy me during my heat cycle."

She clapped her hand over her mouth and gave Porter a horrified look. "Oh my God, I can't believe I just told you that."

He laughed. "People can't resist revealing secrets to the bartender."

"Or it's the whiskey."

"That too," he said cheerfully. "I've been with a few female

3

cat shifters in my time, but never during their heat cycle. Is it really that difficult to keep her satisfied?"

Bria just shrugged. She didn't want to talk to Porter about her heat cycle, especially after how bad her last one was. It was her first heat cycle without a boyfriend and a terrible experience. Raden may not have been able to completely satisfy her urge to mate during the two days that her heat cycle lasted, but having nothing but her own hand and a vibrator to get through the whole thing was pure torture. Near the end, she had almost gone to a bar to find a shifter – any shifter – to help ease her need.

She shivered all over as she remembered the pain, the aching, and the deep, overwhelming desire that nearly drove her mad. She swallowed another mouthful of whiskey, this time thankful for the burn in her esophagus. It helped distract her from the knowledge that her next heat was less than a week away.

She took a deep breath. She would be fine. Now that she knew what to expect, she was better prepared. She'd already purchased a couple of different vibrators and a few other toys. That would be enough.

No, it's not, her tiger snarled like a sulky child. *We need real dick, not plastic.*

She ignored her tiger's whining. What she needed to be concentrating on was finding a damn job. Her savings were almost completely depleted, and unless she wanted to move back in with her parents, she needed to find employment.

"Are you Porter?"

The low and incredibly deep voice to her left made her turn. A hand roughly the size of a baseball mitt rested on the bar. She stared at it for a moment before looking up.

And up.

And then up some more.

The shifter standing next to her was massive. He was well over seven feet tall with a thick chest, broad shoulders, and arms the size of her thighs. His short blond hair was so light it almost looked white, and he had dark brown eyes that gave her a quick once-over before returning to Porter.

She inhaled as Porter smiled at the shifter. "I am. You must be Hudson."

"Yes," the shifter replied. "Nice to meet you."

"Good to meet you too," Porter said. He held his hand out, and Bria watched it be swallowed in the enormous hand of the colossal-sized shifter.

"Why don't you have a seat in the booth over there? I'll grab us both a drink of water," Porter said.

Hudson studied the booth. "Can't fit in it."

Porter hesitated. "Oh, right. Sorry. How about that table over there instead?"

The shifter nodded and gave Bria another cool glance before walking toward the table. He sat down, and Bria wondered if the chair wouldn't simply collapse beneath his mass. Surprisingly, it held his weight. The bouncer, a black bear named Judd, joined him. They shook hands, and Judd clapped him on the back. Judd was a large shifter in his own right, and a normal shifter would have pitched forward with the force of his hand. Nothing on Hudson moved, and she couldn't get over how small Judd looked next to him.

"Jesus, he's bigger than Judd said," Porter said. "I mean, I knew polar bear shifters were big, but I've never seen one in person, have you?"

"No," Bria said. "They're notoriously shy. They never interact with humans and usually avoid shifters, too."

"Fuck, I think he's even larger than Bishop," Porter said.

Bishop was a grizzly bear shifter and, until Hudson, the biggest shifter Bria had ever seen.

"Why is he here?" Bria asked.

"Job interview."

"For a bouncer?" Bria said. "Is Judd leaving?"

"No, I'm interviewing him for a bartender position," Porter said. "Although Judd said he can double as a bouncer if needed."

"Yeah, no doubt about that. You fired Arlo, huh?"

Arlo was a weasel shifter who had worked as a bartender at Bud's bar. To get drug charges dropped against his younger brother, he had fed Vaughn information about Porter that had led to Porter being framed for Bud's murder."

"Actually, no. He quit as soon as Vaughn was dead and Maggie was safe. I talked to Maggie and she wanted me to give him a second chance. She said if my brother were in trouble, I would have done what Arlo did, and he didn't know how dangerous Vaughn was either. Anyway, I agreed, but Arlo quit. I heard he moved out of the city three days later."

"Sorry, Porter," Bria said.

"Yeah, me too. Warren agreed - "

"Warren?"

"He's a part-time bartender. He's been working for Bud for years and is about ninety-five years old. He agreed to cover Arlo's shifts while I looked for a new bartender, but it's been six weeks, and he's threatening to quit."

"Not many applicants?" Bria asked.

Porter shrugged. "I'm just picky. Judd suggested I meet with Hudson, they've been friends for a few years now, and I agreed. I'd better get over there."

"Before you go..." Bria held out her empty glass, and Porter filled it again.

"You're not driving," he said. "Why don't you give me your keys right now."

She handed them over without protest. "I was planning on taking an Uber, Porter. I'm not stupid."

"I know. But you're Kat's best friend, and she'll scratch my eyes out with her pointy jaguar claws if I let anything happen to you. When your Uber gets here, I'll give you your keys back. Deal?"

"Deal." Bria sipped at her whiskey and stared at the shiny surface of the bar in front of her as Porter walked away.

"HEY, BRIA BABY."

"Kit Kat?" Bria stared blearily at her best friend as she sat on the stool next to her. "What are you doing here?"

"Ronin texted me and asked if I wanted to meet him here for drinks when he was done with his shift."

"On a work night?" The whiskey was muddling her thoughts. "It's Thursday, right?"

"Yes. How are you doing?"

Bria stared at the tall and lithe jaguar shifter for a moment before turning her gaze to Porter. "Porter, you asshole. You called Kat, didn't you?"

"No," Porter poured a beer, "I *texted* Kat. Big difference."

"Why would you do that?" Bria said.

"Because you're drinking too much tonight, and you're sad," Porter said.

Bria opened her mouth to argue and stared into her whiskey instead as Porter set the beer in front of Kat and walked away. Kat put her arm around her and leaned her head against hers. "What's wrong, honey?"

"Nothing. Everything." Bria blinked back tears as she stared at Kat. "I'm a loser."

"What? You're not a loser." Kat scowled. "I mean, you are, but you're my loser, and that makes you cool."

Bria smiled a little. "Yeah, okay."

"Are you feeling sad about Raden?"

"No. Embarrassed, but not sad."

"You don't need to be embarrassed. Raden was a fool for breaking up with you. You're amazing, honey, and he will regret letting you go."

"I'm embarrassed because I didn't have the guts to break up with him first." Bria took another sip of whiskey. "I knew it wasn't working, but I refused to admit it to myself."

"Sometimes couples go through rough patches," Kat said. "It doesn't mean that -"

"He was a lion shifter who couldn't satisfy me during my heat. Either there's something wrong with him, or there's something wrong with me. Raden said he'd been with other cat shifters, and there wasn't an issue."

"You believed him just like that?" Kat asked.

"Why would he lie about it?"

"Why?" Kat gave her a look of disbelief. "Bria, honey, I love you, but get your damn head out of the clouds. Why wouldn't he lie about it? You think any shifter alive wants to admit that he can't satisfy his partner during her heat cycle?"

"He said I got really aggressive near the end of my cycle," Bria said.

"So what? That's normal. I told you how much I bite and scratch Ronin. Hell, I'm lucky he's a phoenix shifter who heals abnormally fast, even for a shifter, or he'd have to take a few days off after my heat cycle to heal."

Bria shook her head. "No, you don't understand. Raden said that I became freakishly aggressive, but I was so frustrated by that point, you know? He'd start strong the first day, but even by the end of the day, he'd be almost useless.

So, I would get upset, and I could feel myself getting upset, but it's not like I could control it. The need would take over, and I wanted more than he could give me."

"Honey, he knew what he was getting into when he started dating a cat shifter," Kat said.

Bria stared at the liquid in her glass. "My last heat cycle was so bad, I thought that I -"

"Hello, Kitten."

Bria stopped talking and stared into her whiskey glass as Ronin sat beside Kat. He pressed a kiss against Kat's mouth before grinning at Bria. "Hey, Stripes, how's it going?"

"Super, you?" Bria replied before sipping at her whiskey.

"Can't complain." Ronin took a swig of Kat's beer.

"Honey, could you give us a minute to finish our conversation?" Kat asked.

"It's fine," Bria said before Ronin could reply. "You don't need to leave, Ronin."

"Bria -"

"It's fine," she repeated before sliding off the stool. "I should go, Kat. It's getting late, and you have work in the morning."

Weaving unsteadily, she fumbled her phone out of her purse. It slipped from her hand, but Ronin snatched it from the air before it could shatter on the ground.

"Holy shit, you're fast," Bria said.

Ronin laughed. "Reflexes like a cat."

Kat took Bria's phone before he could hand it to her. "Bria, you're coming home to our place tonight."

"No," Bria said. "It's a weeknight, and I don't need a babysitter. I'll go home and -"

"Ronin, help her to my car, would you, honey?"

"Sure." Ronin slung his arm around Bria's waist. "C'mon, Stripes, let's get your drunk ass back to our house."

"I'm not drunk. I'm just tipsy," Bria said.

"Good night, Porter." Kat leaned over the bar and pecked Porter on the cheek. "Thanks for calling me."

"Night, Kat," Porter replied. "Bria, take care of yourself."

Bria waved her hand in Porter's direction as Ronin led her toward the door.

"WHAT'S WRONG WITH ME, KIT KAT?" BRIA ASKED.

Kat helped her climb into the bed and pulled the quilt to her chin. She sat on the side of the bed before brushing Bria's hair out of her face. "Nothing, sweetie. There's absolutely nothing wrong with you."

"There might be." Bria yawned.

Kat kissed her forehead. "There isn't."

Bria yawned again. "Thanks for letting me stay with you tonight. I love you, Kat."

"I love you too. Get some rest, and I'll see you in the morning."

"Yeah. Hey, Kat?"

"Yes?"

"Ronin's a good guy. I'm glad you have him."

"Thanks, sweetie."

"Does he happen to have a brother? Because my cycle is next week, and I'm not sure I can do another alone."

Kat kissed her forehead again. "Ronin's an only child. Sorry, sweetie."

"Dammit."

Kat laughed and stood. "Good night."

"Night, Kit Kat."

CHAPTER 2

B ria paced restlessly in her bedroom. She'd spent the last few days dreading her upcoming heat cycle, and now that it was here, it was even worse than she had imagined. She stared at the variety of toys on her bed, and her cat yowled in displeasure.

No more toys! It hissed at her. *Give me the real thing.*

She moaned and sat on the bed. She grabbed a vibrator and used it to bring herself to orgasm, but the pleasure was fleeting and did nothing to help the ache. She needed someone to fuck her, or she would go mad. She stood and paced again before dressing.

Bria, no! You can't go out – not like this. You're too far gone to be smart about who you take home. It's only another few hours. You can do this alone.

She ignored her inner voice, and her tiger roared with happiness. She needed someone, and she needed them now.

She grabbed her purse and keys and ran out of her apartment.

BRIA, THIS IS MADNESS.

No, what was madness was trying to finish her heat cycle alone. She stood in the nightclub's parking lot, staring at the flashing neon lights as her cat growled.

"Why is this happening?" she said in a low voice.

She had gone through her last heat cycle alone, and it was bad, but this – this was something so much worse. Spending the last day and a half alone in her apartment, masturbating furiously, still couldn't get rid of that ache, that deep need to have something in her.

Please, Bria, don't do this. Be strong. By tomorrow morning, your cycle will be finished, and you –

Shut up! Her cat hissed.

She was dangerously close to shifting. She closed her eyes and took three deep breaths before walking to the entrance. Her hands shaking, she paid the cover charge as the human bouncer stared curiously at her. She was tempted to grab him and drag him into the alley behind the club. A little bolt of fear ran through her.

Stop it. Get a hold of yourself! The way you're feeling, you'll tear that human to shreds while you fuck him, and you know it. You need a shifter – preferably a powerful one.

And willing – don't forget willing.

Right.

She walked toward the long, curved bar. The music was loud, and she felt every pounding beat deep in her pelvis. It throbbed miserably. The need was now at the point of pain, and she blinked back the tears that were suddenly blinding her.

She made a startled little hiss when she ran into a warm wall of muscle. Unable to stop herself, she pressed her hands against the shifter's chest. She ran her fingers over that hard flesh separated only by the thin fabric of his shirt and purred.

"Sorry, Miss. You okay?" His deep voice sent lust spiraling through her lower body.

Please, God, please God. Don't let me lose control.

She forced her gaze upward, staring into the tiger shifter's eyes as he cleared his throat. She realized with horror that she was moving her hips in slow circles against his pelvis. She whined low in her throat when his hands cupped her hips and stilled her incessant rhythm. Without thinking, she tried to reach for his dick. Her fingers grazed the front of his crotch, and he inhaled sharply.

"Wait." His voice was surprised as he pushed her hand away. "Not -"

She purred to him, reaching for his dick a second time.

He had what she wanted.

What she needed.

He batted her hand away again before staring at the people around them. Oh God, what was she doing? She was so far gone that she was trying to have sex with someone who didn't want her. She tore away from him before she lost it completely and tried to fuck him in the middle of the damn club.

"I'm so sorry." Her voice was raw.

"Wait." He tried to touch her arm.

She hissed at him before backing away. "I – I'm sorry."

She slipped through the crowd toward the bar, each brush of her body against the other shifters and humans, making her cat cry out with need. She found an empty stool and ordered a beer when the bartender stopped in front of her. She sipped at her beer as the music and her pelvis pulsed and thumped. She stared grimly at the top of the bar. She needed to look around, needed to pick out a shifter to approach and proposition.

What if there isn't a shifter who's interested?

There is! There has to be!

"Hello, gorgeous."

Her body tensed. She inhaled before staring at the shifter standing beside her. He was a snake shifter, and she licked her lips as her cat meowed with satisfaction.

"Can I buy you a drink?"

"I already have one."

He smiled at her. With his dark skin and soulful dark eyes, he was handsome enough, and she licked her lips again. She had never been with a snake shifter before, but what did that matter? He would have what she needed. Her eyes dropped to his crotch. He wore incredibly tight pants, and she stared at the bulge in the front of his pants before tearing her gaze away.

The snake shifter hissed happily. Bria flushed bright red as he moved a little closer. "Tiger shifter, is that right?"

"Yes."

"I get the feeling you need something else, other than a drink. Am I right?"

He was so close to her now that she could feel his breath on her face. She moaned. "I – yeah, I do."

"I have what you need, gorgeous. Why don't we go back to your place?"

She nodded, and he hissed in delight. "Good."

He held his hand out, and she reached for it.

Bria, wait! You know nothing about him!

She hesitated, and there was a flash of annoyance in his suddenly-yellow eyes. "What's wrong?"

"Nothing. I just – let me use the ladies' room first, and then we'll go, okay?"

He frowned at her. "Okay, sure, I guess."

"I'll be right back."

She hurried away as her cat snarled in anger. The blaring music faded to a muted hum as she entered the bathroom. She smiled weakly at the woman washing her hands before hurrying into a stall and resting her forehead on the back of the door.

Get back out there! He has what we need! Her cat yowled.

Shut up! Just shut up and let me think!

Think about what? We'll go mad if you don't take that snake shifter home.

Yes, she would. The logical part of her brain retreated against the overwhelming lust and need. She flung open the stall door and blinked in shock at the tiger shifter she had practically dry-humped earlier. He was standing in the now-deserted ladies' room doorway, giving her a silent, assessing look. Her cat studied his long, lean length and made a happy little purr.

Forget the snake shifter. I want him. Give him to me.

"This is the ladies' room," Bria said.

"That snake shifter is dangerous."

She hissed at him. "Get out of my way."

He sighed and glanced over his shoulder. "Listen to me, okay? That shifter makes a living by preying on cats in their heat cycle. Once your heat cycle has ended and you're back to normal, he'll tell you that unless you pay him a whole lot of money, he'll go to the authorities and claim that you raped him."

Her mouth dropped open. "How do you know that?"

"Does it matter?" he asked. "Just trust me, okay?"

"Why should I? I don't even know you," she said.

"I've heard stories about him doing this before, and I believe them," he said patiently. "I know you're finding it hard to think right now, and I know your heat cycle is making you crazy, but you need to hear me. You're making a big mistake."

She hesitated as the normal part of her brain that wasn't crying out for relief rose to the surface. He nodded at the look on her face. "That's right. You can't let him anywhere near you. It's better for you if you go home."

Her cat immediately surged forward, angry and upset and demanding relief. She hissed again at the tiger shifter. "I don't care."

"You do care," he said. "Just try to think past the need for a minute, okay?"

"No!" she snarled and tried to shove past him.

She yowled when he grabbed her arm and yanked her back into the ladies' room. Her claws extended, and she swiped at him, narrowly missing his face as he pushed her into the accessible stall and locked the door behind them.

"Let me go, or I'll rip you to pieces," she growled.

His fangs popped out, and his eyes glowed jade at her. She made a startled meow when he pushed her against the wall and kissed her. She froze for a moment before her cat made a yowling hiss of delight, and her pupils narrowed to slits. She returned his kiss, shoving her tongue deep into his mouth and tearing at his shirt and jeans.

He muttered a curse against her mouth and pushed her hands away before unbuttoning his jeans. She purred loudly when she freed his dick. It was long and thick and delicious looking. He shoved her skirt up around her waist and tore off her panties before lifting her. She wrapped her legs around his waist and made another soft mew of need.

He covered her mouth with his before entering her wet pussy in one hard thrust that had her screaming with pleasure. He fucked her hard and rough, his mouth never leaving hers, as her hips bucked against him and her orgasm rushed through her.

He pressed her into the wall, panting into her mouth. "Better?"

"Again!"

He drove in and out. His cock was so hard and a perfect fit within her that Bria could barely breathe from the pleasure. She mewled as she slid her hands under his shirt. She tore at him with her claws, and he hissed in pain but continued to plunge in and out of her.

"Oh, oh, oh…" She bit him hard on the shoulder, her teeth sinking through the fabric of his shirt and into his flesh.

He growled and slammed in and out of her. She dug her claws into his back as her second orgasm washed over her. She shuddered and shook against him, purring and making high-pitched sounds of happiness as he buried his face into her damp neck and licked the salt from her skin.

"Oh God," she moaned.

"Need more?" He rasped out.

She nodded. A little of the need had dissipated enough that she could feel some shame creeping in. "I'm sorry."

"Don't be." He dropped his mouth onto hers again and kissed her slowly this time. She sucked at his tongue, and he cupped her breast with one large hand, squeezing it as he pushed his cock deep inside of her.

He released her breast and slipped his hand between them, pressing the heel of his hand against her clit. She purred and rubbed herself against his hand, her pussy squeezing his cock rhythmically as he slid in and out of her.

"Harder," she panted.

He cupped his hands around her thighs and held her tightly as he pushed in and out.

"Fuck, your pussy is incredible," he muttered into her mouth.

"Your cock is incredible," she whispered.

He smiled, and his fingers dug into her smooth thighs before he started a rough rhythm that had her gasping with pleasure.

"Oh God, please, please," she whimpered.

Her third and most powerful orgasm yet shuddered through her. She clung to the tiger shifter as fire and lightning coursed through her veins. He rubbed her thighs when she collapsed against him.

He was still hard within her, but the fiery need to be fucked had abated enough for her to think clearly. She licked her lips before whispering, "I'm sorry."

"I told you, there's no need to be sorry. Are you good for now?"

She nodded, but her cat made a disappointed hiss when he pulled out of her and set her on her feet. She swayed, and he steadied her before tucking his erect cock back into his jeans and buttoning them. He grimaced as he adjusted himself, and she felt another trickle of shame.

"I – uh, should go. Thank you," she whispered.

She needed to get the fuck out of there and get back to her apartment before the next wave hit. The slow cycle of need was already starting in her belly, and she felt a moment of panic. What the fuck was happening to her? Her cycle had never been this bad before.

She smoothed her skirt as the tiger shifter watched her carefully. She couldn't look him in the eye, and she moaned in dismay when she realized blood was blooming on his shirt.

"Oh shit, I'm so sorry."

He barely glanced at the bite on his shoulder. "It's fine. It will heal."

"I know, but I… oh God, turn around."

"It's fine. Don't worry about it."

"Turn around." She grabbed him and swung him around, another moan of dismay bursting from her throat. The back of his shirt was soaked in blood, and she yanked it up, staring in horror at the long, deep scratches on his back.

"You need to go to the hospital."

He laughed. "You know I don't. They'll heal on their own."

He turned and frowned when he saw how pale her face was. "Hey, are you okay?"

She swayed again. She felt physically sick over how terribly she had scratched him – another first for her – and he grabbed her upper arms. "Don't pass out on me."

"What is happening to me?" she whispered.

"It's just your heat cycle."

"It's never been like this before," she said. "It's never been this bad. Already, I – I'm starting to feel…"

She closed her eyes and didn't object when he put his arm around her waist. "Come with me."

"Where are we going?"

"Back to my place."

"I can't." She pulled away from him.

"If you don't, you'll be right back at this club. We both know that. Do you want to risk taking someone home like that snake shifter?"

"How do I know you're not like him?"

"I'm not," he said. "I just want to help you with your cycle."

"Fuck. " Bria pressed her fingers to her temples as her pelvis throbbed. The shifter was right. She'd be right back at the club if she didn't go home with him. The way she was feeling, her fingers and a vibrator weren't going to do shit for her.

"Okay," she whispered. "Do you live close?"

"Ten-minute drive."

He took her hand and led her out of the stall. Two women stood beside the sink, staring wide-eyed and slack-jawed at them. Bria turned scarlet. She wondered how long they were standing there and listening, but the tiger shifter simply nodded to them and led Bria into the dark and loud night-club. He walked her quickly through the crowds of people. She kept her head down and tensed when she heard the snake shifter.

"Hey! She's mine."

A hand landed on the tiger shifter's arm, and she pressed her lips together when he growled. "Get your hand off me, asshole."

The snake hissed but released him, and the tiger shifter led her to the exit. She took deep breaths of the fresh air and followed him across the parking lot to his car.

He opened the door, and she climbed in without a word, trying to keep herself from sticking her own damn fingers into her pussy as he started the car. He drove fast, but she moaned in dismay when he had to stop at a red light.

"Please," she whispered. The need was back, throbbing deep in her pelvis like it had never found a moment of satis-faction, and she gave him a helpless look. "Please."

He reached across and slid his hand under her skirt. She spread her legs, crying out when he rubbed at her clit.

She screamed as she orgasmed against his rough fingers. She shuddered and shook and clutched his wrist when he sank two fingers deep into her aching pussy. The light turned green, and he stepped on the gas, keeping his eyes on the road even as his fingers plunged back and forth.

She humped his hand shamelessly, bracing one hand on the ceiling of the car as she rode his hand to another orgasm. She collapsed against the seat, keeping her hand locked around his wrist so he couldn't remove his fingers from her pussy.

"Okay?"

"I need your cock," she gasped. "Please."

"Soon. I need my hand back, baby. Just for a minute."

"No."

"Give me my hand back, and I'll be fucking you in less than five minutes."

"Do you promise?" She was ashamed of the way she whined.

"I promise."

She reluctantly released his hand, growling under her breath when he pulled his fingers free. He licked his fingers and she purred when he smiled at her. "Very nice."

He pulled into a driveway, and she opened the door before he even shut off the car. She ran to the front door, impatiently waiting as he joined her and unlocked the door. She was purring in anticipation and leaped on him when he shut the door.

He hissed in pain and tugged her hands away from his back, ignoring her angry growl of displeasure. "You promised!"

"I know," he said. "But let's give my back a chance to heal."

She snarled, and he squeezed her hand as she dropped her purse and kicked off her heels. He led her down the hallway.

"I'm not waiting for your back to heal," she said heatedly. "I can't wait, so if you're not going to help me, then I'm fucking leaving and you can't stop me."

They were in his bedroom now, and without speaking, he pushed her over the back of the armchair next to the small gas fireplace. He unzipped her skirt before raking it down her legs. He thrust the fingers of his left hand into her pussy as he worked at the buttons on his jeans with his right.

She moaned and drove back against his hand as he moved it rapidly back and forth.

"Your cock!" She gasped. "Give me your cock!"

"I'm working on it, honey," he muttered.

Her yowl of displeasure turned into a moan of pure delight when his fingers were replaced with the blunt head of his cock. He speared into her, nearly lifting her off her feet. She tore at the fabric of the chair, her nails shredding it as he thrust back and forth.

Her orgasm hit her, and as she was shuddering her way through the aftershocks, his hands were unbuttoning her shirt and pulling it from her body. He unhooked the clasps of her bra, and she tossed it impatiently to the floor.

"So lovely," he whispered as she straightened and then squeezed his cock with her inner walls.

He uttered a curse and cupped her breasts, his fingers flicking her nipples as he drove rhythmically in and out of her tight pussy. She squeezed around him and shrieked with pleasure as he pinched her nipples and sent her over the edge again.

"More," she begged. He pulled out of her and lifted her easily.

"Yes." He set her on the bed. "Spread your legs."

She spread them eagerly as he stripped off his clothes and sank to his knees beside the bed. She watched as his dark head dipped between her smooth thighs.

"Oh fuck, that feels so good!" She shrieked when his tongue slid across her swollen clit. He sucked it into his mouth, teasing the sensitive bundle of nerves with his lips and his tongue until she howled her release.

Bria purred and writhed and clutched at his head as he brought her repeatedly to orgasm with his fingers and mouth. Had she ever been with someone this good? Someone who knew exactly what to do?

He spent the next hour with his face buried between her legs and his hands pinning hers to the bed and away from his shredded back. When the sheets were in strips around her body, and she was spent and shuddering, he wiped his dripping face on the sheets before reaching into the nightstand. He unwrapped the condom, rolling it down onto his cock as she stared up at him.

"I feel so much better." She purred as he nudged her thighs apart and knelt between them.

"Good," he said. "I'm glad. Are you ready for me?"

She nodded. She was actually feeling a little sleepy, and her body was a wet noodle, but she wasn't about to deny the man an orgasm when he had just spent the last hour and a half bringing her repeatedly to orgasm.

He slid into her, and she squeezed around him compulsively as he hooked her thigh around his waist.

"So tight," he muttered before his deep, rumbling purr started.

The sound brought a spark of pleasure to her belly, and she arched her hips up to meet each of his downward strokes.

"That's right, baby," he rasped. "I know you're tired, but fuck me with that tight little pussy."

Another shudder of pleasure, and she tugged his mouth down to her breast. He sucked on her nipple, and she moaned as a flash of heat spread through her pelvis. He teased it into a hard, little peak before licking a slow circle around it.

"Can you come once more for me?" The speed of his

thrusts increased. "I want to feel you coming all over my cock."

"Yes, I think so."

"That's my good girl," he whispered. Another sweet shudder of pleasure went through her at his approval.

"Do you need me to rub your clit?" He licked her ear before sucking on her earlobe.

She arched her back, rubbing her sensitive nipples against his hard chest. "Yes, please."

He reached between them, and she tensed a little. She had come so many times that she needed him to touch her clit to come again, but she was also incredibly oversensitive. She mentally prepared herself for the pain that would go with it.

To her surprise, he brushed her clit with just the tips of his fingers and so lightly that it stimulated rather than hurt.

"Oh," she moaned. "Fuck, you are so good at this."

"Thank you." His whisper held a tinge of amusement.

He thrust faster, keeping that light caressing of her clit until she forgot her weariness and was moaning and arching against him, searching desperately for relief.

"I'm close," he panted into her ear. "Your pussy is so hot I can't hold out any longer. I'm sorry."

If she'd had the breath, if she hadn't been so close to an orgasm, she would have told him in no uncertain terms that he had nothing to be sorry about. The shifter had the stamina of a god. Instead, she squeezed her inner muscles around him, and he groaned loudly. The pressure of his fingers increased just enough to make her peak. She cried out, her muscles clenching around his thick cock. He groaned again before he found his release, his body shaking against hers.

He kissed her neck before rolling off of her and disposing

of the condom. Bria, weak and finally sated, stared dreamily at the ceiling.

Get up and go home, Bria. You can't stay the night.

No, she really couldn't, but the tiger shifter was already tucking her limp body under the quilt, and she made a happy little purr when he spooned her. She was warm and tired, and sleeping for an hour or two wouldn't hurt. Besides, she wasn't entirely certain she could walk anyway. The tiger shifter kissed the back of her shoulder, and she purred again. He made a rumbling purr in reply that was oddly soothing.

CHAPTER 3

She woke just before dawn, blinking sleepily at the unfamiliar ceiling as a faint feeling of relief went through her. Her cycle was done, and the pulsing need that had tormented her for the past two days had disappeared. She stretched lazily before wincing. Her thigh muscles had just started screaming at her, and she moved her legs gingerly under the quilt. What the hell did she do to herself? Did she –

She hissed in sudden dismay. Oh shit, she had fucked a stranger last night. She turned her head and stared at the broad back of the tiger shifter. He was sprawled on his stomach, his head buried beneath his pillow, and his large body taking up most of the queen bed.

"Bria, you idiot," she whispered before blinking back the hot tears. She sat up slowly, holding the quilt against her naked chest and watching the shifter for any movement. Deep slashes covered his back, and she bit back her moan of shame. She had done that to him. She had clawed and scratched and bitten him while he fucked her senseless, and she had begged for more.

Feeling nauseous, she slid out from the bed and quietly dressed. As she crept toward the door, the floorboards made a loud squeak. She froze as the shifter snorted and scratched at one of the slashes on his back. He muttered something before sliding his hand back under the quilt. She released her breath in a quiet hiss and eased the door open. She closed it quietly behind her and hurried down the stairs. Her purse and shoes were lying on the hallway floor, and she snatched her cell phone from her bag and ordered an Uber as she slipped out the front door.

TWO HOURS LATER, FRESHLY SHOWERED AND HOLDING A TRAY with two cups of coffee in one hand, she rang the doorbell of Kat's house. The door opened, and still in her robe, Kat smiled at her. "Bria, what are you doing here?"

"I did something really bad, Kit Kat." Bria burst into tears.

"Oh, honey, come inside."

Twenty minutes later, Bria stared into her coffee cup while waiting for Kat to yell at her.

Instead of yelling, Kat said, "Thank God. The way you looked, I thought you had murdered someone or something."

"Did you hear what I said?" Bria asked. "I slept with a total stranger last night. I was completely out of control. I didn't care who he was or if he was dangerous. I let him fuck me in a public washroom while I shredded his back with my claws. Then I went home with him and screwed him six ways to Sunday."

"Well, that wasn't your best idea," Kat said. "But it could have been worse. Sounds like the guy did you a favour by keeping you away from that snake shifter. Do you think he was telling you the truth about that?"

"Honestly? Yes. Now that I'm back in control, there was something off about that damn snake."

She stared at the table. "I just keep thinking – what if I had tried to fuck a human or a shifter who wasn't that strong? The marks on his back were so deep. It must have hurt like hell when I did it."

"You said they were starting to heal, right?"

Bria nodded, and Kat patted her hand. "Then it's fine. Besides, you know better than anyone how resilient tiger shifters are. He'll be completely healed in a day or two."

"I need to go to the doctor," Bria said. "There's something seriously wrong with me."

"There isn't. So, your heat cycle made you sleep with a random stranger. Most cat shifters have been there, sweetheart. You used protection, right?"

"Yes. But I wouldn't have and wouldn't have even cared if he hadn't taken care of it."

"That doesn't mean there's something wrong with you. Our heat cycles make us do crazy things sometimes."

Bria shook her head. "You're wrong, Kat. It's never been like this before. There's something wrong with me."

"Honey, look at me."

Bria raised her gaze to Kat. The jaguar shifter gave her a sympathetic look, and she didn't object when Kat took her hand in a tight grip.

"This is the first time you've been single since you started your heat cycles, yeah?"

Bria frowned in thought. "Yeah, I guess so. I mean, I started dating Kyle in high school, and we were together for nearly eight years, but then I was gone on the pilgrimage for three months."

"But you had sex with Raden during the pilgrimage, right?"

"Yeah. We hooked up maybe two weeks after I got there."

"And you slept with him regularly during your heat cycle?" Kat asked.

"Yes, but what does that have to do with what's happening now?"

"Everything. You know the rumour that heat cycles are much worse when you're not having regular sex, right? Well, it's not just a rumour."

"No," Bria said.

"Yes. It's only going to get worse the longer you go without sex."

Bria's mouth dropped open. "I – are you sure?"

"Very sure," Kat said. "Your first heat cycle without sex was bad, right? And this second one worse?"

"So much worse," Bria said.

"I hate to tell you this, sweetie, but it's not even half as bad as it will get. I was feeling bad about just using Mark for sex during my cycles, so I went three heat cycles in a row without getting laid. By the fourth one, I had Ronin pinned to the floor of my office while I rode him like a damn pony. We weren't even dating – I had barely spoken to him outside of work at that point."

"Oh fuck," Bria dropped her head into her hands before breathing deeply. "Okay, it's fine, it's fine. I just need to find a boyfriend before my next heat cycle."

Kat raised her eyebrow at her. "You're going to find a boyfriend in a month?"

"Yes. What? I can do it. I'm a good-looking girl, right? Maybe I don't have a lot of sex experience, but I can get the goddamn job done. Any guy would be happy to have an unemployed girl who bites and claws like a Tasmanian Devil when she doesn't get sex regularly."

Kat laughed. "Honey, you are awesome, but do you want to start dating some random shifter just so you don't freak out during your next heat cycle?"

Bria sighed loudly. "I don't have a choice. I'm not strong like you."

"You can take the medication to curb your heat."

"No," Bria said. "I won't take it. My aunt has a friend whose daughter took the meds from twenty to twenty-five, and now she's having a terrible time getting pregnant. She wants kittens more than anything, but she can't have them. I don't want that to be me in a few years, you know?"

"I thought you didn't want kittens."

"I don't know for certain. If I meet someone who wants one, I want to have the option at least."

"There is something else you can try." Kat gave her a thoughtful look.

"What?"

"The website that - "

"No way," Bria cut her off. "I'm not trolling that meat market looking for shifters who just want no-commitment-required sex with a horny cat shifter every month. I'm not that desperate."

"I did it."

Bria's eyes widened. "Shut your mouth! You did not, Katarina Frost."

"I did. Well, I didn't have sex with any of them, but I created an account and interviewed three different shifters."

"Holy shit," Bria said. "When did you do this?"

"While you were on your pilgrimage."

Why didn't you go through with it? Were they all losers?"

Kat laughed. "Two weren't great, but the third was good."

"So why didn't you sleep with him?"

"Because it was Ronin that I wanted, even then. Luckily for me, he was happy to help during my heat cycle."

Bria continued to stare at her, and Kat shrugged. "I think you should give it a try. You don't even have to create an account. I still have the third shifter's email, and I'll send it to you. He was a tiger shifter, and honestly, if I hadn't already been half in love with Ronin at that point, I would have given him a try. He was handsome and polite and seemed to care about meeting my needs each month."

"Yeah, and probably fourteen other cat shifters every month."

"He said he didn't help out more than one cat shifter at a time," Kat replied.

"You believed him?"

"Yes. Just email him, Bria. You can meet in a public place, he'll give you references, and you can give them a call. If you're not interested after meeting him, email and tell him. He wasn't offended when I said no thanks. Plus, he said he didn't mind scratching or biting. That'll come in handy for you."

She grinned as Bria flushed. "I – yeah, maybe I will. My mom says it would be good for me to not be in a relationship for a while. She says I've barely spent any of my adult life being single and need to get to know who I really am."

Kat laughed. "God, I wish my mother was like that. She's finally jumped off the 'you're going to die old and alone' train, but now she's hopped on the 'you need to make me a grandmother before I die' train. Ronin delights in teasing her about how he's pretty certain he's sterile. She falls for it every damn time."

"Do you think I need to be single for a while, Kat? I've always been in a relationship and find it lonely not to be in one. I don't know what to do with myself."

"I think you need to do what makes you happy. If being in a relationship makes you happy – then be in one. Just make sure it's the right guy, okay?"

Bria nodded, and Kat took a sip of her coffee. "How's the job hunt going?"

"Good. I have two interviews this week. Both are just reception jobs, but my savings are dangerously low, so I'll take what I can get. Maybe someday I'll grow up and figure out what I want to do with my life."

She took a drink of her coffee and smiled at Kat. "Thanks, Kat. I feel much better."

"Good. Email that tiger shifter, okay? It's better than trolling for total strangers in a bar."

"Yeah," Bria said. "I will."

BRIA PAID FOR HER COFFEE AND MOVED TO THE OTHER END OF the counter. She shifted from foot to foot and tried to calm her racing pulse.

After talking to Kat, she'd gone home, and before she could lose her nerve, she sent an email to Jace, the tiger shifter she'd recommended. She kept it brief, explaining that she received his email from Kat and wondered if they could meet to discuss her heat cycle. Jace had replied within a couple of hours and agreed to meet. His email was short but well-written. Feeling a little sick, she arranged to meet him at Starbucks the next morning.

She smoothed her bright red top and wondered if her jeans were too tight. They did showcase her ass nicely, and she considered it to be her best physical feature. Her boobs were too small to be proud of, but both Kyle and Raden had loved her ass.

She sighed nervously. She hadn't sent a picture to Jace, and he hadn't asked for one, but now she wondered if she should have. What if he didn't like what he saw?

So what if he doesn't? You're still not entirely sure you can go through with this anyway.

That was a good point. She sighed again. She had given him a description of what she was wearing so he could find her at Starbucks. She tentatively searched the people milling about. She didn't see anyone who looked remotely big enough to be a tiger shifter, and some of the nerves eased a little in her belly. She was early, so he likely wouldn't be here for another ten minutes anyway. She smoothed her shirt and picked at a loose thread near the button.

"Bria?"

A hand touched her elbow. The deep, raspy voice sounded vaguely familiar. She turned and raised her gaze to the hazel eyes of the tiger shifter who had fucked her in the bathroom three nights ago.

"Hi, I'm Jace. It's nice to…"

They stared at each other in shocked silence. Bria's pulse pounded in her ears, and she knew her mouth was hanging open.

"Well, this is a bit awkward, huh?" He finally said.

She blinked at him before forcing the words past her dry throat. "A bit awkward? Oh my God, I have to go."

She tried to dart by him, and he placed his hand on her arm, pulling her to a stop. "Wait, don't go."

She closed her eyes and took a deep breath as he waited patiently.

"This was a mistake," she said.

"Just – let's have a coffee and talk, okay?"

It was the last thing she wanted, but she nodded in defeat and waited as he ordered his coffee. She picked hers up, dismayed at the way her hands were shaking. She found a table near the back as he grabbed his coffee and joined her.

"Hi," he said as he sat down across from her.

The table was small - too small - and she sat back when his knees bumped against hers. "Um, hi."

"So, you're friends with Kat?"

She nodded as he sipped at the coffee. "I've only met her once, but she seemed nice."

"Yeah." She stared at the table.

"Bria?"

"I'm sorry I ran out on you the other morning. That was really ungrateful of me, but I was embarrassed and didn't know what to say." She was babbling but couldn't stop. "When I woke up, my heat cycle was done, and I was ashamed of what I had done to you, but I shouldn't have just rudely left. I want to say thank you. You really helped me out."

"You're welcome."

She waited for more and frowned at him when he just took another sip of coffee. "That's it?"

"What else did you want me to say?"

"I don't know - that you're not upset with me for leaving like that."

"Why would I be?"

Her face went red, and she glared at him. "Listen, maybe you're used to just having random, casual sex with strangers, but I'm not, okay? What happened between us was really out of character for me, and I don't want you thinking I'm some kind of – of whore."

"I don't." He gave her a look of confusion. "You were in heat and couldn't help yourself."

"I'm not weak!" she snarled, even though she was terribly afraid that she was.

"I didn't think you were."

Her sudden anger vanished, and she rubbed at her temples. "What a mess."

"It isn't. I think this makes things a lot smoother for us."

"What do you mean?"

"Well, you know what I can do for you during your next heat cycle. I can still provide references, of course, but now you have first-hand knowledge. That will make your decision easier, right?"

"God," she muttered. "I guess now I know why you were so good at it. You do this for a living."

He laughed. "I don't do this for a living, Bria. There's no money exchanged, and as much as I enjoy sex – I can't exactly live off of it."

"Why did you help me?" She asked. "Why did you warn me about that snake shifter, and why did you..."

A small grin crossed his face. A weird tingle of heat went through her belly, and her cat perked up.

"Why did I help ease your need?" he suggested.

"Yeah," she mumbled.

"I told you – I'd heard stories about the snake shifter, and I didn't want that to happen to you."

She pulled compulsively on a strand of hair as he said, "As far as the easing your need goes – I knew it was the only way to keep you from taking the snake home."

She released her breath in a shaky sigh. "Right."

Why was she feeling such disappointment? Did she expect him to confess that he had found her so beautiful and intoxicating that he couldn't resist? She was losing it.

"So, let's talk about how this works. My schedule is flexible, and I can be available for you whenever you require. Is your heat cycle regular?"

"Like clockwork."

"Good. If you choose me, I assure you you're the only one I'll be helping. There won't be other cat shifters."

"Guess that would be pretty tiring for you, huh?" she said.

He smiled a little. "You were a bit more demanding and aggressive than most."

She blushed furiously, and he shook his head. "That's not a bad thing, Bria. I'm assuming you've had a few heat cycles without sex, which makes it much worse."

"This was my second one," she confessed without thinking.

A look of surprise crossed his face, and her blush deepened. "Oh God, I'm a freak."

"You're not," he said. "Besides, I didn't mind."

She licked her lips and didn't fail to notice the way his gaze dropped to her mouth. "How is your back, by the way?"

"Completely healed."

"Good."

He leaned forward. He was wearing a dark suit that clung to his broad shoulders, and she stared fixedly at his red tie as he said, "If you choose me, I like to have an email or text reminder a week before your cycle starts. That way, I can clear my schedule for you. Of course, if it happens early, you can always text me, and I'll work something out."

"It won't," she said. "It never does."

"The preference for most cat shifters I've helped in the past is that I stay with them - either at my place or theirs, completely your choice – through their entire heat cycle. The need is usually less intense if you know you can have me whenever you want me."

Dull heat coloured her cheeks. He was so matter-of-fact about it, so clinical, and she supposed she should have been happy about that. Unfortunately, at this moment, she couldn't get the memory out of her head of his mouth buried in her pussy.

"Of course," he continued, "I'm also happy to be available on an on-call basis during your heat cycle. Also, I have good stamina and am more than willing to delay my gratification until you're completely satisfied."

She didn't reply, and he cleared his throat. "Don't judge me completely on what happened earlier, Bria. I'd had a long day at work and wasn't expecting to be helping a cat shifter through her heat cycle that night. I know my performance was subpar, but I assure you I'll be at the top of my game when you need me."

She blinked at him. If his performance three nights ago was subpar, she wasn't sure she could handle him when he was at the top of his game.

"You were fine," she said.

He winced. "Fine? I need to work on my performance, apparently."

"N-no," she stuttered as her cheeks flamed again. "You were good. Uh, really good. I mean that."

"Thanks." He pulled a piece of paper out from the inner pocket of his suit and handed it to her. Confused, she opened it and stared blankly at it for a moment before her eyes widened. Right. In his email, Jace had asked her to bring a copy of her latest medical tests as well as proof that she was on birth control for him to look at. She fumbled the papers out of her purse and pushed them across the table. Jace looked them over as she studied his.

He handed the papers back to her and smiled. "Thank you. As you can see from my tests, I'm infection free, but I will wear a condom if that's your preference."

"Uh, I'm okay with not wearing condoms," she said.

"All right. Do you have any other questions?"

"What about in between my heat cycles?"

"What about it?" He gave her a confused look.

"Would you – I mean, are you available then as well?"

Surprise crossed his face. "I don't usually have cat shifters asking for me when they're not in heat."

This time, she was positive her cheeks were on fire. She had no idea why she had said that. It had just come tumbling out of her. She realized with sudden clarity that she couldn't do this. She was the relationship type, not the 'fuck them once a month' type, and she was stupid to think she could even try.

He ran his fingers over a small shaving cut on his jaw. "I don't do conventional relationships, Bria. This is why this arrangement works so well for me."

She stood, and he immediately stood as well. "What's wrong?"

"I can't do this with you. I'm sorry for wasting your time." She pushed past the table and fled.

THE TINY TIGER SHIFTER WAS QUICK. BRIA WAS ACROSS THE coffee shop and out the door before Jace could even think of going after her.

"Dammit, Jace, you fucking idiot," he muttered. He sat down, pushed his half-finished coffee aside and stared blankly at the wall. It had rattled him badly when the woman in the red shirt with the amazing ass had turned around. He hadn't expected to see the little tiger shifter from the club again. His tiger had immediately roared its approval, and he had damn near rubbed up against her before he could get control of it again.

He had been ridiculously disappointed when he'd awoken

and discovered she was gone, leaving nothing but healing scratches on his back and destroyed sheets. The woman was dynamite in bed and so responsive to his touch. Her aggression and frantic need had only increased his lust.

Christ, when she had bumped into him at the club, and he had smelled her lust and felt her hips pressing against his groin, he had hardened immediately. He'd instinctively known that she was in her heat cycle, but she had skittered away before he could offer to help.

He had watched, growing angry when the snake shifter had arrowed in on her. It was pure instinct that had made him go after her in the bathroom to warn her. Her need had a strong hold on her by then, and he had, again, acted on instinct when he pushed her into the stall. Her scent, the way her blue eyes flashed fire at him – hell, even the way she had hissed at him - had his dick straining at his jeans.

He wasn't lying when he told her he was tired and muttered another curse. Maybe she would have chosen him if he was a little more attentive and faster to ease her need. But he had shown four houses that day, and there was a mistake with some paperwork that had nearly cost him a sale.

His assistant Rosalie was running on empty, trying to cover her job and reception. He didn't blame her for the mistake, but he had spent a few tense hours calling the bank to fix the error and apologizing to the clients. He wouldn't have even gone to the nightclub that night if he hadn't promised Lincoln he would. Then the damn lion shifter had bailed on him as soon as the first bunny shifter twitched her nose at him.

He reached for his coffee. It didn't matter now. He had blown it with Bria. He didn't know why it bothered him so much. He had three more emails from cat shifters wanting to meet with him. One of them would be a good fit.

I want Bria, his tiger growled sulkily. *Give her to me.*

Way too late. She specifically said she couldn't do this with him, which meant she was probably already choosing from the next one on her list of applicants. He cursed again – why the fuck didn't he make a better effort that night?

CHAPTER 4

Bria opened the door and hurried into the foyer of Kat's office. Along with a wolf shifter named Malcolm Burke and a grizzly shifter named Bishop King, Kat owned a security firm that provided personal protection for paranormals. Over the last year, they had branched out into providing corporate security for paranormals and personal security for humans.

Their receptionist and Malcolm's mate was a human named Willow. She was on the phone and waved at Bria as the door opened again. Bria turned and smiled at the curvy redhead who walked into the office. "Hi, Ava. How are you?"

Ava set the car seat she was carrying on the floor. "I'm good. Just brought Lila in to see her dad during lunch."

Bria crouched next to the car seat before pulling back the blanket. Lila stared at her, and Bria brushed her hand over the baby's bright red hair. "Look at her chubby cheeks. I can't believe how big she's getting."

Ava laughed. "She loves to eat. She might be human, but you can totally tell she's Bishop's kid."

"How old is she now?"

"Almost seven weeks."

Bria touched Lila's cheek with the tip of her finger. "Hi, Lila. Hi, sweet baby."

"Do you want to hold her?" Ava asked.

"Can I?"

"Of course." Ava bent and unbuckled the belt before lifting Lila out of the seat. She handed her over, and Bria kissed the baby's cheek.

"You look just like your mama."

Willow had finished her phone call, and she joined them. "She looks so much like her mama. Hi, Bria."

"Hi, Willow. How are you?"

"Good. You here to see Kat?"

"Yeah, if she's here."

"She is," Willow said as she picked up Lila's hand and kissed it. "How's my sweet Lila girl?"

The door to Bishop's office opened, and the giant grizzly shifter came hurrying out. He was sniffing the air and broke into a huge grin when he saw Ava. He embraced her and kissed her before smiling down at her. "Hi, gorgeous."

"Hi, honey. Sorry to drop by without texting, but I wondered if you wanted to have lunch with Lila and me?"

"Yes." Bishop kissed Ava's forehead before holding out his hands for Lila.

Bria handed him the baby. She looked incredibly tiny in his massive hands, and Bria couldn't help but feel a tinge of worry. Grizzly shifters weren't exactly known for their delicate touch.

She shouldn't have worried.

Displaying a gentleness she hadn't known existed in him, Bishop tucked Lila against his broad chest. The baby stared up at him, and when he made a low rumbling sound of happiness, her face broke out in a toothless grin. She kicked her feet, her grin widening as Bishop gave her his finger to hold. She gripped it tightly, her gaze never leaving his face as he cooed to her.

"How's my baby girl? Has she been a good girl for her mama today? Daddy is so happy to see you. Your daddy loves you. Yes, he does."

Willow started to giggle. "Bishop, you are ridiculously adorable. Did you know that?"

Bishop turned red but continued to coo to his daughter. Lila tried to put his finger in her mouth and angrily cried when he wouldn't let her.

"Uh oh. I think she's hungry again. Do you mind if I feed her before we go for lunch?" Ava said.

"Why don't you feed her in my office while I run to the café and grab us something? We can eat in my office or the boardroom," Bishop said before handing Lila back to Ava.

He left the office, and Ava jiggled Lila and smiled at Bria "How are you, Bria? I haven't seen you since Lila's baby shower. Did you find a job?"

"I'm good. I have a job interview tomorrow and another one the day after that."

"Awesome," Ava said as Lila's face scrunched, and she made a loud, wailing cry. "Okay, sorry to cut this short, but this kid's hunger cry can break glass. I need to feed her."

Bria laughed. "Fair enough. Good to see you again, Ava."

"You too," Ava called as she picked up Lila's car seat and hurried toward Bishop's office.

Kat's office door opened, and Ava waved at her. "Hi, Kat, sorry about the noise."

Kat laughed. "It's fine. Come see me before you leave so I can get my Lila fix."

As Ava disappeared into Bishop's office and shut the door, Kat smiled at Bria. "Hey, sweetie, what's up?"

"Do you have plans for lunch?" Bria asked.

"Nope. I was going to go downstairs to the café."

"Want some company?"

"I would love that," Kat said.

The café on the first floor of the building was crowded and noisy. After grabbing their food, they snagged a small table by the window. Bishop was leaving the café with a bag of food and they waved at him before Kat opened her bottle of water and took a drink.

"What's wrong, Bria?"

Bria glanced around the café before leaning forward. "I met with the tiger shifter this morning."

"Great. How did it go?"

"Kat, it was him."

Kat crumbled some crackers into her soup before stirring it. "It was who?"

"The tiger shifter! From the club! Jace was the tiger shifter from the club!" Bria said.

Kat's spoon clattered to the table. "You're kidding me."

"I'm not," Bria said. "Oh God, Kat, I was so humiliated."

"Seriously? Jace was the tiger shifter you fucked in the bathroom at the club?"

"Keep your voice down."

"Sorry." Kat picked up her spoon and wiped it with her napkin before dipping it into her soup. "I'm just really surprised."

"How do you think I felt? I almost ran out of the Starbucks."

"You didn't, did you?"

"No, Jace convinced me to sit and talk to him."

"Good. How did it go?"

Bria stared at her untouched sandwich. "Embarrassing. I apologized for just attacking him in the bathroom and then running away in the morning, but he said it was fine. It didn't even seem to bother him."

"Well, that's a good thing, right?" Kat said.

"Yeah, I guess."

"So, did you make arrangements for your next heat cycle?" Kat took a bite of soup before wrinkling her nose and adding salt.

"No. Jace told me how it worked, and we looked at each other's medical records, but I told him I couldn't do it."

"What?" Kat stopped sprinkling salt into her soup. "Why would you do that? You already know how good he is in bed. This was the perfect solution."

"I can't do it," Bria said. "I'm not the type of person to sleep with someone when it doesn't mean anything. I want a boyfriend, not a fuck buddy. I humiliated myself by asking Jace if he was available in between heat cycles. I don't even know why I said it. It just popped out, you know?"

"Oh, Bria," Kat said.

"He made it clear in no uncertain terms that he was only interested in me during my heat cycle. He said he doesn't do 'conventional' relationships. It was so embarrassing. I don't even know him, and I was acting like we were on a first date or something. Oh, God."

She buried her face in her hands as Kat reached across the table and squeezed her shoulder. "I'm sorry. I should never have convinced you to try this method."

"It's not your fault. You were trying to help me, and I appreciate it."

They sat silently for a few minutes before Kat said, "So, now what are you going to do?"

"I have two job interviews this week. I'll concentrate on

47

finding employment so I don't have to move in with my parents. Then, I'll download the "Shifter Love" app and try online dating. I have almost a month until my next heat cycle. I can find a boyfriend before then."

"What if you don't?"

"I'll just have to get it through it on my own," Bria said.

"You couldn't before. Do you want to end up at some club trying to bang a random shifter again?" Kat asked

Bria winced. "I'll handcuff myself to the bed if I have to."

"Honey, you should at least consider asking Jace to help you."

"Yeah, I know. I'll give it a couple of weeks, and if I haven't found anyone by then, I'll email Jace again."

"Good," Kat said. "Now, tell me about your job interview tomorrow."

BRIA STUDIED THE SIGN OVER THE SMALL BRICK BUILDING. "Shepherd Real Estate" was written in bold, black letters across the white sign. She stepped out of her car, smoothed her skirt, and walked confidently toward the building. She had pooched the interview yesterday. Even a full twenty-four hours after she met with Jace, she was still shaken by it, and it had shown in the interview. She was determined not to mess this one up. Setting aside the fact that she was running out of money, she needed to regain her confidence by acing this interview.

She stepped into the cool interior of the building. The front desk was empty, but a woman was already walking into reception from the hallway. "Ms. Norsen?"

"Yes," Bria smiled at her as she came hurrying over.

"Hi, I'm Rosalie. It's nice to meet you."

"Nice to meet you, too."

"Can I get you a cup of coffee or a glass of water?" Rosalie asked as the phone rang.

"Water would be good, thank you."

"Okay, just have a seat. Mr. Shepherd is running late, but I'll let Betty know you're here."

She answered the phone as Bria sat in one of the high-quality leather chairs in the reception area. The place was nice, decorated with modern, high-end furnishings, and she studied the art on the walls. Rosalie hung up the phone and punched another button.

"Betty? Ms. Norsen's here for her interview."

She listened for a moment and then hung up the phone. "You'll be meeting with Betty - she's our HR person - and Mr. Shepherd. Mr. Shepherd is on his way, but there's no point in waiting. Follow me, please."

Rosalie headed toward a hallway to the left of the reception area. Bria followed the chubby brunette down the hall until she stopped in front of a glass door. It was a small boardroom with a long table taking up most of the space. A thin, gray-haired woman sat at one end.

As Rosalie ushered her into the room, the woman stood and held out her hand. "Hello, Ms. Norsen. I'm Betty."

The woman was a raccoon shifter. If her scent hadn't given her away, the dark circles under her eyes and her fidgeting would have. Bria shook her hand. "Hi, nice to meet you. Please call me Bria."

Betty indicated for her to sit down. Bria set her purse on the floor and folded her hands in her lap as Rosalie poured a glass of water from the jug on the credenza. She placed it in front of her before leaving.

"I'm so sorry that Mr. Shepherd isn't here yet. He's on his way, but I thought we could get started anyway." Betty's hands moved restlessly, toying with the pen, her water glass, and a pale yellow file folder.

"That's fine with me."

Betty yawned and then gave Bria a chastised look. "Oh, excuse me."

"Not a problem." Raccoons were nocturnal, and Bria was surprised to see one who worked a day job. Most raccoon shifters preferred the night shift.

As Betty pulled her resume from the file folder, Bria took a deep breath.

You can do this, Bria.

"WELL, BRIA," BETTY SAID FIFTEEN MINUTES LATER. "I THINK you'd be the perfect fit in our company. We've been without a receptionist for nearly a month now, and I know Rosalie, in particular, is anxious to fill the position. With your experience as a receptionist, I think you'd do well."

"Thank you," Bria said. "I enjoy being around people and promise to treat each client respectfully."

"That's what we're looking for. We have a few demanding clients who require a little extra babying when they come in. Why, we've got one client that Mr. Shepherd's shown over twenty-five houses to, and they still haven't found the one they want. It's starting to become a bit of a joke among the staff on whether they'll – oh, here's Mr. Shepherd now."

Bria stood and turned around. The smile faded from her lips, but her cat purred happily and made a soft meow of excitement.

"Bria! What – what are you doing here?" Jace stared at her in surprise.

"You're Mr. Shepherd," she said stupidly.

"Do you already know Jace?" Betty asked.

"We, uh, well…"

"We met once before through a mutual friend," Jace said.

"Then you must know how great she is," Betty said.

"Yes." Jace pulled on his tie. "Sorry, I'm late."

"No problem." Bria nearly fell back into her chair. Her palms were sweating, and dismay flooded her body as Jace took the chair next to Betty. She handed him Bria's resume, and he scanned it briefly.

There goes this job.

"We started the interview without you," Betty said. "I must confess, I think Bria would be perfect for the position."

He nodded and placed her resume on the table before staring at her. "Good. When can you start?"

Bria blinked at him in shock as Betty made a particularly large twitch and touched Jace's arm. "Do you not have any questions for her?"

"I trust your judgement." Jace glanced at his watch. "I have another appointment in fifteen minutes. Did you go over salary and benefits with Bria?"

Betty nodded, and Jace glanced at Bria. "Were they acceptable?"

"Um, yes," Bria said.

"Good. Betty, why don't you get Bria to complete the paperwork and set her up with a key card? Can you start Monday?"

"Yes, that's fine," Bria said.

"Good." He stood and gave them both a brief smile before leaving the boardroom.

Bria sank back into her chair as Betty gave her a look of bewilderment. "Well, welcome to the team, Bria."

KAT STARED AT BRIA. "I CAN'T BELIEVE IT. I MEAN – I CAN, but what the hell is happening here? This isn't a small city – how do you keep running into him like this?"

"Forget that part," Bria said miserably. "Now he's my boss. I fucked my boss, Kat!"

"Future boss," Kat corrected. "He hired you, so obviously, it wasn't a problem for him. I told you he was a nice guy. Rejected by you, and he *still* hired you."

"Why?" Bria said. "Why on earth did he hire me to work for him? He didn't even really interview me, for God's sake. He just said fine and left. More importantly – why the fuck did I say yes? Have I lost my mind, Kit Kat? I've lost my mind, haven't I?"

She dropped her head into her hands as Ronin strolled into the kitchen. He kissed Kat before studying Bria. "What's wrong?"

"She had sex with her boss."

"Nice!" Ronin gave Bria a grin of delight and held his fist out. "Welcome to the club, Stripes. We meet every other Thursday. Bring cookies."

She fist-bumped him before sighing.

Kat laughed. "She didn't know he would be her boss, Ronin. She hooked up with him at a club the other night."

"Kat!" Bria said.

"A little casual sex is nothing to be ashamed of," Ronin said cheerfully.

"I only did it because I was in heat," Bria said.

"Cat shifters and their heat cycles – it's my favourite thing about you lovely feline ladies." Ronin gave Kat a flirty grin. "Isn't yours coming up, gorgeous? I need to get some stretches in, make sure I'm limbered up and ready for action."

A small grin crossed Kat's face. "Yes, we wouldn't want you pulling a muscle like you did last time."

"It was pretty painful, but I powered through it. Such is your spell over me, Kitten."

He grabbed his lunch bag from the fridge. "I'm filling in for Garth at the lizard's warehouse tonight, so don't wait up, okay?"

She nodded, and he gave her a slow and lingering kiss. "But if you want me to wake you up when I get home, just say the word."

"Word," Kat said a bit breathlessly.

Ronin winked at her, and she smacked his butt as he left the kitchen.

Kat stood and pulled some chicken from the fridge. "Stay for dinner with me, honey."

"Thanks, I'd like that. What can I do?"

"Start making the salad," Kat said. "Also, try not to worry about working for Jace. You needed a job, and now you have one."

"Yeah, a job where I slept with my boss."

"True, but you didn't know that at the time. Jace is obviously fine with working with you, so there's nothing to worry about. Did you join the Shifters Love site yet?"

Bria grabbed the salad fixings from the fridge. "Yes. I've already had a few emails from some shifters."

"Of course you have, you're gorgeous," Kat said. "Anyone promising?"

"Not yet," Bria said. "But I don't have time to be picky."

"Yes, you do. If you don't find someone, you can use -"

"I can't use Jace for my heat cycle. He's my boss now."

"I wasn't going to suggest Jace," Kat said with a raised eyebrow. "But it's interesting that you went right to that. Are you regretting turning Jace down?"

"No," Bria lied. "But even if I was, it's too late now. I'm not fucking my boss."

"I know. But I was going to say that if you don't find someone to date in the next couple of weeks, you can use the website to find someone. There are bound to be more shifters like Jace on there."

"Yeah," Bria cleaned the mushrooms and sliced them. She wouldn't tell Kat this, but if she didn't find a boyfriend before her next heat, she really would chain herself to her headboard. She couldn't use that website to pick a shifter to sleep with. She just couldn't.

"JACE? HELLO...PAY ATTENTION TO ME."

Jace looked up from his laptop and gave Rosalie an apologetic smile. "Sorry."

"What's going on with you?" Rosalie leaned back in her chair and tapped her pen against her chin.

"Nothing."

"You've been acting weird since interviewing that Norsen woman this afternoon."

"No, I haven't."

"Yes, you have."

"No, I haven't."

Rosalie gave him an exasperated look. "Fine, you haven't. Can you pay attention to me long enough to get through this month's budget report? It's after six already, and I'd like to get out of here."

He winced. "Sorry. I know you've been working a lot of

overtime this last month. But we hired Bria, and she's starting on Monday. Once she's trained, things should get easier for you."

She nodded, and he scratched at his lean abdomen. "I really do appreciate all the extra work you've been doing, Rosalie."

"I know. I didn't mean to snap. I just have plans for tonight."

"Ooh, going on a date, Rosie-girl?"

Lincoln strolled into his office without knocking, and the scent of Rosalie's desire immediately washed over Jace. He ignored it as the lion shifter grinned at his assistant. "Who's the lucky guy?"

Her face bright red, Rosalie shook her head. "Uh, not a date. I have a dentist appointment."

"Oh. You sure know how to party on a Friday night." Lincoln dropped into the seat beside her and gave her a panty-melting grin. "I like your outfit today, Rosie."

"Th-thank you."

Jace groaned inwardly when the scent of her need increased. He knew Lincoln could smell it, too. He wanted to kick his best friend when Lincoln reached out and pulled on a lock of Rosalie's curly hair. "Thanks for getting me a coffee this morning."

"No problem." She chewed on her bottom lip and stared at Lincoln's mouth.

"Rosalie?" Jace said. There was no reply, and he repeated her name.

"Uh, yeah?" She dragged her gaze from Lincoln's mouth. "What's wrong?"

"Nothing," Jace said. "Why don't you head out? We'll finish going over the budget report Monday morning. Okay?"

"Right, okay." She stood and smoothed her hand self-consciously over her dark blue skirt. Lincoln turned and watched her leave.

"See ya later, Rosie girl."

"Bye, Lincoln."

Jace glared at Lincoln when Rosalie was gone. "Knock it off, or I'll fire you for sexually harassing your coworkers."

"What?" Lincoln gave him an innocent look. "Rosalie likes it when I flirt with her."

"It's still not appropriate, and I want you to quit doing it."

"Fine," Lincoln said. "But when Rosalie is super cranky because I'm not paying attention to her, it's your problem."

"Having sex with a fellow employee is a shit move."

"Yes, but according to our employee handbook, it's not a 'get your ass fired' move. What are you doing?" Lincoln asked when Jace started typing.

"Sending an email to Betty asking her to revise the employee handbook."

Lincoln laughed. "Forget it, Jace. I wouldn't sleep with Rosalie anyway. The woman is way too tame for me. I need someone who won't freak out when I bring out the handcuffs."

A flash of blue was in his peripheral vision, and Jace groaned. Fuck, had Rosalie heard Lincoln? He inhaled, but Rosalie's scent still lingered in his office, and he couldn't tell by the scent if she was standing in the hallway.

"Then stop flirting with her and leading her on," Jace said in a low voice. "I mean it, Lincoln."

His best friend just shrugged before scrolling through his phone. "Hey, who was that hot little number in the green skirt in the boardroom earlier?"

Jace tensed. "New receptionist."

"Excellent," Lincoln said with a grin.

"Stay away from her. I mean it."

Lincoln studied him for a moment. "What's wrong?"

"Nothing," Jace said. "Long day."

"Come out and have a drink with me."

"Thanks, but I'm heading home."

"Boring," Lincoln said. "Text me if you change your mind. I'll be at Bud's."

CHAPTER 5

"Feeling overwhelmed yet?" Rosalie asked as she and Bria walked toward the office kitchen.

"Surprisingly, no. You're good at training," Bria said.

"Good." They passed a cluster of cubicles, and Rosalie said, "Hey, Sam?"

The squirrel shifter with the sand-coloured hair popped up like a gopher from her cubicle. "Yeah?"

"Can you listen for phones? Bria and I are going to have lunch."

"You bet."

As they walked into the kitchen, Bria said, "Sam is the assistant to the agents, right?"

"Mostly right," Rosalie said. "She helps Rhonda, Derek and Warren, but I help Jace and Lincoln. Hey, Ivan. Thanks for getting Bria set up in the system so quickly."

"No problem, Rosie." Ivan held out his fist and Rosalie bumped it with her own. Rosalie was tall and curvy, over six feet tall in her short and sensible heels, but she still had to reach up. The office IT guy was a giraffe shifter and close to eight feet tall. His blond hair stuck up in short spikes, and like most giraffe shifters, his face and long, thin limbs were covered in freckles.

"If you have any computer issues, just let me know, Bria," Ivan said.

"Thank you."

"Yep. Welcome to the office." He grabbed a salad from the fridge and, ducking to get through the doorway, left the kitchen.

Bria grabbed her lunch from the fridge as Rosalie heated hers in the microwave. When they were sitting at the small table in the corner of the kitchen, Bria said, "Are you the only human in the office?"

"No, Derek is human too. Rhonda is an ostrich shifter, Warren is a wolf shifter, and Lincoln is a lion shifter. You can tell by scent what Sam and Betty are, right?"

"Yes."

Rosalie took a bite of her pasta. "It's quiet in the office today. Most of the agents are doing showings, but they have their weekly meeting tomorrow, so you'll meet everyone then."

"Sounds good," Bria said.

"You're a tiger shifter like Jace?"

"I am."

"Cool." Rosalie hesitated, and Bria gave her an encouraging look, but Rosalie took a bite of pasta instead of speaking.

"How long have you worked for Mr. Shepherd?" Bria bit into her sandwich.

"Two years," Rosalie said. "Jace is a good guy and a great boss. A little disorganized sometimes, but still great. You'll like working for him."

"Is he going to be in the office today?"

Rosalie took a sip of water. "Probably not. He had a lot of client meetings this morning and a networking event this afternoon. I doubt he'll return to the office when that's finished."

"Oh, okay." Bria took another bite of her sandwich. She wasn't disappointed that Jace wasn't in the office today. She wasn't. In fact, the less she saw of him, the better.

"Can I ask you a question?" Rosalie asked.

"Sure," Bria said.

"All right, and just let me know if I'm overstepping, okay?"

Bria nodded, and Rosalie said, "When you're at home, do you shift into your tiger form or spend most of your time in human form?"

Bria grinned, and Rosalie flushed. "I'm sorry. Is that too personal of a question?"

"No. I spend most of my time in my human form, even at home."

"Is that what most shifters do?" Rosalie asked.

"I think it depends on the shifter," Bria said. "My dad spends a lot of time in his tiger form, but my mom rarely shifts. I can't even remember the last time I saw her shift. She does shift, just not usually in front of others. We have to spend some time in our animal forms, or we get...weird."

"Do you have any siblings?"

"No. Tiger shifters aren't known for their big families. If we even want kittens, most of us only have one, maybe two, at the most. We like our space."

"What about lion shifters? Do they like to have big families?"

"That's kind of tough to say. Female lion shifters love

61

kittens and are great mothers, but male lion shifters are a little on the," she hesitated, "wild side. Not many of them want to settle down, you know?"

"Yes." Disappointment coloured Rosalie's voice. "So, male lion shifters never get married or commit to one woman?"

"Some do," Bria said. "I was dating a lion shifter for a while, and he wasn't your typical lion shifter."

"Not typical, how?"

"Well, he was ready to settle with one woman and, um, honestly? He wasn't super kinky in bed. Most lion shifters love the kinky stuff, but Raden had pretty normal tastes in bed."

"So," Rosalie poked at her pasta with a fork, "if a woman wanted to attract a lion shifter, she needs to be kinky in bed. Is that right?"

"It helps. Obviously, there are exceptions to the rule, but if he's a typical lion shifter, then yeah, it helps if you're open to trying new things in the bedroom."

"Okay."

"Is there a lion shifter you're interested in?" Bria asked.

"What? No, no, that's not it," Rosalie said. "I just – I'm curious about shifters, that's all. I've never even dated a shifter before, although I'm, you know, open to that. There aren't a lot of shifters on the online dating app I use. I think they stick mostly to the Shifters Love one, but humans aren't allowed to sign up for that site."

"I just signed up on Shifters Love," Bria said.

Rosalie grinned at her. "Been on any dates yet?"

"No, but I've had a couple of messages from a squirrel shifter and a wolf shifter."

"A squirrel shifter?" Rosalie gave her a look of surprise. "Do tiger shifters date prey animals?"

"Not usually," Bria said. "Again, there are exceptions, but if a prey shifter is looking to date a predator shifter, they usually like to be dominated. I'm not into that."

She laughed at the look on Rosalie's face. "Sorry, did I share too much?"

"No, not at all. I hope I'm not coming across as being too nosy. I'm interested in shifters and their lives, but I've never felt comfortable talking to Betty or Sam about it." She lowered her voice and glanced at the doorway of the kitchen. "They won't admit this, but neither are very fond of humans."

"I don't think you're being nosy," Bria said. "If you have any questions about shifters, just ask me, and if I have questions about humans, I'll ask you. Deal?"

"Deal," Rosalie said.

As Rosalie reached into her lunch bag for an apple, Bria finished the last of her sandwich. She'd never been friends with a human before. Willow and Ava were the first humans she'd hung out with, but she wasn't sure they were at the friend stage. But she was already fond of Rosalie and could see her becoming a friend. The woman was very sweet.

"Well, it must be my lucky day. Two gorgeous ladies in the kitchen." A deep voice purred.

The musky smell of lion filled the kitchen, and she stared at the large blond man standing in the doorway. He smiled at her as his dark green eyes dipped to her chest before back to her face. He ran a hand through his shaggy hair and strolled into the kitchen, dropping into the chair beside Rosalie with lazy grace.

"Lincoln, this is Bria, our new receptionist."

Rosalie's voice was a little breathy. Bria knew she had a thing for Lincoln even before she smelled Rosalie's arousal.

"Nice to meet you, Bria." Lincoln held out his hand, and

Bria shook it. He held onto her hand for a beat too long and she had to fight not to roll her eyes in front of him. She could already tell he was a typical lion shifter, full of swagger and bullshit.

"You're tiny for a tiger."

Bria didn't reply. After a lifetime of teasing about her small stature, she was over the remarks about her size.

"I didn't know you were coming in today, Lincoln," Rosalie said.

Lincoln gave her a flirty grin. "I was close to the office and couldn't resist popping in to say hello to my favourite girl. How's your day, Rosie-girl?"

Bria contained her urge to make a retching noise as Lincoln sat back in the chair and rested his hand on his upper thigh next to his crotch. His pants were tight, but she refused to look at the bulge in his pants like he so obviously wanted.

Beside her, Rosalie took a glance at his crotch and then flushed when Lincoln tugged playfully on a dark curl. "Your hair looks pretty today."

"Thank you. Um, my day is good. I've been training Bria."

"Good, good." Lincoln glanced at his phone. "Do you think you could do me a favour, Rosie? I have my dry cleaning here, but I need to meet a client this evening. Could you drop it off for me after work? It's in the direction of your place, right?"

"Oh, um, I was going to my mom's for dinner after work, and she lives in the opposite direction," Rosalie said.

Lincoln cocked his head at her before nodding. "Sure, okay. Thanks anyway. I just thought my favourite girl could help me out."

"You know what? I can do it," Rosalie said. "My mom won't mind if I'm a little late for dinner."

"I knew my best girl would help me out. I'll throw the clothes on your desk, okay? Oh, and can you pick up my shirts while you're there? I've got five of them waiting for pick up."

"Sure, happy to help." The scent of Rosalie's arousal increased when Lincoln leaned forward and kissed her cheek.

"Thanks, Rosie-girl. I owe you."

"No problem."

Lincoln stood. "I should get going. I have another showing in half an hour." He smiled at Bria. "Nice to meet ya, tiny tiger."

"It's Bria," she said.

"Right. Sorry. I like to give nicknames."

"I prefer to be called Bria."

He grinned at her. "Message received. Bye, Bria."

"Goodbye."

Lincoln winked at Rosalie. "See ya, Rosie-girl."

"Bye, Lincoln."

When the lion shifter was gone, Bria smiled at Rosalie. "So, you like Lincoln, huh?"

Rosalie paled and dropped her half-eaten apple on the table. "What? No, of course not. Why would you say that? I do favours for everyone in the office. It doesn't mean I like him."

"No, I – sorry, I could just smell your... when he came in, your scent changed and was... uh, never mind. I'm being stupid."

Rosalie stared at her. "What about my scent?"

"Nothing," Bria said. "Your scent was nothing."

"No, you said my scent changed. What do you mean by that?"

Cursing her stupidity, Bria lowered her voice. "When Lincoln came in, I could smell your attraction for him."

Rosalie gripped the edge of the table as her face paled even more. "What? You can what?"

"It's no big deal. Shifters are used to smelling other shifters' and humans' arousal. Half the time, we just block it out, you know?"

"Oh my God," Rosalie whispered. "So, any shifter can smell... Jace – *my boss* – smells that I..."

"Some shifters have better senses of smell than others. Tigers actually don't have that great of one, at least not compared to, like, a lion or -"

"Lion?" Rosalie went from white to green. "Lions have a great sense of smell?"

"Shit." Bria leaned forward. "Okay, yeah, lions have a good sense of smell, but it's no big deal, Rosalie. I promise you. Shifters are used to it."

"Oh. My. God. Lincoln knows. He can smell it on me, and he knows that I, that I... oh no, this can't be happening."

Rosalie lurched to her feet, and Bria stood up. "Rosalie?"

"I have to go home. I'm not feeling well. Just answer phones and ask Sam if there's something you don't know."

The curvy brunette ran out of the kitchen. Feeling sick to her stomach, Bria sank into her chair. Fuck, she'd screwed up.

JACE LOCKED HIS CAR AND WALKED TOWARD THE OFFICE. Yesterday was Bria's first day, and he hadn't purposely avoided going into the office. He was busy yesterday. Sure, he had slipped out of the networking event early and could have returned to the office, but a workout at the gym seemed smarter. He'd been slacking on his workouts lately.

Yeah, that's it. So, why are you sweating through your dress shirt at the thought of seeing Bria again?

He ignored his inner voice. He would keep things professional with Bria. Maybe a big part of him regretted his decision to hire her, but it was too late now. If she occasionally smelled his need for her, so what? It's not like it would be a surprise to her. They'd had sex, for God's sake.

That thought brought on an image of Bria naked and moaning. Her legs spread wide as he licked and sucked her clit. God, her little pussy was the sweetest he'd ever tasted. His cock was hardening in his pants, and he groaned inwardly. What the hell was he doing? Thinking about Bria naked was the last thing he should be doing.

He thought about the boring network event, the mountain of paperwork he never seemed to get to, and the pain-in-his-ass client he was meeting with this afternoon. By the time he'd crossed the parking lot to the office, his half-a-woody was gone. He pulled open the door and stepped into reception.

"Good morning, Bria."

"Hello, Mr. Shepherd."

He stopped at the desk and smiled at her. "You can call me Jace."

"Right, okay."

"How was your first day?"

"Uh, good." She chewed on her bottom lip, and he could smell the faint scent of her anxiety.

Shit. He was making her nervous. "Good. Where's Rosalie?"

"She's, uh, at her desk. Listen, Jace, I screwed up yesterday. I told Rosalie that -"

"Jace?"

Rosalie walked out of the hallway and into reception.

His smile of greeting died on his lips as he stared at his assistant. Her curly dark hair was piled on top of her head in an untidy bun, and she wasn't wearing makeup. Her shirt was badly wrinkled, as if she'd just grabbed it from the laundry, and cat hair covered her dark pants.

"Rosalie? What's wrong?"

"Your two o'clock appointment cancelled. Rhonda wants to know if you can meet with her at ten to go over her commission for the Warrant house sale, and," she plucked an envelope from the pile of folders in her arms and handed it to him, "this is for you."

He studied his name written on the front in Rosalie's neat handwriting. "What is it?"

She didn't reply. She looked tired, and the skin under her eyes was puffy as if she'd spent the night crying. When she tried to walk away, he touched her arm. "Rosalie, wait."

She turned and stared at him. "What is it?"

"Tell me what's wrong."

"Nothing's wrong."

"What's in the envelope?" Why did he have such a bad feeling in the pit of his stomach? He glanced briefly at Bria. She looked like she was going to vomit as she stared at Rosalie.

Rosalie glanced at Bria before shrugging. "Whatever. I might as well tell you. It's my letter of resignation. I'm quitting."

"What?" Panic flooded through him, and he squeezed the envelope in one fist. "Rosie, you can't quit."

"I can, and I am."

"No! Whatever's wrong, we'll fix it. Okay? Just tell me what's wrong and -"

"Nothing's wrong." Her voice broke, and he watched as tears dripped down her face. She wiped angrily at them. "I just – I can't work here anymore."

"Of course you can," he said. "I can fix whatever's wrong. I swear."

"No, you can't!"

He stepped back. Rosalie's usual low, calm voice was shrill with anxiety, and he didn't think he'd ever seen her on the verge of losing her shit like this.

"Rosie, please, let's just talk."

"I don't want to."

"Please. You owe me at least that."

She wiped at the tears still flowing down her cheeks "Fine. Let's talk."

"In my office," he said. "I'm just going to get a coffee and meet you there. Okay? Do you want a coffee?"

"No, I don't want a coffee." She turned and stalked out of reception.

"Fuck," Jace muttered. He stared at the envelope in his hand. "What the fuck is happening?"

"Jace?" Bria's soft voice made him twitch. He'd forgotten she was there.

"What is it?"

"This is my fault."

He stared at her. "How?"

"Yesterday, we were having lunch, and Lincoln came into the kitchen. I could smell Rosalie's need for him, and when he was gone, I..."

"You what?"

"I didn't know that she didn't know shifters could smell a person's arousal," Bria said in a tiny voice. "When she found out, she... she kind of lost it and went home."

"Oh shit," he said.

"I'm so sorry. I feel unbelievably stupid. Rosalie was upset that you knew she liked Lincoln and that he knew and -"

"Yeah, okay." He started to leave, and Bria stood up hurriedly.

"Jace, wait! Let me talk to her, please?"

"I think you've done enough."

She flinched, and he muttered a curse under his breath. "Sorry. That wasn't fair. I didn't mean it. I just... I'm fucked if Rosalie quits."

"Let me talk to her. I'll fix this. I promise."

He studied her for a moment. "Okay. Go talk to Rosalie."

"What about phones?"

"I'll answer them." He moved behind the desk.

Bria gave him a look of surprise. "You'll answer them?"

"It's my company. Why wouldn't I?"

"Right."

"Go on. Talk to Rosalie and convince her not to quit."

"I will," Bria said.

She hurried away, and Jace sunk into the reception chair. Christ, what a shit show today was turning out to be.

"NOTHING YOU CAN SAY WILL CONVINCE ME NOT TO QUIT, Jace." Rosalie was staring out the window with her back to the door. "Just be happy that I gave you two weeks' notice."

"Rosalie?" Bria said tentatively

She swung around. "What are you doing in here?"

"I asked Jace if I could talk to you." She shut the door and sat in the chair across from Jace's desk. "Will you sit and talk with me?"

Rosalie stared out the window again before turning and dropping into Jace's chair. "Yeah, okay."

"I'm so sorry about yesterday. I feel awful for upsetting you. I shouldn't have said what I did. It's none of my business who you like."

"I don't care if you know I like him, okay? Don't take this the wrong way, but you're just the receptionist. I don't give a shit if you can smell my – my," her face flushed, "arousal for Lincoln."

She pounded her fist on Jace's desk. "Do you know I was going to talk to Jace about getting my real estate license next year?"

"That's great," Bria said.

Rosalie laughed bitterly. "Except I just found out that he knows I'm nothing more than a horny human who can barely think straight when his goddamn best friend walks into the office."

"He doesn't think that."

"You don't even know him," Rosalie said. "I have spent the last two years trying to prove to him and everyone else in this office that I would make an excellent agent. It was for nothing because they all know I – I want to screw Lincoln! That's not exactly professional work behaviour."

Bria grabbed a tissue from the corner of Jace's desk and handed it to her. "Rosalie, I know you don't want to believe this, but it is no big deal to shifters. We smell all sorts of things every single day about other shifters and humans, and we just learn to ignore it."

Rosalie wiped her face, and Bria leaned forward. "Sam has a crush on someone in the office."

"What? She does?"

"Yes. I smelled it this morning when Sam saw him, and she knows that I know, and all the other shifters know, too. Do they treat her differently?"

Rosalie shook her head. "No. I mean, I don't think they do."

"They don't, and they won't. Smelling arousal is no different to us than smelling hunger or anxiety. I promise you, Jace does not think differently of you because he knows you like Lincoln. Just like he doesn't think differently of Sam."

"Okay, maybe he doesn't. But what about Lincoln?" Rosalie's cheeks flushed bright red. "All this time, whenever he's around me, he smells... God, I want to die of embarrassment. I can't work with him anymore."

"I know it's weird, and I'm sorry, but quitting isn't the answer. Shifters are everywhere in this damn city. Finding a job where there aren't any won't be easy. What if, at your new job, you develop a crush on one of your coworkers? Are you going to quit that one too?"

"I won't develop a crush on someone else."

"Fair enough. Still, I know I just started here, but it's obvious that you run this place. Jace is freaking out. Hell, I can smell his anxiety from here. If you quit and start over, it'll take you much longer to get your license, right? Not to mention, Jace will probably stalk you and beg you to come back for the next six months."

A small smile crossed Rosalie's face. "He would be up shit creek without me."

Bria reached across the desk and squeezed her hand. "He would be."

Rosalie sighed. "I don't think I can face Lincoln. I can't help my reaction when I'm around him, Bria. I try, but..."

"Lincoln doesn't need to know that you know he can smell your attraction to him," Bria said.

"I know he's taking advantage of me with all the personal shit he gets me to do for him," Rosalie said abruptly. "I've seen the women he dates, and I'm not his type."

"Lion shifters don't have a type. They love women. All women. Trust me on this."

"They do have a type. Maybe not physically, but they like women who are wild and kinky in bed and," a bitter laugh escaped from Rosalie's throat, "that's not me. I've slept with one guy – a human – and we didn't exactly set the bed on fire together. Half the time, he couldn't even make me – fuck, sorry. I'm sharing way too much."

"That's okay. I don't mind," Bria said.

"I know I'm wasting my time with him, I do, but you can't help who you love, right? I know he likes women who know what they're doing in bed and are up to trying crazy things. I want to be that type of woman."

"Or," Bria said, "maybe it's none of that, and he doesn't want to date a coworker."

"There's no policy against dating a coworker," Rosalie said. "Trust me, if I believed he wasn't asking me out because I was a coworker, I would have quit long ago. I overheard him just the other day telling Jace he wouldn't date me because I'm not kinky enough for him."

Another bitter laugh. "I wanted to argue, wanted to get Lincoln alone and tell him that I was plenty kinky only... I'm not. He mentioned handcuffs to Jace, and I'm surprised he didn't see the glow of my face in the hallway. I want to try new things in bed, I do, but not with someone who is already expecting it from me. I'd look like an idiot."

Bria shrugged. "Learning something new doesn't make you an idiot."

"Yeah, I guess. I just – it doesn't matter because Lincoln wants someone who is already kinky in bed, not someone who's willing to learn to be kinky."

"I think," Bria hesitated and then decided to forge ahead, "the bigger concern is that lion shifters aren't really into settling down."

"Some of them are. You said your ex was ready."

"Yes, but Lincoln seems like a typical lion shifter to me. They start great in a relationship when it's new, and the sex is hot and heavy, but they get bored easily."

"Maybe a girl just needs to be open to lots of sex and different, like, positions and stuff," Rosalie said.

Bria hid her frustration. She'd already decided that Rosalie was way too good for Lincoln and hated the idea of the arrogant breaking the sweet human's heart. "It really has nothing to do with their partner, you know? A woman could have sex with them seven times a day, and they'd still get bored and want to move on. They can't help it. It's their nature."

"But not all of them," Rosalie said stubbornly.

"No, not all of them." Bria knew when to admit defeat, and like it or not, Rosalie was in love with Lincoln.

"Did you – I mean, in the kitchen yesterday did you smell anything on Lincoln? Was he, uh, turned on by me even a little?"

"Um..."

"Shit. Forget I asked that. I know he isn't attracted to me."

"I'm sorry. But just because I didn't smell anything yesterday doesn't mean he isn't," Bria said.

"Yeah, maybe."

"Please don't quit, Rosalie."

Rosalie rubbed at her forehead. "I'm not going to quit. I love working for Jace, and just thinking about leaving makes me sick to my stomach."

Bria grabbed her hand again. "I'm really glad you aren't quitting, and not just because Jace will fire me if you quit, and I'll be broke and have to live with my parents like a loser."

Rosalie smiled a little. "Now, I need to apologize to my boss and ask for my job back."

"You won't have to ask. Jace doesn't want you to leave. I'll go back to reception and tell him to come see you, okay?"

"Okay. Thanks, Bria."

"I'm sorry again, Rosalie. I hope we can still be friends."

"We are. None of this is your fault. I should have done some research on shifters and figured it out for my damn self," Rosalie said.

Bria stood and walked to the door before opening it. "I'll send Jace in right away."

"Thanks."

"ROSALIE?" JACE STEPPED INTO HIS OFFICE AND CLOSED THE door. Rosalie was sitting in the chair across from his desk, and he sat in the chair beside her. God, he hoped she wasn't still crying. "Rosie? You okay?"

She gave him a faint smile. "Yes. Very embarrassed."

"Don't be. Shifters don't -"

"Yeah, Bria told me. Shifters don't care when they can smell a human's arousal." Her face was beet red, and she looked like she would cry again.

"I'm attracted to Bria," he blurted.

She gave him a startled look. "What?"

"I'm attracted to Bria, which means that when I'm around her, she and any other shifter within twenty feet can smell that I'm attracted to her. You're not the only one in the office this kind of shit happens to."

"Why did you hire her if you're attracted to her?" She asked.

"Because it's like Bria said, it isn't a big deal."

Did he sound sincere? God, he hoped so. He was only partially lying to Rosalie. Normally, it wasn't a big deal for a shifter to know you found them attractive, even if they were your receptionist.

Unless you'd seen said receptionist naked, tasted the sweetness of her mouth, had your dick buried deep in her very wet, very tight pussy and wanted desperately to be back in her very wet, very tight pussy.

"Jace?"

"Sorry, what?"

"I asked if I could have my job back. I don't want to quit. I was just upset and -"

"Rosie, you don't have to ask for your job back. You know the office would collapse in on itself like a dying star if you left."

Her laugh sent relief coursing through him. "Yeah, it really would."

He hesitated and said, "I can set Lincoln up with a home office. Ask him not to come into the office unless there are meetings or -"

"No. That's not fair to him, and besides, he doesn't know that I know... I don't want things to get any weirder than they already are, okay? I know he's your best friend, but please don't tell him that I know he can smell my attraction to him."

"I won't. I promise."

"Thanks." She stood and gave him another faint smile. "I'd better get back to work. Sorry for all the drama this morning."

"It's fine."

"Bria's doing really well. I know it's only her second day, but she's smart and picks things up quickly."

"Good, I'm glad."

He waited until Rosalie left his office before moving to his chair and sinking into it. He stared out the window. Bria was smart and doing a good job…it wasn't a mistake to hire her.

No, not at all. Every boss should hire someone they've seen naked. It's a brilliant idea.

He groaned and quickly opened his email. He needed to stop thinking about a naked Bria.

CHAPTER 6

"Oh crap, did I forget to tell you Fridays were casual?" Rosalie grabbed a mug from the cupboard and set it next to Bria's.

"No." Bria poured coffee into both mugs before setting the pot back. She smoothed her dress self-consciously as she studied Rosalie's t-shirt and jeans. "You told me."

"Oh." Rosalie added cream to her coffee before pouring some into Bria's.

It was early Friday morning, and no one else was in the office yet, but Bria still lowered her voice. "I have a date tonight after work."

"Nice," Rosalie said. "With who?"

"A wolf shifter from the Shifter's Love app. We've been texting back and forth for a few days now, and he hasn't once misspelled 'your' or asked for a nude or sent me a dick pic, so I'm meeting him at Bud's."

"What's Bud's?" Rosalie asked.

"It's a shifters-only bar. Well, it's supposed to be shifters-only, but I know the new owner, and he's fine with humans coming to the bar. He doesn't advertise it because he knows that a lot of the shifters like that it's just shifters. But Porter – the owner - is mated to a human."

"Oh. So, you're meeting him for dinner and drinks?"

"I am."

"Well, you look gorgeous, and he won't be able to resist you."

JACE STOOD IN THE HALLWAY OUTSIDE OF THE KITCHEN WITH his hands clenched into tight fists. His tiger was growling and snarling, and he tried to calm it as he listened to Bria tell Rosalie what Bud's Bar was.

She's ours! His tiger growled. *She belongs to us, not some stupid wolf shifter.*

Knock it off, you idiot! He snapped at his tiger. *She's not ours, and I'm not interested in anything more than sex. Stop it with the 'she belongs to us' shit. I'm not in the fucking mood.*

"Is there a reason you're standing in the hallway looking like your head is about to explode?" He was knocked into the wall when Lincoln clapped him on the back. "Oh, sorry, buddy. Sometimes, I don't know my own strength."

"Shut up, Lincoln," Jace said.

He followed the lion shifter into the kitchen, nearly running into his back when he stopped abruptly.

"Tiny ti – Bria, you're looking lovely today."

"Thanks, Lincoln."

Jace stepped around Lincoln and forced a smile at Bria and Rosalie. "Morning, ladies."

"Morning," Bria said.

Rosalie was staring into her mug of coffee, and she visibly twitched when Lincoln dropped his arm around her shoulders. "Hey, Rosie-girl. I like your T-shirt."

"Thank you," she said. "I better get to work. Busy day."

She ducked out from under Lincoln's arm and hurried out of the kitchen. Lincoln frowned and sniffed the air as he studied Rosalie's retreating form. When she was gone, he poured himself a coffee.

Jace watched as Bria grabbed her lunch bag from the counter and bent to stuff it into the fridge. God, she looked good. Her dark hair was braided, and her dress matched her eyes in colour. It clung to her firm ass, and he glared at Lincoln when he caught the lion shifter staring.

Lincoln shrugged and added sugar to his coffee as he continued to stare at Bria's ass. She straightened and shut the fridge door. "Well, I should get to reception."

"Right. Hey, uh, any plans for the weekend?" Jace asked.

"I'm going to Kat's place on Sunday. How about you?"

"Not too much this weekend. Some work. What about tonight? Plans for tonight?"

Fuck, could he sound any more pathetic?

Bria flushed and picked up her coffee mug from the counter. "I do have plans, yeah. Um, dinner with a friend."

"Good. Anyone I know?"

His tiger made a low growl of anger at his stupidity. He wanted to argue, but he *was* sounding like a fucking idiot.

"No," Bria said. "Uh, no, I don't think so."

"Right. Okay, well, bye."

"Bye." She gave him an uncertain look and left the kitchen.

He ignored his urge to bash his forehead against the wall to see if it knocked some fucking sense into him and grabbed a mug from the cupboard.

Lincoln was leaning against the counter and staring at him.

"What?" Jace poured a cup of coffee.

"That was a train wreck, dude. Like, I watched that train coming down the tracks and then just...boom." Lincoln shook his head. "You used to have game with the ladies. What the fuck happened?"

"I don't know what you're talking about. I was just making small talk with an employee."

"Sure. Hey, did Rosalie seem different to you?"

"No."

Lincoln ran a hand through his shaggy hair. "Really? You don't think she's been a bit standoffish this week?"

"No."

"All right. See you in the meeting at ten."

"What are you doing tonight?"

"If I'm lucky, some hot little shifter who likes taking it up the ass."

Jace scowled at him. "Seriously, Lincoln?"

"What? You asked, I answered. Why? You wanna do something?"

"I don't know. I don't have any plans. I was thinking of maybe going to Bud's and having dinner and a few drinks."

"Oh, fuck yes," Lincoln said. "I'm in."

"Good. I'll meet you there after work."

"Fuckin' A, my friend. Fuckin' A."

Jace grabbed an apple from the fruit bowl and walked to his office. He shut the door and collapsed into the chair behind his desk. He tossed the apple on his desk and stared at his monitor. His tiger was making low growls of happiness, but his stomach was rolling with nausea.

What the fuck was he doing?

Going to Bud's tonight was absolutely the wrong thing to do. So, why was he doing it? Bria wasn't his, no matter what his tiger tried to say. Besides, he didn't want Bria to be his.

He didn't – no, he couldn't – be in a relationship again, not after what happened to his brother.

Your brother? What about you? It runs in the family, you know. It's hereditary, and if you think it was just your brother who was unlucky, you're fooling yourself. You remember what it was like when you and Tabitha broke up, don't you? You remember how it felt. How you felt. How scared your parents were. They were sure you would end up like Jonah. They were right to be afraid. Weren't they?

He stood up, almost knocking his chair over, and strode jerkily to the window. His back was sweating, and he could feel the heat rising up his neck. The nausea in his stomach surged upward, and he swallowed down bile. It was almost five years since his brother had...he swallowed more bile. Nearly five years, and he still wanted to throw up whenever he thought about it.

He took a deep breath and leaned his forehead against the window. He wasn't going to Bud's tonight because of Bria. He was going to spend time with his friend. Bud's would be crowded on a Friday night, and he probably wouldn't even see Bria.

"GOD, YOU ARE THE TINIEST TIGER I'VE EVER MET."

Bria forced a smile. Okay, so it was the first time Patrick, the wolf shifter, lost points with her. Of course, it was only ten minutes into their date.

"How tall are you?"

"I'm 5'3"."

"Shit." Patrick whistled under his breath. "When you shift, are you normal size?"

She frowned at him. "Why does it matter?"

"It doesn't. I was just curious." Patrick took a swallow of beer. "It's busy in here."

Bria sipped at her wine. "Bud's has gotten busier the last few months."

"Yeah, because that new owner is a human-loving idiot. He's a disgrace to wolf shifters. It doesn't even bother him that humans are stinkin' the joint up. I guarantee you, poor old Bud is rolling in his grave right now."

"Bud let humans in here." Bria could feel her temper rising, and she tamped it down with effort.

"He didn't," Patrick said. "Trust me. I knew Bud and -"

"Bria?"

Feeling a perverse sense of glee, she stood and hugged Porter. He grunted in surprise but returned her hug. "Hey, I just wanted to stop and say hi."

"Hi." She smiled at Patrick. "Patrick, this is Porter, the new owner of the bar and a good friend of mine. Porter, this is Patrick."

"Nice to meet you." Porter held out his hand, and Patrick stood and shook his hand.

"Uh, good to meet you too. I like what you've done with the place."

"Thanks, it's getting there. Bria, good to see you again. I'll send Tori over in five minutes to get your food order, okay?"

"Sounds good. Thanks, Porter."

Porter kissed her cheek before returning to the bar. Bria sat down and smiled stiffly at Patrick. He gave her a sheepish look.

"So, uh, you know the new owner."

"I do."

"Sorry, Bria. I tend to run off at the mouth sometimes. Can we start over?"

Bria studied him silently, and he gave her a small smile. "Just one more chance?"

"Sure," she said.

"Great. So, what do you like to do in your spare time?"

"Jace! Hey, Jace!"

Jace locked his car and turned around. Rhonda, Sam, Derek, and Rosalie were walking across Bud's parking lot.

"Hey, what are you guys doing here?"

Sam gave him a surprised look. "Lincoln invited us. He said you wanted to go for some food and drinks. Was he wrong?"

"No," Jace said. "I'm glad you came."

He trailed after them as they walked toward the entrance. Rosalie fell into step beside him. "Lincoln didn't tell you he was inviting us, did he?"

"No, but it's fine. The more the merrier. Although," he lowered his voice, "I'm surprised you decided to come."

She shrugged. "What can I say? I'm addicted to that stupid lion shifter."

He put his arm around her and gave her a quick, rough squeeze. "He's a fool, Rosie."

"Maybe. Is it really okay for Derek and me to go in here? Bria told me a little bit about Bud's this morning. It's technically a shifters-only bar, right?"

"Yes, but sometimes humans go in with shifter friends. You'll be fine."

Ahead of them, Sam smiled up at Derek. "You should maybe take my hand, Derek. This is a shifters-only bar, but humans are allowed in if they're with a shifter."

"Sure." Derek took her hand, and the scent of Sam's

excitement and need washed over Jace. God, he hoped Derek wasn't about to get some squirrel shifter sex tonight. The last thing he needed was two of his employees having sex.

But it's okay for you to have sex with Bria?

Had. I had sex with her. Before she worked for me.

"Jace?" Rosalie nudged him with her elbow before whispering, "Derek's the one that Sam has a crush on, isn't it?"

He nodded, and Rosalie said, "I'm a little surprised. I thought Sam didn't care much for humans."

He was saved from answering by the loud swell of voices as Rhonda opened the door to Bud's.

The bouncer was standing near the door, and he sniffed at them as they walked past. His forehead wrinkled as Lincoln joined them.

"Rosie-girl! You made it!" He put his arm around her shoulders and pulled her against his side. "Stick with me, sweetheart. Humans aren't always welcome here. Isn't that right, Judd?"

The bear shifter just shrugged. "It ain't a problem."

Lincoln stroked Rosalie's arm, and Jace could immediately smell her desire. He blocked it out and scanned the bar as they followed Sam, Rhonda and Derek to a table. As he suspected, the bar was busy, but he had no problem spotting Bria. She was sitting in a booth against the far wall, and his tiger snarled. The wolf shifter had reached across the table and was holding her hand.

It was a little alarming how quickly his tiger was losing his shit. He sat beside Rosalie and tried to soothe his tiger, inwardly groaning when Rhonda said, "Hey, Bria's here!"

She leaned across the table and shouted, "Bria! Hi!"

He glanced up just in time to see Bria snatching her hand from the wolf shifter's. She said something to him, and he studied their table before nodding. She slid out of the booth and walked to their table.

"Hey, Bria," Rhonda said. "Why don't you and your friend join us for drinks?"

"Oh, um...."

"Rhonda," Sam said, "they're on a date. Isn't that right Bria?"

Bria gave him a quick look. "Well, I mean, sort of..."

"Either you are, or you aren't," Rhonda said with a laugh.

Bria peeked at him again. "We are."

"Well, have fun, tiny tiger," Lincoln drawled. He still had his arm around Rosalie's shoulders, and Jace hated how happy and flushed she looked. He loved his best friend, but Rosalie deserved better. Lincoln would never be the man she wanted him to be.

"Thanks," Bria said. "I'll see you guys on Monday."

She left, and Jace smiled at the rabbit shifter, who bounced up to the table. "Hey, handsome. I'm Tori, and I'll be your waitress tonight. You guys need anything," she traced one finger down his biceps, "just holler, and I'll hop on over What would you like to drink?"

"Just a beer," Jace said.

"You bet, hon."

"Holy crap!" Derek's mouth dropped open, and he stared at the bar. "What the hell kind of shifter is that?"

They all turned and stared at the bar. Jace studied the giant shifter standing behind the bar. He was massive, the glass of beer in his hand looked more like a shot glass, and he had short blond hair and broad features that practically screamed, 'I like to fight.' Tattoos covered his arms, and he somehow looked both bored and pissed off simultaneously.

"That's Hudson,' Tori said. "He's, like, a polar bear shifter and so grumpy. But he's, like, a really good bartender, so Porter won't fire him."

"Wow," Sam said. "Why is he working here? Polar bears hate being around crowds."

Tori just shrugged. "Even a polar bear's gotta make money, right?" She winked at Lincoln. "Hey, Lincoln. You're looking good tonight."

Lincoln dropped his arm from Rosie's shoulders." Hey, sweet bunny buns. How's my favourite server?"

"Can't complain," she said. "You want your usual?"

"Yeah." His gaze drifted over the rabbit shifter's small but perky tits, and Jace could almost see Rosie's good mood deflating.

As Tori took everyone else's order, Jace stole another glance at Bria. The wolf shifter was holding her hand again. His tiger roared and tried to surge forward. Sweating, he pushed it back and tore his gaze from Bria and her date.

Fuck, he was in trouble.

ROSALIE STUDIED HERSELF IN THE BATHROOM MIRROR. HER cheeks were too red, and it was obvious that she was close to tears.

Get it together, Rosie!

She was surprised Lincoln had paid so much attention to her when she first arrived. Surprised but also flattered and a little turned on and stupidly happy. The first ten minutes, she had even let herself fall into a little fantasy that she and Lincoln were dating. He'd made it easy to slip into fantasy, what with his arm around her shoulders and how he had whispered to her that she looked pretty tonight.

It hadn't lasted long. There were a lot of shifters at the bar.

A lot of very pretty female shifters.

Twenty minutes after they'd sat down, Lincoln was gone. Saying he spotted a friend, he'd left their table and hadn't returned. She'd seen him over the next hour or so, talking and chatting with other male shifters and flirting with every female shifter that drifted into his view. She wasn't surprised that Lincoln would ignore her and flirt with every woman at the bar. So why did it hurt so much?

It's because you're a human. Lincoln isn't ever going to date you, Rosie. Get it through your head!

"No, it's because you're not kinky enough in bed," she muttered to her reflection. "Change that, and you have a chance. You're too shy and too timid, Rosalie. Be different!"

Yes, be different. Simple. Easy. No problem.

Suddenly exhausted, she grabbed her purse from the counter before leaving the bathroom. She didn't want to watch Lincoln flirt anymore. She opened her bag as she walked down the hallway and started rummaging for her keys. She wanted to go home, get into her pajamas, and curl up on the couch with Mr. Pibbles and not think about –

She ran head-first into a solid wall of muscle. There was a loud grunt above her, and she staggered back. She stared at Bria's wolf shifter date. "I'm so sorry."

He sniffed at her before sneering, "Watch where you're going, human."

"I'm sorry," she repeated as she scooted around him.

"You know," the shifter grabbed her arm, and she squeaked in alarm when he turned her to face him, "Bud's Bar is a shifters only bar."

"Th-that's not true," she said. "My friends said humans could come in here."

"Your friends gave you bad advice." The man took a step closer. "You should leave before something bad happens to you. Pretty little thing like you – who knows what shifters would use you for."

Her heart hammering in her chest and her mouth dry, she yanked her arm free and took a stumbling step backward. The man grinned at her, and she stared in sudden terror at the fangs protruding from his mouth. She took another step back and ran into a second unforgiving wall of hard flesh and muscle. Her terror was like a living, breathing thing inside of her as she whipped around and stared at the giant standing behind her. It was the bartender named Hudson, the one that Tori said was a polar bear shifter, and she peered up at him as the wolf shifter behind her made a low growl.

"You okay?" The bartender rumbled. His voice was deep. She could almost feel it vibrating out from his chest like thunder.

"Help me," she whispered.

He frowned and studied the shifter behind her. She moved closer to Hudson, crowding against his big body before staring at the wolf shifter.

"Get the fuck out of here," Hudson said to the shifter.

The shifter glared at him. "What did you say?"

"Leave the bar now."

"You can't kick me out. I didn't do anything."

"I heard what you said to her," Hudson said.

"She's a fucking human. Who the fuck cares what I said to her?" the wolf shifter said.

"I care. Leave the bar now."

"She's the one who should leave. This is a fucking shifters bar."

"Last chance," Hudson said.

The wolf shifter snarled. His body swelled, and dark fur

sprouted on his face. Rosalie moaned and pressed herself against Hudson. She wrapped her arms around his waist and stared disbelievingly at the polar bear shifter when he laughed.

"You think you can take me on, wolf shifter? I'll tear you to pieces and eat your guts for my breakfast."

The wolf shifter growled as his skin rippled.

"Go on," Hudson said. "Shift. I haven't been challenged in a long time and miss the taste of blood."

The bear shifter hadn't moved a muscle, but the wolf shifter suddenly stepped backward. He stared uncertainly at Hudson and then at Rosalie as the fur faded on his face.

"Pity," Hudson said, "I hate cowards."

The shifter flushed dully but didn't say anything.

"Get out," Hudson said.

The wolf shifter made a soft growl and pushed past them. When he was gone, Rosalie let her breath out and gave Hudson a shaky smile. "Thank you. Thank you so much."

The bear shifter looked decidedly uncomfortable. With embarrassment, Rosalie realized that she'd wrapped her arms around his waist and was clinging to the giant shifter like a praying mantis.

"Oh God, I'm sorry." She released him and stumbled back.

"I don't like to be touched." The shifter's voice was terse.

Her face flamed red. "I'm so sorry. I don't normally grab onto strangers – I'm sorry. I was scared."

God, she sounded like a complete idiot.

"Go back to your shifter friends," he said.

"Okay. Um, thank you again." She studied his face for a moment. He wasn't exactly handsome. His features were a little too craggy and rough to be considered handsome. But something was appealing about him. Maybe it was his size.

She was over six feet in her heels, and few men made her feel small.

She felt small next to him. Small and delicate.

Her gaze drifted to his chest. He was wearing a t-shirt with the words "Bud's Bar" printed on it. His shirt was too small, the letters distorted by the sheer width of his chest. One massive hand came up and scratched at his stubble covered throat. His hand was twice the size of hers. If they put their hands together, palm-to-palm, she wasn't sure her fingers would even go past his palm to his fingers.

Had she ever seen anyone as big as this man? She didn't think so. She knew Ivan was taller, but the giraffe shifter was also thin and spindly. A strong wind would blow him over. The giant standing before her would be as unmoving as a boulder.

Her gaze dropped to his flat abdomen. The too-small t-shirt left nothing to the imagination. Every muscle in his abdomen was clearly defined against the white fabric and looked as hard as granite. She wanted to touch them to see. Instead, she clenched her hand into a fist as she stared at his belt and then -

"Lady, go back to your friends." His voice was impatient.

She snapped her gaze back to his face. She'd been three seconds away from ogling his crotch like a damn pervert. What the hell was wrong with her?

"Yes, of course. I'm sorry. Thank you."

Annoyance was written into the lines of his face. He made a 'go on' gesture with his hand, and she turned, almost running out of the hallway and back into the bar. She would tell Jace and the others that she had a headache and go home. As she weaved past shifters, trying to ignore how they sniffed at her, she realized the wolf shifter still sat with Bria.

She hesitated only a moment before marching over to

their booth. The wolf shifter gave her a startled look before his mouth turned into a hard line.

"Bria, I need to talk to you privately," Rosalie said.

"Sure," Bria said. "Patrick, can you excuse me just for a minute?"

"We're on a date," he said. "Can't you talk to your little work friend later? It's kind of rude to leave."

Rosalie's fear of the wolf shifter turned to anger. "Fine, I'll tell her right here. Bria, this asshole you're on a date with threatened me in the hallway outside the bathroom."

"What?" Bria stared at Patrick. "You threatened her?"

"Of course I didn't. Why would I do that?" he said.

"Because you don't like humans," Rosalie said. "He threatened me and grabbed my arm. Said I should be careful because I was a human, and who knew what shifters would do to me in a place like this."

"You dick," Bria said to Patrick.

"She's lying," Patrick said. "You're seriously going to believe this bitch human over me? What fucking kind of shifter are you?"

"Fuck you." Bria gave him a scornful look and slid out of the booth. Before she could stand, Patrick grabbed her forearm and squeezed.

"Don't you walk away from me. I've paid for your drinks and goddamn dinner, and you owe me."

Rosalie stepped back when Bria's eyes went from blue to golden yellow. Her pupils had narrowed into slits, and when she grinned at the wolf shifter, Rosalie could see the way her eye-teeth had lengthened into fangs.

"Let go of me, Patrick," she growled.

The wolf shifter bared his fangs at her as a dark beard grew on his face. "You owe me, you little bitch and I -"

"Take your hand off of her."

The voice was a low, angry growl next to her. Despite the way it was oddly familiar, the sheer rage in it still frightened her badly. Rosalie stumbled away from the sound and straight into the big, broad body of Hudson.

She tore her gaze from Hudson and looked toward that familiar voice, gasping when she realized it was Jace who had spoken. She stared at him as he took another step toward the booth. She'd never seen Jace like this. His eyes were bright green, his pupils dark slits, and his upper body looked bigger, almost distorted somehow.

He was Jace.

But not Jace.

The Jace/not Jace growled, a sound of pure anger that sent fear rocketing through her. Without a single ounce of shame, she flung her arms around the polar bear shifter's waist again and clung to him like a frightened kitten.

"I told you to leave." Hudson's voice reverberated above her.

The wolf shifter ignored Hudson. He stared unblinkingly at Jace as the tiger shifter stepped closer. "Take your hand off of her. I won't ask again."

"And if I don't?" Patrick said.

Jace bared his fangs at him. "I'll kill you, wolf shifter."

Judd joined them. "What's the fucking problem here?"

"No problem," Jace said. "This asshole was just leaving."

The wolf shifter studied him for a moment before releasing Bria's arm. She slid out of the booth, and Jace immediately pulled her into his embrace. She didn't object, letting him slide his arm around her waist in a possessive grip.

"Leave," Hudson said.

"Yeah, I'm leaving," Patrick snarled. He slid out of the

booth, and Rosalie made a low moan of fright when his hot gaze fell on her. "Fucking human bitch."

He stepped toward her, and the heavy arm of the polar bear shifter circled her waist. Hudson pulled her up tight against his body, a low growl erupting from his chest.

"Buddy, you are getting on my last fucking nerve," Judd said. "Get the fuck out now, or I swear to God, I'll fucking ban your ass from this place for life."

The wolf shifter snarled at him, and Judd growled, his big body swelling.

"You want to fucking do this?" Judd said. "You think you can beat me?" His body swelled even more, and Patrick gave him an uncertain look before pushing past him.

"Fuck you, and fuck this place."

He stalked toward the door, Judd following closely behind him.

Feeling slightly shaky, Rosalie leaned against Hudson's hard warmth and smiled up at him. "Thank you."

"You're touching me again," he said gruffly.

The polar bear made a valid point, but she wasn't going anywhere even if she did let go. Hudson's arm was still around her, his hand holding her against him like she belonged to him.

"Lady, you're touching me," he repeated.

She stared at his big hand cupping her hip for a second before saying, "Um, you're touching me too."

His hand tightened almost painfully before he muttered something she couldn't hear and released her. He pulled free of her grip and stepped back so fast she would have fallen if Jace hadn't caught her by the upper arm.

"You okay, Rosie?"

"Yes, thank you." She watched the polar bear shifter retreat to the bar before turning around. "Are you okay?"

Jace still had his arm around Bria's waist, but when Rosalie's gaze lingered on his arm, he dropped it and stepped away from Bria.

"Fine. Sorry, I didn't mean to frighten you."

"That's okay. I just - sometimes I forget that you're a shifter." She gave him a faint smile. "Bria, are you all right?"

"Don't worry about me." Bria took Rosalie's hand and squeezed it. "Did that asshole hurt you?"

"No, the bartender helped me in the hallway, so, um, I was fine." Her gaze wandered back to Hudson. He was standing behind the bar, and when he saw her staring at him, he glared irritably at her before turning away.

"Okay, well, I guess I'll go home and block Patrick's number from my phone," Bria said.

"Stay and have a drink with us," Jace said.

"I don't want to intrude."

"You're not. It's an office get-together. Right, Rosalie?" Jace said.

"It is. C'mon, Bria, it's still early. Have a drink with us," Rosalie said.

Bria hesitated before nodding. "Okay. Thanks."

"You know those two are going to have sex tonight, right?"

Jace studied the way Sam had her body pressed up against Derek's. Bud's Bar had a small, almost minuscule, dance floor tucked near the back. Sam and Derek and a few other couples were swaying to the music.

"No, they're not," he said.

Derek reached down and squeezed Sam's ass. The

squirrel shifter grinned at him, and Jace groaned when they kissed.

"That is definitely a we're-having-sex-tonight kiss." Amusement laced Bria's voice.

"Great." Jace tipped his beer bottle to his mouth and drank the last swallow. It was just him, Bria, Sam, and Derek left. Rosalie had only stayed another half hour before she said she had a headache and left. He had no doubt that her leaving had more to do with watching Lincoln shove his tongue down a redheaded fox shifter's throat. Rhonda had left soon after. Watching Sam and Derek flirt while Bria made small talk was more than awkward. He was relieved when Sam convinced Derek to dance with her.

"Rosalie said there was no rule about coworkers dating," Bria said. "Was she wrong?"

"No, but it's a complication that the office doesn't need. What if they start dating and then break up?"

She shrugged. "Maybe they'll remember they're adults and not make it weird at work."

"Doubtful."

"If you're so against coworkers dating, why don't you have a firm rule against it?"

He had meant to update the employee handbook. He really did. Except now Bria was working for him and...

And you want to date her.

No, I don't!

"Jace?" Bria touched his forearm.

"I'll be asking Betty to update the employee handbook in the next month or so."

"Oh."

They sat silently for a moment before Jace cleared his throat. "Sorry about earlier. I hope I didn't scare you like I scared Rosalie."

"Why would it scare me?"

Fuck, he couldn't even hold a normal conversation with Bria. Lincoln was right – he was a goddamn train wreck.

"It wouldn't. Of course, it wouldn't," he said. "Sorry."

"I should be saying thank you. It was nice of you to come over and help out," Bria said.

"You probably had it under control, but I…"

How exactly was he supposed to end that sentence? Just casually say that he knew she had it under control, but the minute he saw the wolf shifter grab her arm, his tiger had lost his goddamn mind?

Truthfully, he had no memory of stalking to Bria's table. His tiger was firmly in control at that point. Jace was certain if the wolf shifter hadn't released Bria, his tiger would have torn the shifter's throat out. His tiger was losing it and –

He shouldn't have touched my mate.

His face paled. Oh shit. This was bad. Really fucking bad. If his tiger was already thinking of Bria as his mate, he was fucked.

She's not our mate! Knock it off, you moron.

She could be our mate.

His tiger sounded like a sulky kitten.

"Jace? Your eyes are glowing. What's wrong?" Bria's soft hand touched his arm again, and his tiger roared happily and retreated.

"Nothing," he said. "Just, uh, my tiger is a little amped up right now. It's been a while since I've shifted."

A complete lie. He'd spent most of last night in his tiger form.

"Oh, okay. Well, thank you for your help."

"You're welcome. You're going to block him, right?"

"Yes, and report him to the dating app. Maybe they'll kick him off Shifter's Love."

"You're using Shifter's Love to find a date?" he asked.

She flushed at his tone. "Yes. So what? Everyone meets their significant other online now."

"Significant other?"

Bria's flush grew brighter. "You know what I mean. I want to be in a relationship, and I won't find a boyfriend sitting at home night after night. Besides, this is no different from you using the Heat Me Up app. Heat Me Up is a really stupid name for it, by the way."

"I didn't name it."

"No, but you use it."

"Who's being judgmental now?" he said.

She rubbed at her temples. "I'm not being judgmental."

"You are. Besides, technically, you use Heat Me Up as well."

"I don't!"

"You do. You got my name from Kat, who got my name from Heat Me Up. So, you've used the app."

"Fine, I've sort of used the app, and I'm being judgmental. But so are you with the Shifters Love thing."

He wanted to argue, but telling Bria it was jealousy making him act this way didn't seem like a great idea. "Yeah, okay, I am."

"We just want different things, right?" Bria said. "You want sex without commitment, and I want sex with commitment. Neither of us is a bad person for wanting what we want. Agreed?"

"Agreed," he said. "So, are you talking with any other guys?"

She stared at him, and it was his turn to flush. "Sorry, that isn't any of my business."

"There's a cougar shifter and a coyote shifter who both

have potential," she said. "What about you? Do you have a cat shifter lined up to help out?"

"I met with a tiger shifter yesterday."

Her eyes flared a bright yellow for a split second before returning to blue. "Oh, that's good. It's, um, good that you can help her out."

"I'm not. It wasn't going to work with my schedule," he said.

"I thought you said your schedule was flexible."

"Not this time."

He was lying again. He could have made it work. The tiger shifter he'd met with yesterday was gorgeous, with long red hair and green eyes. She'd had a typical tiger shifter body - tall and athletic looking with toned thighs. Her six pack was clearly visible through her t-shirt.

Unfortunately, he suddenly only seemed to find smaller-than-average tiger shifters with dark hair and blue eyes appealing.

He'd ended the meeting after fifteen minutes.

Don't forget how you changed your account on Heat Me Up to inactive as soon as you got home last night.

He ignored his inner voice. He had changed it to inactive because he was busy right now. It had nothing to do with Bria.

"I should probably get going. It's getting late," Bria said.

"It's not that late. What are your plans for tomorrow?"

"I don't really have any. I might stop by my parents' place for lunch."

"They live here in the city?" he asked.

"They do."

"That's nice. Do you have any siblings?" Jace asked.

"Nope, only child. How about you?"

"I had an older brother."

"Had?" Bria grew still.

"He died five years ago."

Bria's hand covered his. He immediately linked their fingers together, and she squeezed gently. "I'm very sorry."

"His name was Jonah. He, uh, he was a really good guy. There were only eighteen months between us, so we were pretty close growing up."

She squeezed his hand again. "I'm sorry. Was it an accident or..."

"Hey, guys!"

Jace jerked his hand free of Bria's when he heard Sam's voice. The squirrel shifter held Derek's hand, and her face was flushed. He could smell both hers and Derek's arousal.

"Derek and I are heading out. Thanks for buying the drinks tonight, Jace."

"You're welcome."

"Okay, well, bye." Sam waved at them and pulled Derek toward the door.

They sat in silence for a moment before Bria said, "Jace? Your brother... was it -"

"You're right, it's getting late, and we should go." Talking to Bria about his brother was a mistake. He couldn't get to know her outside of the office.

I want her.

He ignored his tiger's growl. He wanted Bria too, wanted her so badly he had half a goddamn woody every time he was around her, but it wasn't going to work. She had made it clear she didn't want him to help her with her heat. Either she would have a boyfriend by then, or she'd go back to Heat Me Up and find a shifter there. She could act like she wouldn't, but there was no way she could go through a heat alone. Her need to mate during her last heat had been more intense than he'd ever seen before.

An image of Bria beneath him, her fangs sinking into his shoulder and her claws raking his back while she climaxed around his cock, flooded through him. His orgasm with her had been one of the best ones of his life, and that was why he was so desperate to be back between her legs. His tiger might be acting like a love-struck idiot, but he knew exactly what he wanted, and it wasn't a relationship.

Bria was already standing, and he hated the look of hurt on her face.

"Bria, I'm sorry, I -"

"You have nothing to apologize about. Good night. I'll see you on Monday."

"I'll walk you to your car."

She hesitated, and he said, "Not a choice."

"Okay. Thanks."

CHAPTER 7

"Kat? I'm here." Bria removed her jacket and hung it in the closet before walking to the kitchen. "You would not believe what happened on my date on Friday. The guy was a total – oh, hey, Bishop."

She smiled at the grizzly shifter sitting at the table next to Kat. Lila was in his arms, and she was sucking on her fist and staring up at him.

"Hey, Bria. How are you?" he said.

"I'm good."

She sat down across from him as Kat stood. "You want some tea, honey?"

"I can get it," Bria said.

"Sit and relax." Kat grabbed a mug and popped a teabag into it.

"Is Ava here?" Bria asked.

Bishop shook his head. "She's at home having a nap. Lila was up most of the night with a fever."

"Poor baby." Bria reached out and stroked Lila's leg. "She's feeling better?"

"Yeah." He bent his head and kissed the baby's forehead.

She smiled around her fist, and Bishop nuzzled her cheek before making a low growl. Lila kicked her feet in excitement and dropped her hand. Her smile widened until Bria could see all of her gums.

She laughed. "Lila sure loves her daddy, huh?"

"She does." Kat handed her the mug of tea before kissing Lila's head. "She loves her Auntie Kat, too. Isn't that right, Lila?"

She purred to the baby, and Lila's eyes widened at the sound before she smiled again.

"I should get going," Bishop said. "Lila will be hungry soon, and I'm interrupting your visit with Bria."

"You're not," Kat said. "You're welcome to drop by anytime, honey. You know that."

"Hey, Stripes." Ronin strolled into the kitchen. "What's happening?"

"Hi, Ronin."

"You heading out?" Kat asked.

"I am. But first..." Ronin held his hands out for the baby.

Bishop hesitated, and Ronin laughed. "Don't hog the baby, big guy."

"Don't drop her." Bishop handed Lila over.

"Your daddy needs to have a little faith in Uncle Ronin, doesn't he?" Ronin kissed Lila's cheek before cradling her in one arm and taking a selfie.

"What are you doing?" Kat asked as Ronin handed Lila back to Bishop.

"Texting this picture to your mom."

"Ronin, don't you dare."

Bria laughed, and Ronin grinned at her. "You think I should send Eleanor the picture, right?"

"Yep."

"Bria, don't encourage him," Kat said.

Ronin hit a button on his phone. "Done."

He tucked his phone into his pocket and gave Kat an innocent look when her phone started to buzz. "Who could that be?"

Kat hissed at him, but he just grinned and kissed the tip of her nose. "Later, Kitten."

He left, and Bria sipped her tea as Kat said, "Bishop was just telling me that he and Ava are thinking about buying a new house."

"Oh yeah?" Bria said.

Bishop nodded as he placed Lila into the car seat and buckled her in. "Yes. We need a bigger place now that we have Lila. The house next to Mal and Willow is for sale."

"I told Bishop that you worked for a real estate agent. Any chance you could set up a meeting with Jace?" Kat asked.

"Sure. I'll talk to him tomorrow and schedule an appointment this week if you'd like. Do you want me to text you or Ava?"

"Ava," Bishop said. "She's easier to get a hold of during the day. You can get her number from Kat. Thanks, Bria."

"You bet."

Bishop bent and kissed Kat on the cheek. "Bye, Kat."

"Bye, honey. Tell Ava I said hello."

Bishop left, and when the front door shut, Kat sank into the chair beside Bria. "So, how was your date with the wolf shifter?"

"Terrible," Bria said. "We met at Bud's, and it was going okay initially. Then he threatened Rosalie and then told me I owed him for buying dinner, and then Jace just about shifted and tore him apart."

"Wait, back up. Why were Jace and his assistant on your date with you?"

Bria laughed. "No, they weren't...let me start from the beginning."

"Okay, so Jace came to your rescue like a tiger in shining armour, and then you spent the rest of the date drinking with him. But you're not banging him," Kat said.

"Kat! He's my boss. Of course I'm not having sex with him."

"You want to though. Even just talking about how he went after the wolf shifter got you all hot and bothered. I could smell it."

Bria flushed. "You know I'm attracted to him. But, he doesn't want a relationship and he -"

"Then why did he rescue you from your dickhead date?"

"Well, because he's a nice guy. He saw that I was in trouble."

"Right, that's it."

"It is," Bria insisted. "Is he attracted to me? Yeah, just like I'm attracted to him. That doesn't mean he wants to date me. In fact, he's made it clear he doesn't want to date. Which is why I'm going out with a coyote shifter on Saturday."

"Seriously?" Kat said.

"Yes. I need to find someone before my next heat and I'm running out of time, Kit Kat. If I don't have a boyfriend, I really will have to chain myself to, like, the radiator or something."

"Or, just use the app," Kat said. "I know how that makes you feel, but it's better than sleeping with a random shifter you find at the bar. Right?"

"I guess."

"Did you download the app?"

"I did, but I haven't set up an account or anything."

"Set it up right now, and we'll look at a few shifters together." Kat took Bria's empty mug to the sink and rinsed it before adding a teabag. "I'll make us more tea."

"It could work out with the coyote shifter. He seemed nice."

"If it does, then you can delete your account on Heat Me Up," Kat said. "But if it doesn't…"

"Fine." Bria pulled out her phone and set up her account as Kat made them tea. By the time she put the steaming liquid in front of her, Bria was scrolling through the app.

"He's good looking." Kat studied the bear shifter. "Pretty eyes."

Bria just shrugged. "He's okay. I'm not really into dating bears."

"It's not dating," Kat reminded her. "You can't think about it like that. Be right back. I gotta pee."

She left the kitchen, and Bria scrolled through a few more shifters. She drummed her fingers on the table, checked the doorway for Kat, and then used the search function to type in Jace's name.

What the hell? His account was there, with a brief bio and a picture of him, but it said 'inactive' in the space for his email.

"His account is inactive? Since when?"

She jumped and hissed in fright at the sound of Kat's voice. She held her phone against her chest so Kat couldn't see it. "You scared me, Kit Kat."

"Sorry." Kat sat down and sipped at her tea. "You don't need to hide the screen. I saw that you were looking at Jace's profile. When did he go inactive?"

"I don't know," she admitted. "He told me Friday night

that he met with a shifter the day before, but it didn't work with his schedule."

"He told me his schedule was flexible," Kat said.

"He said the same thing to me. I don't know why that's changed."

"I think I do."

"It has nothing to do with me," Bria said.

"No? So, why is his account inactive all of a sudden?" Kat asked.

"I don't know. It's busy at work. Maybe his schedule actually is too full."

"Maybe," Kat said. "So, did you see anyone else with potential, or did you just stare at Jace's profile the whole time?"

Bria set her phone down and picked up her tea. "Let's talk about something else, okay? When are you and Ronin getting married?"

"Now you sound like my mother."

Bria laughed. "Who would have thought your mother would be anxious for you to marry a bird shifter?"

"I know, right? Ronin has won her over completely. Do you know where he was going this afternoon? A football game with my father. Even Dad thinks he's great," Kat said.

"I'm happy for you, Kat."

"Thanks, honey."

"Also ridiculously jealous," Bria said.

Kat leaned forward and took her hand. "You'll find the right guy for you. I know it."

"Maybe." She stared into her tea. She was terribly afraid she had already found the right guy – he just didn't want her the way she wanted him.

"Hi, Bria."

Ava walked into the office, and Bria smiled at her.

"Hi, Ava. How are you?"

"I'm good. Bishop and I have a two o'clock meeting with Jace."

"Great. Have a seat." Bria stood and moved around the desk. "Can I get you a cup of coffee or a glass of water?"

"Water, please."

"Sure. Where's sweet Lila today?"

"She's with my mom for a few hours," Ava said.

"Jace is running about ten minutes behind but is on his way."

"That's fine," Ava said as Rosalie walked into reception. "Bishop texted me that he's still five minutes away." She smiled at Rosalie. "Hi there."

"Rosalie, this is my friend Ava. Ava, this is Jace's assistant Rosalie."

"Nice to meet you," Rosalie said. "Bria, I'm just running out to the post office. Be back in about half an hour."

Rosalie left, and Bria smiled at Ava. "I'll grab your water. Be right back."

When she returned with the water, Ava stood near the desk, and Bria groaned inwardly. Lincoln stood next to her. She hurried forward and handed Ava the glass of water.

"It's nice to meet you, Ava Lewis." Lincoln's voice was a husky purr.

"It's nice to meet you as well," Ava said.

"So," Lincoln's gaze drifted to Ava's bare left hand before returning to her face, "what's a pretty little human like you doing in our office?"

Ava gave him an amused look. "Buying a house. Isn't that why people usually come to your office?"

Bria choked down her laughter as Lincoln's cheeks went

red. "I've already got the perfect condo in mind for you. Two bedrooms, one bath, in the heart of downtown. Close to the hottest nightclubs and best restaurants in the city."

The door opened, and Bishop strode into reception. Bria waved at the giant grizzly, but he ignored her. His lip was curling, and he was sniffing the air. No doubt he could smell Lincoln's arousal just like she could. Deciding the lion shifter could use a lesson in manners, Bria kept her mouth shut as Bishop moved silently behind him.

Lincoln reached out and tugged on a lock of Ava's red hair. "What do you say? I could set up an appointment for you to look at it. It's perfect for a single girl looking for a little fun. Maybe we could have dinner afterward and -"

The deep growl made the lion shifter freeze. He sniffed the air before turning. Bishop loomed over him, his face red and his hands in fists. "Touch my mate again, lion shifter and your head will hang on the wall of my home."

Lincoln held his hands up and took a step to the right. Bria could practically see the steam rising from Bishop's ears as he wrapped one beefy arm around Ava's waist. He drew the curvy redhead into his embrace and glared at Lincoln.

Lincoln cleared his throat. Bria couldn't smell any fear coming off the lion shifter. She couldn't decide if Lincoln was incredibly brave or incredibly stupid as he grinned at Bishop. "My apologies. I didn't know she was your mate."

"She carries my scent," Bishop growled at him.

"True. She does have a rather thick scent of grizzly on her." He lifted his left hand and pointed to his ring finger. "But when a lady hasn't got a ring, she's not truly mated, is she?"

Bishop snarled, and his beard thickened. "She belongs to me."

"Honey, stop." Ava patted Bishop's chest. "He's just trying to get you riled up now."

Lincoln grinned. "Maybe just a little. It was nice to meet you, Ava."

He shoved his hands into his pockets, winked at Bishop, and walked out of reception. Bishop was still growling under his breath, and his shirt strained against his shoulders. Ava rubbed his chest again.

"You're mine," Bishop said to her. "Mine."

"Yes," she said. "I'm yours, honey. Relax, okay?"

"If he touches you again -"

"He won't."

Bria watched as Ava smoothed her hand over his chest a third time and smiled at the angry grizzly shifter before pressing a kiss against his mouth. He relaxed, and his body returned to its normal size. He gave Bria a sheepish smile. "Uh, hi, Bria. Sorry about that."

"It's fine," she said. "I was just telling Ava that Jace is on his way. I'll take you to the boardroom, okay?"

"Sure." Bishop took Ava's hand, his gaze lingering on her ring finger. As she led them to the boardroom, Bria had a feeling that it wouldn't be long before Ava wore a wedding ring.

"How are your mom and dad doing?" Lincoln gave him an uncharacteristically somber look as Jace climbed into the car.

"They're doing okay. We went to his grave today and then walked along the river. Jonah used to love swimming there."

"I remember."

Jace stared out the windshield. "Mom said to say thank

you for the flowers. It means a lot to her that you remember what today is."

"You and I have been best friends since we were kids," Lincoln said. "I'm not going to forget Jonah's birthday."

The lion shifter backed out of Jace's driveway and drove down the street. "Why don't we forget about going to the club and just buy some beer and chill at my place tonight? We can watch the game."

"No, I want to go to the club."

"It's not that I'm trying to discourage you from getting your rocks off with a random shifter, but is your brother's birthday the night to do it? Besides, isn't that why you joined Heat Me Up? So you could fuck shifters without having to do the whole pick up random chicks at a bar?"

"I turned my account inactive."

"Seriously?"

"Yes."

"Why?" Lincoln turned left at the lights.

"It's really busy at the office right now."

"No busier than usual. Plus, it's like two days a month. If you'd rather work instead of enjoying two days of non-stop fucking with a hot cat shifter, there is something seriously wrong with you. Are you having issues with the old twig and berries?"

He glanced at Jace's crotch. "No shame if you are. The number of guys who can't get their twig to stand up is surprisingly large. I hear, three out of five -"

"I'm going to a club tonight for the sole purpose of getting laid. There's nothing wrong with my dick."

"Again, I question whether your brother's birthday is the night to do it," Lincoln said. "You're hurting, and you're vulnerable tonight and -"

"What have you done with my best friend?"

"Nothing. I can be sensitive and understanding. I mean, usually, it's because I'm trying to get into a shifter's pants, but I can make an exception for you, my little snookums." Lincoln grinned.

"I want to get drunk and find some random shifter to have sex with. It's the perfect way to end an awful day."

"Jace -"

"Enough, Lincoln. You have no idea what this is like. I don't need your goddamn advice on how to get through the birthday of my dead brother."

Lincoln didn't reply, and Jace sighed. "Fuck. I'm sorry. That was a shitty thing for me to say. I didn't mean it."

"It's fine, man. I just don't want you to do something you'll regret."

"I won't."

"All right. Hey, are you sure you want to go to Club Delight? We usually go to Trinity," Lincoln said.

"I'm sure. I'm tired of Trinity."

He wasn't, but he sure as hell couldn't go back to Trinity any time soon. Going to Trinity to pick up a shifter didn't feel right. Not when the last time he was there, he'd fucked Bria in the bathroom.

Is that the only reason it doesn't feel right? Are you seriously going to fuck some other random woman when the one you want is Bria?

He blocked out his inner voice. He couldn't have Bria and needed to get used to the idea. What better way than by sleeping with someone else?

I want Bria. Give her to me, his tiger growled.

Fuck, his tiger was going to drive him insane.

WELL, THE DATE WITH THE COYOTE SHIFTER WASN'T AS disastrous as her date with Patrick, but it was not going well. Bria sipped at her drink and checked her watch again. Yeah, he wasn't coming back. It had been forty minutes since Ron had excused himself to use the bathroom. She'd been ditched.

She finished her drink and watched the humans and shifters dancing for a few minutes before sliding off the stool. The club was busy tonight, and she was getting a bit of a headache from the loud beat of the music. She didn't even know why Ron had suggested the club for a first date. They could barely even hear each other over the music. Maybe he'd suggested it because it would be easy to sneak away when he found her boring as hell.

She picked her way through the crowd of people and headed toward the exit. At least she wasn't at Club Trinity. She would have given him a hard no if Ron had suggested that one. She didn't think she could ever go back there. Not with the memory of fucking Jace in the bathroom lingering in her head.

She left the bar and took a deep breath of the night air. It was hot and stuffy in the club, and -

"Jace, we are leaving."

She spun around, staring wide-eyed at Lincoln and Jace. The lion shifter was practically dragging Jace out of the club. Her hands flew to her mouth when Jace punched the lion shifter in the mouth.

"Goddammit, Jace!" Lincoln roared. Blood trickled from his mouth, and he dodged Jace's second swing. The tiger shifter was swaying back and forth, and she could see how his body was starting to swell.

As the humans and shifters waiting to enter the club watched with amusement and trepidation, Lincoln grabbed Jace's arm again. "Listen to me, you ass. My cousin is at the fucking hospital, and I need to go. I don't have time for your bullshit."

"So then go," Jace snarled at him before shaking free. "I don't need you babysitting me."

"Like hell, you don't. You're already shitfaced and in no shape to be alone. Now get your striped ass in my goddamn car."

"No."

Lincoln growled with anger. "You think this is what Jonah would want? You think he'd want you getting drunk on his birthday and then fucking whichever random female finds you pathetic enough to throw a pity fuck your way?"

"Fuck you!" Jace shouted. "Don't you dare fucking say his name again, or I'll kill you, Lincoln! Do you hear me? I'll fucking kill you!"

"You can try," Lincoln snarled as a golden-coloured beard grew on his face.

Without thinking about it, Bria ran forward. Jace and Lincoln were on the verge of shifting, and she worried they would try to tear each other apart.

"Jace!" She grabbed Jace's arm, and he swung around. His snarl of anger switched to loud purring. He pulled her into his embrace and rubbed his face against her throat.

"Hi, baby." He purred into her ear before rubbing his face against her throat again.

"Hi," she said. Lincoln was staring at them, and she patted Jace's back. "Let me go."

"Don't wanna," he mumbled before threading his hand into her hair. He pulled her head back to mark the entire length of her neck before rubbing his face against the curve of her jaw.

"Jesus, Jace," Lincoln groaned. "Bria, I'm sorry."

"It's fine," she said. "Jace, let me go."

He let go of her reluctantly. He was still purring, and Lincoln rolled his eyes. "You're gonna be fucking humiliated tomorrow."

"How drunk is he?" Bria asked.

Jace nearly knocked her over when he staggered behind her and rubbed his big body against her. Lincoln grabbed her arm to steady her, and Jace snarled at him before yanking Bria out of his grip. He pressed her back against his chest and wrapped his arm around her waist. He rubbed his face repeatedly against her hair before licking her neck.

"Stop," she said.

He growled like a sulky kitten but stopped licking her. He refused to release her, though, and she ignored his erection pressing against her ass. "How drunk is he, Lincoln?"

"Very." Lincoln wiped the blood from his mouth. "Dammit, Jace, stop marking Bria, you idiot."

Jace growled at him before marking Bria's throat again. He purred to her, and she swallowed down her answering purr as Lincoln's phone buzzed. The lion shifter glanced at it and muttered a curse.

"What's wrong?" Bria asked.

"My aunt is texting me. My cousin was in a car accident and is at the hospital. I told my aunt I'd meet her there, but I need to get Jace home first. Except he's refusing to leave the club."

Bria rocked forward as Jace gently headbutted the back of her skull before sweeping aside her hair and licking the back of her neck.

"You smell good," he said before purring to her again. She gasped when he gave her throat a hard nip with his fangs.

"Jace!" Lincoln said. "Quit biting your receptionist!"

Jace licked away the small trickle of blood flowing down

her skin as Lincoln said, "He's not usually like this, I swear. It's a rough day for him. It's his brother's birthday and…"

"I know about his brother," Bria said.

"Really?" Lincoln gave her a look of surprise. "He doesn't usually talk about Jonah."

"He, um, he mentioned it the other night. Listen," she said as Lincoln's phone buzzed again, "go to the hospital. I'll get Jace home."

Lincoln shook his head. "You'll never convince him to leave the club. He's itching for a fight, and if he gets in a fight with someone, you could get hurt."

Jace was still licking his bite on her throat, and Bria touched his arm around her waist. "Jace, it's time to leave. I'll drive you home because Lincoln has to go to the hospital. Okay?"

"Sure." Jace licked the bite again and pressed his dick against her ass.

"Are you fucking kidding me?" Lincoln said.

Bria almost giggled at the look of exasperation on Lincoln's face. "Go, Lincoln. I'll get him home."

"I'll help you get him to the car," Lincoln said.

"I don't need help," Jace said. He took Bria's hand and staggered toward the parking lot.

She tugged him toward her car and smiled at Lincoln when he followed them. "I hope your cousin is okay."

"Me too. He's a cheetah shifter, so he should heal fine, but he's my aunt's only kid, and she is freaking out."

"You're close to your aunt?"

"Yeah. Are you sure you don't mind giving Jace a ride home? I can call him an Uber or -"

"No Uber." Jace leaned down and nuzzled Bria's neck. "I'm taking Bria home and fucking her."

"Oh God," Lincoln groaned again. "Okay, that's it. I'm taking you home, you asshole."

"I'm not fucking you. You're way too hairy," Jace said.

Bria burst out laughing, and Jace grinned at her. "I'm funny."

"No, you're an idiot, and you'll be so fucking embarrassed tomorrow," Lincoln said.

"He probably won't remember." Bria unlocked her car.

"Again, I'm really sorry." Lincoln opened the door. "Jesus, this is weird."

"What's weird?"

"Normally, I'm the one being inappropriate, and Jace is apologizing for me."

She laughed again as Jace purred and leaned down to lick her throat.

"Are you sure you're okay with taking him home?" Lincoln asked.

"Fine," Bria said. "I can handle a drunk tiger shifter."

Jace licked her throat. "I'll be a good boy, little tiger. I promise. I'm going to make you feel so good again."

"Again?" Lincoln arched his eyebrow at her.

She shrugged. "Jace is drunk and doesn't know what he's saying."

"Yeah," Jace said, "I'm horny."

She laughed. "I said drunk."

"And horny," he said.

"C'mon, get in the car." Lincoln helped Jace into the car and buckled him in before shutting the door.

He patted her on the shoulder. "Thanks, Bria. I owe you."

"It's no problem."

The car door opened and Jace leaned out, held in place by his seatbelt. He bared his fangs at Lincoln. "Don't touch her! She's mine!"

"Yeah, yeah, calm down, ya dick," Lincoln said. "Can you even remember where you live?"

"I remember," Jace said. "Bria, do you remember?"

She cleared her throat. "I'll get directions from you. Goodnight, Lincoln."

"Goodnight, Bria."

She shut the passenger door and waved to Lincoln. As she climbed into the driver's seat, she hoped the lion shifter was distracted enough not to think too much about what Jace said. She started the car and drove in the direction of Jace's house. He placed his big hand on her thigh and rubbed.

"Hi, baby."

"Hi, Jace."

"How come you were at the club?"

"I was on a date."

He growled, and his hand tightened on her leg. "With who?"

"A coyote shifter named Ron."

"Ron is a stupid name."

She laughed. "There's nothing wrong with the name Ron."

He snorted. "Where is stupid Ron?"

"I don't know. About an hour into the date, he ditched me."

"Are you kidding me?"

"Nope."

"He's an idiot with a stupid name."

"Thanks. I'm sorry you're having such a bad day."

He shrugged. "Jonah's birthday is always bad. I miss him."

"I'm sorry, honey." She patted the hand on her thigh, and he linked their fingers together.

"I decided I was going to get drunk and then get laid by a random shifter."

The little growl was escaping her mouth before she could stop it.

He grinned at her. "I like that you're jealous."

She didn't reply, and he squeezed her hand. "Jonah would have thought it was a dumb way to celebrate his birthday, but I didn't care. I didn't want to think about it anymore, you know? I was with my parents all day, and even after five years, they…"

He stopped and stared out the passenger window for a while. She drove in silence and didn't pressure him to talk. When they were nearly at his house, he said, "Anyway, that was my plan. Only halfway through the night, I realized I didn't want to fuck some random shifter. I wanted to fuck you again. Which I thought was impossible. Except here we are, driving to my house to have sex. I can't wait to fuck you again, little tiger. I think about your tight little pussy way more than I should."

He squinted at her neck. "Sorry, I bit you. My tiger loses control when he's around you."

"It's fine. It'll be healed by tomorrow."

"I can't wait to taste your sweet pussy again."

She ignored the slow burn of lust in her belly as she pulled into his driveway and shut the car off. "Okay, let's get you in the house."

"Yes, let's." His voice was eager.

She climbed out of the car and hurried to his side. He'd already unbuckled his seatbelt, and she steadied him when he climbed out of the car. "Put your arm around me."

"Yes, ma'am." He slung his arm around her shoulders, and she guided him to the front door.

"Where are your keys?"

"Front pocket." He yawned.

She slid her hand into his pocket, grabbed his keys and

opened the door. He kicked his shoes off and took her hand. "C'mon, let's get you naked."

She steadied him as he slowly climbed the stairs. He yawned again but put his arm around her waist when they entered his bedroom and leaned down to nuzzle her neck. "I want you so much, little tiger."

"We can't have sex. You're too drunk."

He made an admittedly adorable growl of disappointment. "I'm not that drunk."

"You are."

"I'll make it good for you, little tiger. I promise," he coaxed. He cupped her breast and licked her throat again before purring. "Take off your clothes, and I'll eat your pussy."

"No," she said. "I don't want to have sex tonight, Jace."

He immediately let go of her and stepped away. "Okay."

She hated the hurt look on his face. "Because you're drunk. Not because I don't want you."

He purred again. "So, when I'm sober, we'll fuck. Right?"

"Uh, sure, maybe. Let's get you undressed and into bed."

"Okay."

He followed her to the bed, and she helped him out of his t-shirt. Fuck, his body was incredible. She ignored her urge to lick his chest and, instead, unbuttoned his jeans. She pulled them down, and he sat on the bed with a heavy thump before yawning again. Ignoring the way his dick pushed at his boxer briefs, she took off his jeans and his socks and placed them in the laundry hamper.

"Okay, climb in," she said.

"Will you lie down with me?" He asked. "I won't try to have sex with you. You can trust me."

"I know." She lay on the bed beside him and rubbed his back when he curled beside her and put his arm around her waist. She cuddled him, listening to his deep, raspy purr, unaware she was purring back to him.

"Thanks for giving me a ride home, Bria."

"You're welcome. Will you tell me how your brother died?"

His purring cut out. "He committed suicide."

"I'm sorry." She held him closer.

He rubbed his cheek against her upper chest. "The day before he died, we had dinner together, and I knew something was wrong, but he – he wouldn't admit it. I should have pushed him harder, should have made him tell me the truth."

"It's not your fault, honey."

"That's what my therapist said." He lifted his head and squinted at her. "Do you think I'm weak for going to therapy?"

"Of course not. Why would I think that?"

"Tabitha did."

"Who's Tabitha?"

"No one. Never mind. I'm really thirsty. Do you think you could get me a drink of water?"

"Yes." He rolled away from her, and she stared at his naked back before sliding off the bed and going downstairs to the kitchen. She found a bottle of water in the fridge and brought it upstairs.

She stopped in the doorway of Jace's bedroom and stared at the tiger lounging on the bed. He was massive in size, and his fur shone in the moonlight coming in through the window. He stared unblinkingly at her with his jade coloured eyes before chuffing.

She glanced at her watch. "It's getting late."

He chuffed again and made a yowling, low-pitched noise.

"Okay. Just for a little while."

She set the bottle of water on the nightstand and climbed onto the bed next to the tiger. She laid on her back, and he purred happily and relaxed beside her. His tail flicked back and forth as he rested his giant head on her chest. She stroked his cheeks and the top of his head before scratching around his ears.

His purr grew louder, and she smiled a little. Tiger shifters purred way more than regular tigers. In fact, most regular tigers couldn't really purr at all. When she was younger, she wondered why tiger shifters could roar and purr. But when she'd asked her dad, he had shrugged and said it was just another thing that made shifters unique from the regular animals.

She stroked the fur on Jace's shoulders and scratched his neck. His head was getting heavy, but she didn't ask him to move. He needed this, and she liked being able to help him. Liked it a little too much.

Don't read too much into this, Bria. He's drunk and sad and not thinking clearly. He doesn't want a relationship.

She sighed inwardly and stared at the ceiling as Jace purred. Yeah, she knew that. So, why was she happier lying in bed with a drunk Jace who only wanted her for sex than she'd been for her entire relationship with Raden? She closed her eyes and continued to stroke Jace's soft fur. He was already asleep. She would stay another half hour and then leave.

CHAPTER 8

"Guess who I just finished talking to on the phone?"

Bria glanced up from her computer screen and smiled at Rosalie. "Who?"

"Your friend Ava. They sold their house on Monday and put in an offer on a house yesterday. It was accepted this morning."

"Wow, that's quick. They just met with Jace last week," Bria replied.

"Sometimes it works out that way." Rosalie set the file on Bria's desk. "Can you make copies of the documents in their file for me? I hate to ask, but I'm swamped, and Ava and Bishop will be coming in this afternoon to sign the paperwork with Jace."

"Of course. I don't mind at all." Bria picked up the file. "So, uh, Jace is coming in this afternoon?"

"Yeah, and it's about time. It's Thursday, and he hasn't been in the office since Monday morning. Even then, he met with you for ten minutes and left. I've had stuff waiting for his signature all damn week."

Bria tried not to look guilty. She was pretty sure Jace was

avoiding the office this week because he was avoiding her. First thing Monday morning, he called her into his office and apologized for Saturday night. He admitted that he didn't exactly remember what happened but remembered enough to know he'd acted inappropriately.

She'd assured him it was fine and not a big deal, but he had left shortly after his apology and hadn't returned to the office.

"Bria?"

"What?" She gave Rosalie a blank look.

"I asked what you and Jace were meeting about on Monday."

"Oh, uh, just going over my, uh…"

Shit. She had nothing.

Rosalie gave her a curious look. "Going over your what?"

"Ladies, who wishes it was Friday?"

The scent of lion permeated the reception. Lincoln strolled in through the front door, and Rosalie smiled happily. "Hi, Lincoln."

"Hi, Rosie-girl. How are you?"

"Good, thanks."

He stood next to her. "You're smelling particularly good today, Rosie."

Rosalie darted a glance at Bria and flushed. "Uh, thanks. You smell nice, too."

"Bria, how are you?" Lincoln smiled at her.

"Fine, thanks." After seeing how he was with Jace Saturday night, she liked the cocky lion shifter a little more than before, but she still hated the way he flirted with Rosalie. There was no scent of arousal coming from Lincoln, and she would be very surprised if he ever showed any interest in dating the curvy human.

"Hey, Rosie, could you help me with some paperwork I

need to scan and email? I hate to ask last minute, but..." He gave her a warm smile, and the scent of Rosalie's arousal rushed over Bria.

"Sure, I don't mind. Do you want to do it now?"

"I always want to do it with you now, Rosie-girl." Lincoln's grin widened when Rosalie's flush deepened.

"Right," Rosalie said a little breathlessly. "Um, okay, well let's head back to my desk then."

"Sure. Later, Bria."

"Bye, Lincoln."

She waited until they were gone before taking the file Rosalie had given her to the photocopier. She needed to speak with Jace about taking Monday and Tuesday off. She'd decided to email him, but now that she knew he was coming in today, she would speak to him in person.

Her stomach churned with nerves. Her heat started on Sunday, and she didn't have anyone to help her. Her plan to have a boyfriend by her next heat had seemed so easy a month ago. That was before her disastrous dates with Patrick and Ron. In desperation, she'd gone for dinner Tuesday night with the squirrel shifter who kept messaging her. He was nice enough, but when, over dessert, he'd made it clear that he wanted her to dominate him in the bedroom, she'd turned him down and gone home.

Last night, she'd scrolled through the Heat Me Up app, finding fault with various shifters for stupid reasons until she'd thrown her phone down and gone to bed. Right or wrong, she couldn't use the app. She would need to be strong and use her hand and some toys to get through her heat. Maybe it wouldn't be as bad this time.

She didn't need Jace's help, she didn't.

I want Jace. Give him to me, her tiger said in a sulky voice.

God, her tiger was going to drive her insane.

OKAY, BRIA. YOU CAN DO THIS.

She took a deep breath and knocked on Jace's office door. He had come into the office half an hour ago. She was on the phone, and he nodded to her before disappearing into his office and closing the door.

"Come in."

"Hi. Could I speak to you for a moment?" She hovered in the doorway.

He looked up from the computer screen. "If you can make it quick? I'm meeting with Ava and Bishop in a few minutes."

"I won't take up much time." She closed the door and crossed to his desk, standing next to one of the chairs and holding the back of it in a white-knuckled grip.

"Thanks for referring them to me, by the way," Jace said. "It's office policy that an employee will get a bonus if they refer a client who purchases a home. I'll ask Betty to cut the cheque for the next pay period."

"Thank you." She gave him a nervous smile.

"So, what's up?"

"Uh, I need to take next Monday and Tuesday off work. Could you approve my request?"

He stared silently at her, and she hurried on. "I know I haven't been working here very long, but it's my heat cycle," her face flushed, but she carried on grimly, "and so I need the time off. It might not be all of Tuesday. My cycle will start Sunday, so I could possibly come in on Tuesday afternoon, depending on what time it ends."

She ran out of breath, stopping the flood of words pouring out of her, and silently thanked God for it. She fidgeted anxiously. She'd be in trouble if Jace didn't give her the time off. She couldn't see him during her cycle, not with how her tiger acted around him. She'd be climbing him like a tree in front of everyone and not giving one damn who saw it.

"Of course," he said abruptly before turning back to his computer screen. "Don't worry about coming in on Tuesday. Just book the entire day."

"Oh, I don't mind coming in if it's - "

"It's fine. You'll need to rest afterward."

"Right," she said.

She continued to stand there, and he gave her an impatient look. "Is there something else?"

Maybe you could take Monday and Tuesday off, too, and spend them with your face buried in my pussy?

For one horrifying moment, she thought she had spoken out loud, but he was still staring at her with that impatient look.

"Uh, no. Thank you, Jace."

"You're welcome." He looked away, clearly dismissing her, and she turned and stumbled toward the door. She pulled it open.

She was such an idiot around him. A complete and utter –

His hand shut the door with a bang, and she whipped around. He was standing behind her, so close she could see how his pupils dilated as he dipped his head and inhaled. "Who did you find, Bria?"

"I – I'm sorry?" She stifled her soft moan when he pressed her into the door with his large body.

"Who did you find to help you through your cycle? What type of shifter will ease your heat?"

"Oh, um, I didn't. I mean..."

She was completely unaware that her hips had pressed against his groin and were moving in slow circles. He growled under his breath. He cupped her ass in one large hand, and her tiger purred happily.

"Does he know you like to bite? Can he handle it when you use your pretty little claws on his back?"

"Jace," she moaned.

He brushed his mouth against hers, just a light touch that shouldn't have brought a rush of wetness to her pussy, but did. She tried to return his kiss, her hips still pressing rhythmically against his, and he wrapped his hand in her hair and pulled her head back.

She hissed at him, and he grinned before nudging her thighs apart. She spread them willingly, moaning when he lifted her to her tiptoes and pressed his erection directly against her throbbing pussy.

"Please kiss me," she whispered.

"His name, Bria. Tell me who's taking my place between your thighs, and then I'll kiss you."

"No one. I told you I couldn't do that."

"No, you said you couldn't do that with me." He leaned away from her, and she hissed in displeasure.

"You can't go through your heat cycle alone," Jace said.

"Yes, I can," she argued. "I can handle it."

"No, you can't. You wouldn't have gone to Trinity's during your last one if you could. It's dangerous for you to try."

"I'm stronger than you think. Last time, it was just really bad, all right? This one will be better."

"Why?" His eyes flashed anger, and his hand tightened on her ass. "Have you been fucking someone else this last month?"

"No, of course not. You know I don't have a boyfriend."

"You don't need a boyfriend to fuck."

"Well, maybe I do, okay?" She shoved at his arm. "Let go of my ass."

He did, and she ignored her tiger's disappointed whine.

"You need someone to help you, Bria."

"No, I don't. I have vibrators and my own damn fingers, and I don't need -"

He growled again and shoved his body against hers, pinning her to the door. "Do you honestly believe a vibrator in your tight pussy will be better than my cock? Better than my tongue? I remember how many times I made you come with my tongue, little tiger. Do you?"

"Yes," she whispered.

"I still remember how sweet you tasted," he growled. His eyes had turned bright green, and his pupils had become dark slits. "I remember how you pulled my hair when I sucked on your perfect, pink clit. How you begged me not to stop."

She moaned, and he slid one big hand under her shirt and cupped her breast through her bra. "Just think about how good it will feel to have me for your entire heat cycle. To know you could ride my dick whenever you wanted. To know that all you have to do is ask, and I'll be on my knees and eating your sweet pussy until you're screaming my name. I have what you need, Bria. Let me help you."

There was a knock on his door before she could scream the 'yes' hovering on her lips.

"Jace?" Rosalie's voice drifted through the door. "Ava and Bishop are here. I've put them in the boardroom."

"Thanks, Rosalie," Jace's voice was hoarse. He cleared his throat as he stepped away from Bria. "I'm just finishing up a quick meeting with Bria."

Grimacing, he adjusted his cock through his pants and crossed the room to sit at his desk.

Bria smoothed down her hair and opened the door. Thanking God that Rosalie was human and wouldn't smell her need for Jace, she smiled at her. "Sorry, it's my fault."

Rosalie frowned at her. "Are you sick? Your face is bright red."

"No, I'm fine. Just feeling a little warm."

She slipped past the brunette and hurried back to reception.

"ARE YOU SURE YOU'LL BE OKAY?" ROSALIE GAVE BRIA a worried look.

"Yes," Bria said. "The office is closing in twenty minutes. I can handle twenty minutes on my own."

Rosalie studied her for a few minutes. "It doesn't seem fair to leave you alone just because I want to skip out early on a Friday. But I told my mom I would meet her at the mall before five and - "

"I'll be fine. Go, Rosalie." Bria kept her hands clenched in a tight fist below the desk.

"Lincoln is still here, but he's holed up in his office, and he wouldn't be of any help if you had questions." Rosalie pulled on a tendril of her hair. "But you have my cell phone, so if there was an emergency..."

"I'm sure there won't be an emergency at quarter to five on a Friday afternoon. The phone hasn't even rung since three. You need to go before you're late."

"Are you sure you're okay today?" Rosalie asked. "You've been quiet all afternoon, and you're pale. The flu is going around, but I thought shifters didn't get sick."

"I'm not sick. Just a bit tired."

Please leave. Oh God, please leave.

"Okay. Well, have a good weekend, and I'll see you on Monday, all right?"

"You bet."

"Remember, just call me if you need any help."

"I will. Bye, Rosalie," Bria said.

The moment Rosalie was gone, Bria gripped her stomach and leaned over. She rocked back and forth for a few minutes before standing and walking to the kitchen. She passed Lincoln's office, but thank fuck, his door was closed. She could hear the faint sound of his voice as he talked on the phone. She poured a glass of water and drank it all in three large gulps before gripping the counter tightly.

Ten more minutes, Bria, ten more minutes.

For the first time, her cycle had come early. She had refused to believe it at first, ignoring the ache in her belly and pelvis, but by three, it was impossible to ignore.

She was in heat and deep trouble.

Jace isn't here, don't worry.

Thank fucking God. After meeting with Ava and Bishop yesterday, Jace left the office again. He'd shown up this morning at eight with donuts and coffee for the office. He'd spent the entire morning in his office with the door closed, but she considered that an improvement over the last few days.

Luckily for her and her hey-why-don't-I-come-early heat cycle, Jace left at noon to show some houses and hadn't returned. She checked the clock on the microwave – eight minutes to five. All she had to do was get through the next eight minutes, and then she could go home.

Where you'll spend the next two days in agony.

She ignored the errant thought. Her hand shaking, she tucked a stray lock of hair back into her hair clip. She would worry about the next two days later. Right now, she still had eight minutes to get through, and she couldn't forget that Lincoln was still in the building. Sure, he was in his office, but what if he left when she did? What if she took one look at him and jumped on him? She needed to be fucked, and her cat wouldn't care who it was, just that they had a nice, thick cock.

I don't want that stupid lion. I want Jace. Give him to me, her cat suddenly hissed.

Yes, Jace. Fuck, she wanted him. Her pussy throbbed, and liquid coated her panties as she imagined him with her right now. He would bend her over the table and fuck her until this horrible, all-consuming grip of need loosened. She could almost feel his cock pumping in and out, feel his fingers gripping her hips. Her fangs popped out, and her nails lengthened to claws. She would claw him and bite him when he made her come, and he wouldn't -

"Hey, Bria? I'm heading out. Have a great weekend and…"

Lincoln had joined her in the kitchen, and her eyes widened in horror. He could smell her heat. She knew that without a doubt. She refused to turn around, hanging onto the counter's edge like it was a lifeline as the scent of Lincoln's lust drifted to her.

"Bria?"

"Good night, Lincoln." She tried to sound bright and cheerful. "Have a – a great weekend."

"Bria, let me help you."

He was directly behind her now, and she flinched when he pressed his hand against her lower back and rubbed slowly.

"No, thank you. I'm fine."

"You're not fine," Lincoln said in a low voice. "Why did you come to work during your heat cycle?"

"It – it's early, but I'm fine."

He rubbed her back again, and she stiffened and tried to draw away. "Please don't touch me."

"I can help you, gorgeous." He leaned forward and pressed his lips against her neck. "Let me."

Get rid of him! Find Jace and take what belongs to us! Her cat was positively snarling at her.

Lincoln moved to her side and placed a possessive hand on the back of her neck. "Don't you want to feel better, gorgeous?"

JACE STUDIED THE EMPTY RECEPTION DESK BEFORE GLANCING at his watch. It was just before five, so he was pretty certain Bria hadn't left. He hadn't needed to return to the office after his last showing, but he had anyway.

It wasn't because he wanted to see Bria, he told himself. Nor was it because he wanted to try to convince her one last time to let him help her through her heat on Monday and Tuesday. His cock stirred in his pants as he thought of Bria alone in her house, touching herself and sliding a vibrator into that deliciously tight pussy.

What if it isn't enough? What if she goes back to Trinity and finds someone else?

His tiger roared angrily at the thought, and Jace winced. Maybe he could hang out at the nightclub, and if Bria showed up, then he could –

For fuck's sake, Jace! What the hell is wrong with you? She doesn't want your help, remember?

Yeah, he remembered. It was driving him crazy.

His tiger suddenly snarled. It had caught the now familiar scent of Bria's need, and it snarled again when it caught the scent of Lincoln's lust as well. His tiger surged forward, making his pupils contract. He ran to the kitchen. He stopped in the doorway, his tiger howling at him to kill Lincoln, and watched as his best friend placed his hand on the back of Bria's neck.

"Don't you want to feel better, gorgeous?" Lincoln asked.

He stood frozen to the spot with his hands in tight fists. His tiger shook with anger, and he controlled his tiger fiercely as he tried to take over.

"No, thank you," Bria whispered.

Lincoln's fingers rubbed at her neck. "No one needs to know. I'll be very discreet. I know you don't have a boyfriend. Do you want to spend the next two days of your heat alone? Let me give you what you want."

He leaned down to kiss her, but before Jace could even take a step into the kitchen, Bria snarled. She shoved Lincoln away from her with a strength that belied her small size.

"I said no!" She growled at him before baring her fangs. "Stay away from me."

"I'm just trying to help," Lincoln said. "I promise I'm not -"

"Go home, Lincoln," Jace said.

Lincoln turned toward Jace, and Bria stiffened. She swung around to face the cupboards as Lincoln gave Jace an easy smile. "Hey, man. I was just talking with Bria about her -"

"I know what you're talking to her about. She's not interested, and you need to leave her alone."

Lincoln studied Bria for a moment. "Bria, I'm sorry. I didn't mean to offend or upset you. I did just want to help."

"I know." She was still facing the cupboards. "Good night, Lincoln."

Lincoln gave him a considering look, which Jace ignored. The lion shifter strode from the kitchen. Jace waited until he heard the front door shut. "You said it never came early."

"I – it never has before," Bria whispered.

Every part of him was screaming to go to her. To set her on that counter and fuck her until the thick blanket of her need had lessened. She was in agony. He could see it in how she shook and clung to the counter desperately.

We can take her now. She's too far gone to say no, his tiger growled.

He clenched his hands into fists again. He wouldn't do that to Bria. He couldn't take advantage of her obvious need for him now that she was deep in her heat. She had refused him before, and to take her now when she couldn't think clearly would make him the biggest dickhead on earth.

He blew his breath out in a harsh rush. "Go home. I'll lock up."

She nodded, still facing the cupboards, and he left the kitchen and walked to his office. He shut the door. It would be better for the both of them if they didn't see each other again before she left.

THE MOMENT SHE HEARD JACE'S DOOR CLOSE, BRIA BOLTED for reception. She shut down her computer but had to try twice, thanks to her madly shaking hands. Her cat yowled miserably. It didn't want to go home to her apartment and her vibrator. It wanted Jace's hard flesh and his wet, hot tongue. She clenched her hands into fists and walked toward the front door.

Leave, Bria. Just be strong and leave.

Instead of leaving, she reached out and flipped the open sign to close before locking the door. She walked to Jace's office and opened the door without knocking. Her cat meowed happily as she stepped into the room. He was sitting at his desk with his hands clenched into tight fists. She couldn't stop her soft purring when he looked at her.

They stared silently at each other as the seconds ticked by.

She cleared her throat, trying not to cry as pain and need pulsed in her belly. "I just wanted to tell you that I won't need Monday and Tuesday off after all."

He gave her a sympathetic look, and she bit her inner cheek to stop herself from begging him to help her.

If you weren't going to beg, why did you come in here? her cat snarled.

"Will you help me, Jace?" she whispered.

He didn't reply, and she couldn't bite back her moan of dismay. "I'm sorry. I'll go."

She reached for the door handle, and her cat purred triumphantly when Jace said, "Lock the door, Bria."

Her hands shaking violently, she turned the lock before giving him a silent, pleading look. He stood and walked to the small couch. "Come here."

Purring loudly, she ran to him as he reached for the buckle on his belt. She shimmied out of her jeans and panties and left them on the floor. He kicked off his shoes and removed his pants, socks and briefs. Already erect, he sat on the couch, and she licked her lips in anticipation as he patted his lap. She straddled him eagerly, high-pitched trills of excitement spilling from her lips as he cupped the back of her neck and guided her down onto his dick.

"Oh God," she moaned when he entered her. "Oh God, it feels so good."

She bounced on him, purring loudly as he tugged her shirt over her head. He leaned forward and kissed between her breasts before unhooking her bra and pulling it away from her body. She continued to bounce as he held her hips and watched her naked frame ride him.

"Christ, you are so fucking hot, Bria."

"You. Too." She panted. "Naked, want you naked."

He yanked off his tie and unbuttoned his shirt. Her hips still moving in fast, tight circles, she helped him out of his shirt before tracing his chest with her nails. He moaned, and she sank her claws into his flesh as her orgasm hit her in a sweet rush of bliss.

"So good," she groaned. She leaned forward and licked at the puncture wounds as he pulled the clip out of her hair and dropped it to the floor. He wrapped her hair in one big fist and tugged firmly.

"Again?"

"Yes, please," she moaned. "Again, and again, and again."

He lifted her without pulling out, and she hooked her legs around his hips as he carried her toward his desk.

"You're so damn strong." Her voice was thick with desire, and he grunted when she bit him on the shoulder.

"Gentle, Bria."

She licked the bleeding bite mark. "I'm sorry."

He set her on the desk and pushed her back until she rested on her elbows. He stared at where they were connected, and she mewled with need.

"I've wanted to fuck you on my desk since the day you started working for me," he confessed.

"Then fuck me," she snarled.

He grinned and wrapped one large hand around the back of her neck. He pulled her into a sitting position as he pumped back and forth and kissed her hard. She returned his kisses frantically, gasping and moaning into his mouth as he thrust into her wet, tight pussy.

"You're allowed to come twice more, and then we need to leave. We can't run the risk of someone catching us."

"No," she whined. Embarrassed but unable to stop, she clutched at his thick neck. "No, I – I can't go through this alone. Please don't make me."

"I won't, but we can't stay at the office. We'll go back to my place, all right?"

She nodded and then moaned when he started to fuck her with hard, impatient strokes. She was on the verge of another orgasm when he stopped. She hissed in anger, and he flinched when she bit his chest. His hand tightened in her hair, and he pulled her head away.

She licked his blood from her lips and growled at him. "Don't stop!"

"Why did you say no to Lincoln?"

She thrust her hips against him, and he pushed her back onto his desk, pinning her smaller body down with his large one and capturing her wrists before she could claw his back.

"Please fuck me, Jace." Her anger turned to pleading.

"I will, baby. But first, you have to tell me why you refused Lincoln." He moved his pelvis lightly, just enough to make her purr, and then stopped.

"Fuck me!" She dug her heels into his lower back. "You fuck me right now, Jace!"

"Soon," he said.

She writhed against him, trying to force him to move before finally snapping, "I don't want Lincoln, I want you!"

JACE'S TIGER ROARED HAPPILY WHEN BRIA ADMITTED SHE didn't want Lincoln. He pressed a kiss against her mouth. "I want you too."

He released her wrists and propped himself up above her. He fucked her roughly, not caring when his coffee mug slid off the desk and shattered on the floor. She was making desperate cries of need, and he growled and arched his back when her claws tore into the smooth skin of his back.

She came all over his thick cock, and it took all of his willpower not to come deep inside of her when her pussy squeezed around him. He was determined to make a better impression this time so she would be ready and needy for him whenever she was in heat. But fuck, it had never been this difficult to hold back his orgasm before.

He pulled out of her and flipped her to her stomach on the desk, shoving her legs apart and lifting her hips before sliding his cock deep into her warmth. She arched her back, and he pressed his hand against the back of her neck, pinning her upper body to the desk as he thrust back and forth. Her nails tore deep grooves into his desk as she panted and thrust her ass against his pelvis.

When she came for the second time, screaming his name and shuddering around him, he hurriedly pulled out of her before he could give in to his own pulsing need to come. He backed away as she shoved herself from the desk and grinned wickedly. "I want more."

"I said two, Bria. Now we need to go."

She traced the claw marks on his desk before giving him an adorable pout. "Just one more. Pretty please?"

"At home. Get dressed."

He started to dress, growling his displeasure when Bria hopped up on his desk and slid her hand between her thighs. Purring, she rubbed at her clit, and he cursed under his breath before dropping his shirt to the floor again.

"Bria," he warned as he walked toward her, "we need to go."

"I know," she panted. "Just let me give myself another, and then we'll go. I won't make it to your place if I don't."

He dropped to his knees in front of her, and she gave a soft yowl of delight before draping her legs over his shoulders. He buried his face between her thighs, and she clutched at his head, arching her back as he sucked firmly on her swollen clit. She rocked against his face, meowing and purring in that hoarse voice that made his tiger nearly insane with need.

When she came, he licked away her cream before sucking and licking at her clit again. He wasn't entirely certain one orgasm would be enough to prevent her from attacking him in the car. He needed to completely satisfy her before they left the office. She crowed with pleasure and cupped her breasts, pulling on her nipples before tightening her thighs around his head.

Twenty minutes and three orgasms later, he sat back on his heels and stared up at her. "Better?"

"Yes," she purred. "Thank you, Jace."

"You're welcome, baby." He stood and caught her by the shoulders when she started to lay back on his desk. "Get dressed. We need to leave."

"Right," she said dreamily. "Back to your house."

She grabbed him and kissed him on the mouth before licking his lips and cheeks clean. "Will you fuck me when we get home?"

He nodded, and she purred happily. "Lots and lots of fucking, right?"

A small grin crept across his face. God, she was insatiable, and he fucking loved it. "Yeah, baby, lots of fucking."

JACE UNTIED BRIA'S WRISTS FROM THE BEDPOST AND RUBBED the marks on her wrists before massaging her hands. He had been forced to use his tie to restrain her to keep her from completely ripping his back to shreds. He picked up the glass of juice he had brought from the kitchen before sitting her up. She leaned naked against the headboard and smiled hazily at him.

It was Saturday afternoon, and Bria's heat showed no signs of slowing down. He handed her the glass. "Drink this."

She drank obligingly and then purred when he picked up the plate of raw meat from the nightstand. "Are you hungry?"

"Starving!" She dug into the meat with relish. When his stomach rumbled, she grinned at him and fed him some meat before sharing her glass of juice. "I hardly ever eat raw meat. God, this is so good."

When they'd finished the meat, she reclined against the pillows and gave him a sweet look. "Thank you."

"You're welcome. I'm going to have a quick shower, all right?"

She nodded, her eyes already beginning to drift shut. Jace guessed he had about three hours before she was hungry for him again. He kissed her forehead as she turned and burrowed under the covers.

He would have to buy new sheets. He grinned to himself. Bria had shredded through all three sets before he'd gotten smart and tied her to the bed. Being restrained had ratcheted up her desire to an all new level, and she didn't hold back her screams and growls of pleasure. He supposed he was lucky his neighbours hadn't called the damn cops.

He stroked her back, pulling another warm purr from her throat, before heading to the primary bathroom. He studied his bitten, scratched and bruised chest in the mirror before turning and staring at his back. God, the little tiger had sharp claws. If he hadn't restrained her, his back would be hamburger by now. It would take longer than usual to heal from the deep slashes.

He smiled again as he turned the shower on and ducked under the hot spray. He would have to restrain her much earlier during her next heat. He didn't mind scratching and biting. It often heightened his desire, but even he had his limits. She was the smallest tiger shifter he'd ever met but she was feisty as hell. He flinched as the water rained down on his back. Hell, feisty might be a bit too tame for her.

He showered quickly, washing the dried blood from his back and chest before drying off and sliding into the bed next to Bria. She didn't move, and he curled on his side, studying her smooth back before tracing his finger down the curve of her spine. He would pick up some silk scarves, maybe even handcuffs, before Bria's next heat.

How do you know she'll come to you for her next heat? This cycle came early and took her off guard. It's the only reason she asked for your help. If you hadn't returned to the office, she'd be in some other shifter's bed right now.

His tiger growled at the thought. Trying to soothe it, he moved closer and wrapped his arm around her slender waist. She tucked into him, purring in her sleep, and he kissed her neck before closing his eyes.

He woke a few hours later to the feel of Bria's warm, wet tongue sliding across his chest. He groaned when her small hand wrapped around his cock and fisted him into hardness. She purred and straddled him, rubbing her wetness against his cock before sliding him deep inside of her. Despite her slender size, she took him easily, and he caught her wrists before she could sink her claws into his abdomen.

"I love your cock," she said breathlessly as she rode him. "It's the best cock ever."

His rumble of laughter turned into a harsh moan when she squeezed him with her inner muscles. "You're so thick. I've never been with anyone as big as you."

He groaned as she squeezed him again. "You'll fuck me every heat. Say it."

"I'll fuck you every heat." He braced his feet on the bed and met each of her thrusts.

She tried to pull her wrists free and growled at him when he wouldn't let her go.

"No, baby. No more scratching." He tightened his grip on her wrists and stopped her when she tried to rake her claws across his stomach.

"You're mine," she said.

"I'm -"

Holy hell, what was he doing? He clamped his mouth shut and tried to distract her with a few rough thrusts of his pelvis.

She hissed at him. "Mine. Say it."

He flipped her onto her back and entered her with one hard push. He caught her wrists and pinned them above her head. She hooked her legs around his waist and hissed again at him.

"Say it!"

He bent his head and sucked on one perfect pink nipple in a desperate attempt to distract her and to stop himself from saying he was hers. She arched upward, making low moans and purrs before coming hard around his cock.

He fucked her into three more orgasms before she whispered, "Better."

He released her wrists, and she moved her hands to his waist. Sated for now, she didn't sink her claws into him, and he propped himself on his hands above her. He plunged in and out of her with quick, hard strokes before climaxing. Her pussy gripped him tightly, and he moaned her name before burying his face in her neck. He licked her damp skin and purred to her. She purred back before licking the bite marks on his shoulder.

When he rolled off of her, she gave him a sleepy look of contentment. "So good, honey."

"Go to sleep, baby," he said. She curled into him, and he tried not to wince when her hand brushed his back. Ten minutes later, she was fast asleep, and he was still staring at the wall. She had said he was hers. She hadn't meant it. Cat shifters always got possessive and weird during their heats. Still, his immediate urge to agree with her, to tell her that he was hers, was unnerving.

You know that's bullshit. None of the other cat shifters you've helped during their heats ever got possessive of you.

Bria hadn't meant what she said. Just like he hadn't meant to nearly agree with her. They had both just gotten caught up in the moment, nothing more.

CHAPTER 9

Bria blinked at the bright afternoon light streaming into the bedroom before stretching gingerly. Her entire body was sore, with a particularly deep ache in her pelvis and thighs.

She lay quietly for a moment. Her heat cycle was over and now that the overpowering need had disappeared, she could feel every ache and pain in her overused body. God she needed to do more yoga or something. She had never hurt this badly after her heat cycle before.

You've never had this much sex before.

That was a good point. The last two days were a bit hazy – all right, really hazy – but she remembered enough to know that she and Jace had more sex than she thought was possible. The need to take and claim him had been so intense. A little shiver ran down her spine – what was happening to her? Her previous heat cycles had never been like this.

It's just because you aren't having sex regularly, that's all. You're not a freak.

Right – so why did she feel like such a freak?

She glanced behind her. Jace was burrowed under the covers with just the top of his dark hair sticking out. She felt a wave of affection that made her stomach twist with nervousness. She was not starting to feel something for her boss – that was just the lingering effects of her heat cycle. She really should have a shower and go home. Jace had to be tired of her by now.

She eased out of the bed. She wouldn't run away like she did the last time. She was an adult, for God's sake. She would make him breakfast. It was the least she could do after he had helped her for the last two days, and then she would make a graceful exit after breakfast.

She stumbled on her first few steps to the bathroom. A ribbon of sheet was wrapped around her calf and she unwrapped it before lifting the quilt and peeking at the sheets. She would have to buy him new ones. These were destroyed.

Nearly an hour later, Bria hummed softly as she turned the bacon in the frying pan. She was feeling much better after her hot shower, and the ache in her pelvis and thighs was more bearable now. She'd borrowed one of Jace's t-shirts and touched the smooth material before grabbing some eggs from the fridge. She started to sing, her alto voice filling the small kitchen, as she placed the eggs on the counter before turning the bacon again.

She thought of Jace asleep in the bedroom, his naked body cocooned in the warmth of his bed, and a thread of lust went through her. Maybe after eating, she could convince him to have a quickie before she returned to her own home.

God, Bria. What is wrong with you? You just had a marathon round of sex with him for the last two days, and you want to sleep with him again? Have some self-control, for God's sake. He's not going to want you again.

Probably not, she mused as she picked up an egg, but maybe if she pretended she was still in her heat cycle, he would let her have her way with him again. Hell, she could focus on his pleasure this time – he would like that.

The details of the weekend were hazy, but she knew from experience that she wouldn't have gone down on him or given a moment's thought to his pleasure. It was all about her during her heat cycle, and normally, that didn't bother her. In the past, there had always been the in-between times of her heat cycle to focus on her partner's pleasure. But if she was only going to be with Jace when she was in heat, well – that didn't seem entirely fair to her. She really needed to maintain better focus during her heat. She would try during the next one, try to remember that Jace needed pleasure as well.

Who says you'll be with him during your next heat cycle? He only helped you because you begged him, remember?

Her face flushed with embarrassment. That was true, but Jace had been clear about being willing to help her.

Yeah, and you rejected him. Just because he took pity on you this time doesn't mean he will the next time. Even if he does – is that really what you want? Do you want to be that girl who uses a guy once a month to scratch an itch? You want a relationship, but Jace doesn't. You're better off concentrating on finding a nice shifter who wants you for more than –

"Well, hello there."

The unfamiliar voice made her squeeze the egg in her hand. It cracked, and its insides slithered into the sink. She dropped the shell in the sink and whipped around. She stared wide-eyed at the man and woman standing in the kitchen, and her tiger made a warning growl.

The man held his hands up. "Easy there, girl." He sniffed in her direction before glancing at the woman standing beside him. "She's small for a tiger shifter, huh?"

"Who are you?" Bria asked.

"I'm Robert Shepherd, and this is my mate, Velma. Who are you, and what are you doing in my son's kitchen?"

The man raised his eyebrows at her as Velma said, "I think it's obvious what she's doing, Bobby."

"Bria? Is that bacon? I'm starving." Jace strolled into the kitchen wearing nothing but a pair of pajama bottoms.

Bites, bruises, and claw marks covered his chest, and bile rose in Bria's throat. He looked like he had been through a battle of epic proportions. Her cheeks burned with shame as Jace blinked in surprise at the couple standing in the kitchen.

"Mom? Dad? What are you doing here?"

"Honey, your chest!" Velma said in a horrified voice. "What happened?"

"I think it's obvious what happened, Velma," Jace's father snickered.

Both his parents stared at her, and Bria turned bright red.

"What are you guys doing here?" Jace repeated.

"We were supposed to have lunch an hour ago," Velma said. "We were worried when you didn't show up and decided to check on you. You weren't answering your cell phone."

"Sorry, I forgot, but you can't just walk into my house without knocking." Jace ran a hand through his dark hair.

"We didn't realize you had company," his father said.

"Um, I," Jace glanced at Bria, "this is Bria. Bria, these are my parents, Robert and Velma."

"Oh, we've met," Robert said cheerfully.

"Right." Jace stared blankly at his bruised and bitten chest. "I'll just, um, grab a shirt."

He turned, and Velma's horrified gasp echoed through the small kitchen. "Oh, Jace!"

She turned an accusing stare to Bria.

Bria couldn't hide her own look of horror. Jace's back was even worse than his chest. It was completely covered in deep slashes, and her pulse beat thickly in her ears as she stared at the torn flesh and bruising. What the fuck had she done to him?

"It's fine, Mom." Jace left the kitchen.

Bria, blinking rapidly to hold back the hot tears, gave his parents a sick lock of embarrassment. "I should go. I'm sorry."

She ran from the kitchen and hurried into Jace's bedroom. He was in the bathroom, and she dressed quickly before grabbing her purse.

"Bria? What are you doing?" He came out of the bathroom, pulling a shirt over his head. She flinched again at the sight of his chest.

"I'm so sorry," she said, "I didn't mean to hurt you so badly."

"You didn't. It's already starting to heal."

"It was worse?" Her stomach roiled, and for one moment, she thought she would barf all over his bedroom floor.

"It's okay." He gave her a look of alarm. "Bria, sit down. I need a minute with my parents, and then we'll talk about -"

"No," she said. "I need to go. I can't... I mean I shouldn't stay any longer. Thank you for helping me. I'm so sorry about hurting you like that."

"You don't have your car here. Let me give you a ride home."

"I can call an Uber." She gave him another sick smile of shame. "Please tell your parents I'm sorry for making you miss your family lunch."

"BRIA, WAIT!"

Jace cursed as Bria ignored him and ran out of the bedroom. He punched the wall when he heard the front door slam shut. He took a few minutes to calm his tiger before returning to the kitchen. His mother was cooking some eggs while his father sampled a piece of bacon from the frying pan.

He grinned at Jace as he crunched the bacon down. "She seems nice. Tiny for a tiger shifter but apparently quite the wildcat."

Jace blushed, and Velma whacked his father with the spatula. "Bobby, you're embarrassing him. Grab some plates from the cupboard."

As his father grabbed the plates and utensils, she smiled at Jace, but he could see the uneasiness lurking beneath her smile. "So, are you and Bria serious?"

"No."

"You're sure?" his dad asked. "She looked pretty comfortable in your kitchen."

"We're not serious. I was helping her through her heat."

He didn't miss the look of relief between his parents. His stomach churned, but he understood why they were relieved. After what happened with Jonah, he couldn't blame them. Not to mention how he had been after he and Tabitha ended things. It was no surprise that his parents were cautious about him dating.

"Are you driving with us to Ashley's engagement party this weekend?" His father ate another piece of bacon.

"No. I'll take my car," Jace said.

"Are you driving up Friday night or Saturday morning?" His mother added two eggs to a plate as the toast popped up.

"Probably Saturday morning." Jace buttered the toast and added it to the stack on the table.

"Why don't you drive up Friday night, and we'll have dinner at that restaurant – Bobby, what's the name of it again?"

"Franco's," Bobby said.

"That's right, Franco's. Your aunt says they have amazing pasta." Velma put eggs on the remaining two plates before placing the bacon on the table.

"I have a showing on Friday afternoon. I may not be finished in time to drive up and meet you for dinner."

"All right, but make sure you leave in plenty of time on Saturday morning," Velma said.

Jace joined his parents at the table and quickly ate a piece of toast and most of his bacon. He really was starving. Starving and tired and more than a little sore.

His tiger made a low growl of satisfaction. He had pleased his mate well this weekend.

Shit. He stared at the food on his plate. His appetite had disappeared, and nausea had taken its place. His tiger was still calling Bria his mate. He was so screwed.

"Velma, did you tell him?"

"Not yet."

"Tell me what?" Jace glanced at his mother.

"Marilyn will be at the engagement party."

He groaned and pushed his plate away before standing and pouring himself a cup of coffee. "Why? Ashley and she aren't friends."

"No, but their mothers are," Velma said.

"You should bring Bria," his father said.

Jace's mouth dropped open as his mother said, "Why on earth would he do that? They're not even dating."

She turned to Jace, the anxiety evident in her voice. "You're not dating her. Right, honey?"

"No, I'm not," he said.

"I know," Bobby said. "But Marilyn doesn't know that. He could use that wee tiger shifter to fend her off."

"Marilyn outweighs that little thing by sixty pounds. She's big even for a female lion shifter." Velma ate some eggs before sipping at her coffee.

Bobby shrugged. "After seeing Jace's chest and back - my money is on the wee tiger shifter. Think about it, son. You know Marilyn is like a dog with a bone when it comes to you. If you show up with a date, it'll help cool her off. She doesn't have to know that Bria means nothing to you."

Jace didn't reply, and his father glanced at his mother. "You know what, forget I said anything. It's a dumb idea."

"It'll be fine," Velma said. "Just be polite to Marilyn."

"And when she tries to corner you in the bathroom for a quickie, duck and run," Bobby said.

"Dad!" Jace glared at him. "Seriously?"

"Why does he get so grossed out when I bring up sex around him?" Bobby said to Velma with a grin. "It's like he thinks we don't have sex or even know what it is."

"Keep talking about sex, and I'm kicking you out of my house," Jace said.

His father laughed as Velma patted Jace's arm. "It'll be fine, honey. Maybe Marilyn has a mate now."

"Maybe I should just skip the engagement party."

"You have to go," Velma said. "You and Ashley have been close since you were kittens. She'll be so upset if you miss the party."

Jace dropped into his chair and drank more coffee as his father stole the bacon from his plate. "Yeah, I know. I'll be there."

"KAT? WHAT ARE YOU DOING HERE?" BRIA STARED IN SURPRISE at her best friend.

Kat lifted the bottle of wine she was carrying. "Sorry to just show up, but I bring wine."

Bria laughed and stepped aside so Kat could come in. "You know you can come by whenever. Where's Ronin tonight?"

"He joined Garth's monthly poker game."

"It's on a Sunday night?" Bria hung Kat's coat in the closet.

"They had to reschedule from last night. Garth's mom needed his help with something. So," Kat followed her into the kitchen of her small apartment, "have you found anyone?"

"Found anyone for what?" Bria grabbed a couple of wine glasses and the corkscrew.

"Your heat. It starts tomorrow." Kat plopped down in a kitchen chair. "Wait, am I getting your cycle mixed up with my sister's? I could have sworn yours started tomorrow because it's always a week before mine."

"No, you're right. Only, it came early for the first time in my life." Bria poured wine into the glasses. She handed one to Kat and sat next to her. She winced and shifted on the chair before taking a sip of wine.

"It came early?"

"Yep. Friday afternoon."

"Shit, were you at work?"

"Yeah." She crossed her legs and winced again before rubbing at her thighs.

"That's not good."

"It really wasn't."

"So, who was the shifter from Heat Me Up that helped you?"

155

Bria took another drink of wine. "Why do you think someone helped me? Maybe I took care of it myself."

Kat laughed. "Sweetie, no cat shifter winces like that when they've handled the problem themselves. Also, you look both unbelievably tired and satisfied at the same time. You had loads of sex this weekend. I know it. You know it. Why are you being so secretive about who helped you?"

"I'm not being secretive."

"Uh, yeah, you are. Who was it?"

"Fine. It was Jace, all right?"

Kat stared at her. "Jace? Your boss helped you through your heat cycle again?"

"It's not like we planned it." Bria drained her glass of wine and poured herself another glass. "It was starting, but I didn't believe it because my cycle never comes early. So, I kept telling myself it wasn't happening. Only it was. By three, I couldn't deny it anymore, and by five, I was in agony. I couldn't even think straight, and my tiger kept yowling at me for relief."

"Shit, did you attack Jace in front of the entire office?"

"No, he wasn't even there. Lincoln – the smarmy lion shifter I told you about – was the only one left in the office."

"Wait," Kat leaned forward and tapped one long red nail against the table, "Jace wasn't there, but Lincoln was. But you didn't fuck him, you fucked Jace."

"It's kind of a long story."

Kat poured herself some more wine. "I have nothing but time. Start talking."

"IT'S NOT FUNNY, KAT."

Kat laughed again. "It's sort of funny. I can only imagine

the look on his parents' faces when he strolled into the kitchen all shredded flesh and puncture wounds."

"Did you think it was funny when your mom walked in on Ronin making you breakfast after you banged him for forty-eight hours straight?"

"Ooh, point taken, girl. Yeah, maybe not so funny."

Bria rubbed at her forehead. "I looked like a psycho cat slut."

"You didn't."

"I did. His chest and back, Kit Kat – it'll take more than a day or two to heal from what I did to him."

"Okay, but he will heal, so don't sweat it. Will you ask him to help you with your next heat?" Kat asked.

"He's my boss."

"At this point, is that even an issue? You've already had sex with him."

"I did kind of make him promise that he would fuck me for every heat," Bria said.

Kat laughed. "I'm sure that was a real hard thing for him to promise."

Bria rubbed her aching thighs. "He was so good at it. We had so much sex I lost track of how many times I came. He never once couldn't get it up or complained when I made him go down on me. The difference between him and Raden – hell, even Kyle – was unbelievable. The need was really bad again, and he just handled it. You know?"

Kat nodded and took a sip of wine. "I'm glad for you, sweetie. Having a partner you can rely on during your heat makes such a difference."

"I tried to make him say he was mine," Bria said abruptly.

Kat stared at her. "Shit. You didn't."

"I did." Bria gave her a miserable look. "When I woke up this afternoon, I didn't remember half of what I had said to him – you know how things are a bit hazy when you're first coming out of your heat - but I've been remembering stuff in bits and pieces all day. After I made him tell me he'd fuck me every heat, I told him he was mine and tried to force him to say it. He wouldn't, though."

"I'm sorry."

"It's fine. He shouldn't have said it. It's just – it's embarrassing that I did that. He's been upfront about not wanting a relationship, and I keep saying dumb stuff to him. It's why I can't sleep with him during my next heat. I want more than he can give me, and that's not fair to either of us."

"No, I guess it isn't. Are you sure Jace doesn't want to date? Last weekend, you were in his bed and cuddling him." Kat asked.

"I'm sure. He was just drunk and feeling sad about his brother. I don't know if I told you this part or not, but he mentioned a woman named Tabitha. When I asked him about her, he shut down and wouldn't talk about it."

"Ah, so it's the old 'gun shy about relationships because his heart has been broken in the past' scenario," Kat said. "Lame."

Bria shrugged. "I guess so. I don't know for sure, but I think it's a safe bet."

"You're going back to the Shifter Love dating app, then?"

"Yeah. I haven't had good luck yet, but there's bound to be someone normal there. Right?"

Kat slugged back the rest of her wine. "At least seventy-five percent normal."

JACE STOOD AND PACED RESTLESSLY IN HIS OFFICE. IT WAS always busy on Mondays, and today was no different. He was out of the office for most of the day at different showings, and when he finally showed up there, Bria could hardly look at him. She looked tired and worn out. He had to stop himself from calling her into his office several times to talk.

The others hadn't noticed the tension between them. Well, maybe Rosalie had – she was weirdly perceptive for a human – and he decided it would be best to let another day or two pass before he tried to speak to Bria. He didn't want to wait, though. He wanted to sit her down and reassure her that he was fine. God, the look on her face when she had seen his upper body. He should have been smarter and hidden it from her.

He glanced at his watch. It was just after five, and Bria would be gone by now. He could leave without having to walk by her, without having to smell the scent of her embarrassment and shame. He traced the deep gouges in his desk before cursing under his breath. He hated that she felt that way. Even worse, his tiger had been growling and grumbling all day for him to simply pick up Bria and take her home. To take her to his bed and show her, in a very precise and very intimate way, that he wasn't upset with her.

His jaw clenched, and he stared at his desk again. He really should have Rosalie order him a new desk. He'd kept the gouges hidden by paperwork this afternoon, but sooner or later, she or someone else in the office would notice them, and he'd need to devise an excuse. But he liked seeing them, liked remembering the way Bria had purred and moaned as he fucked her against the desk.

Fuck. It was ridiculous to want Bria again. He'd just spent the last forty-eight hours between her soft thighs, and there was no way he should want to be back there already. Besides the scratches and puncture wounds from her claws and teeth, his body had already healed from the other aches and pains. But he had seen Bria wince when she sat down and noticed how she walked a bit stiffly. She wasn't completely healed yet.

Besides, now that her heat was over, she wasn't interested in just having sex with him. She'd gotten what she needed. It would be another month before she wanted him again if she didn't find a boyfriend between now and then.

There was a soft knock on the door, and he spat out a 'come in.'

The door opened, and Bria stuck her head into the room. "Hi. Can I talk to you for a minute?"

"Yes. Shut the door."

She held a large bag in her hand, and he stared at it curiously as she shut the door and approached his desk.

"I thought you had left already," he said.

"I wanted to speak to you first." She glanced at his door. "Lincoln and Rosalie are still here, so I'll make this quick."

"About yesterday – I'm sorry you had to meet my parents like that. I know it was embarrassing."

"Oh, uh, that's okay. It wasn't your fault." She picked at the handle of the bag. "How are you feeling today?"

"Fine. It really was much worse than it looked. You shouldn't -"

"Are they healed?"

"Yes."

She eyed him suspiciously. "Let me see."

He hesitated, and she sighed. "Yeah, that's what I thought."

"I told you that I didn't mind scratching and biting."

She bit at her bottom lip. "If you hadn't – hadn't restrained me, I would have really hurt you."

"But you didn't, and next time, I'll be quicker to restrain you." He flinched at his words, wondering if she would reject him immediately, but she was staring at the bag in her hand and didn't seem to hear him.

"I bought you these." She pulled two packages of sheets from the bag. "To replace the ones I ruined."

"You didn't have to do that."

"I wanted to. I also have this."

She pulled a large jar from the bag, and he stared at it. "What is it?"

"It's a salve for your chest and back. It will help you heal faster."

"Where did you get it?"

She had placed it on the desk, and he picked it up and examined it.

"I know a place downtown. It's a shifter store with ointments and salves for different things. It will help. Will you use it?"

He nodded, and she gave him a look of relief. "Good. Start using it right away, okay?"

"I will."

"Okay, well, uh, have a good night."

"You too." He watched her walk toward the door, more turned on than he should have been by the sight of her ass in her tight skirt. His tiger growled happily when she paused at the door.

"Do you have someone to – I mean – how will you put it on your back?"

He grinned at her. "Well, Lincoln is still here. I'll ask him to rub it into my back. I'm sure he'll love the idea."

His pulse sped up when the smile curved across her lips. "I'd rather you didn't show Lincoln your back. He knows I was in heat on Friday, and it won't take him long to put two and two together."

"Rosalie, then. She'll be horrified, but I'll tell her the job description has changed."

"No!" Her sudden growl made him twitch. "She is not to touch you."

He didn't reply, and she flushed before striding forward. "Take off your shirt. I'll put some salve on it before I go home."

"Yes, ma'am." He gave her a flirty little grin, then yanked off his tie and dropped it on the desk. She stared at it and he wondered if she remembered that it was the tie he had used to restrain her to the bed. It was stupid of him to wear it today, but he couldn't resist.

"Do you like my tie, Bria?"

That delightful flush deepened, and he knew if he took off her shirt, the flush would cover her small but incredible tits. Fuck, he wanted to suck on her nipples right now. Instead, he unbuttoned his shirt and held the jar out to her.

She was staring at his broad chest, at the still-healing marks on his tanned skin. Did she even remember how it felt to be underneath him, to have his cock slamming into her tight pussy repeatedly? He knew some cat shifters remembered very little during their heat, but he had no idea if Bria was one of them.

"Bria?" he prompted.

"Sorry." She took the jar, and he took his shirt off and draped it across the desk before turning around. "Oh God, it hasn't healed at all."

"Of course it has. Stop feeling bad."

Shame replaced the obvious scent of her desire. He made sure not to move a muscle when she tentatively rubbed the salve into the slashes on his back. The salve was cold, but her hands were warm, and he tried not to groan with pleasure while she rubbed the salve into his back.

"All finished."

Her voice was a little hoarse, and he turned around, hoping she wouldn't notice how his cock tented his pants. She would smell his desire, but there wasn't anything he could do about that.

She bit her bottom lip as she stared at his chest. "Um, do you want some help with the front?"

"That would be very helpful."

She swallowed, her throat making a dry click, and scooped out a large amount of salve. She spread it over her fingers as he sat on his desk and spread his legs. She hesitated before stepping between them, and he held back his groan when her thighs brushed against his. She smoothed the salve over his chest, concentrating on each bite mark and scratch with studious regret as the scent of their mutual desire hung thickly between them.

When her fingers scraped across one flat nipple, he inhaled sharply, and she gave him a worried look. "I'm sorry. Did that hurt?"

"No, little tiger," he rasped. "It doesn't hurt. Keep going."

She licked her bottom lip before stroking his chest with her soft, warm hands. She gasped when his big hands cupped her ass, and he pressed her against his hard dick.

"I – is that better?" she whispered.

"Not yet," he growled. "I need more."

"Okay," she almost moaned. Her hands rubbed across his collarbone, and she gasped again when he slid his hands inside her skirt and gripped her bare ass.

He squeezed the firm flesh before tracing the thin strip of material between her ass cheeks. This time, she did moan, a soft sound that set his skin on fire with need.

"I feel so bad about doing this to you." She pressed her mouth against a particularly deep bite mark on his shoulder.

"You shouldn't." He squeezed her ass again.

"I feel like I should make it up to you, somehow."

"Maybe you should." He bent his head and sucked on her bottom lip.

She purred, and his cock throbbed at the sound.

Her purring fucking did him in every time.

"What do you want me to do?" She licked his mouth, and he groaned.

Despite how much time they had spent mating over the weekend, he wanted her again with a desperation that would have been funny if it hadn't been so ridiculously pathetic.

"You can go with me to my cousin's engagement party this weekend."

She blinked in surprise at him as he gave her his own look of shock. Where the fuck did that come from?

She pulled away from him. He let go of her ass with regret, and she folded her arms across her torso. "You want me to go with you to a family thing?"

"Yes. My cousin Ashley is getting married, and we're having an engagement party for her. My entire extended family will be there."

It was the wrong thing to say. Bria's eyes widened, and she took another step back. "Your entire family?"

Goddammit.

"Yes, but there will also be friends there. One of them is a lion shifter named Marilyn."

She gave him a blank look, and he forged ahead. "I've known Marilyn since we were kittens, and she, uh, has a bit of a crush on me."

Her eyes flashed golden fire before returning to their normal blue. "So what? You want me to go with you and pretend to be your girlfriend, so Marilyn leaves you alone?"

He nodded. "Yes, that's exactly what I want. I know I

sound like an asshole, but I have tried everything else with her – including flat-out telling her I will never be interested in her as anything more than a friend. The woman is relentless."

"Do you think me posing as your girlfriend will make a difference then?"

"I do. When Tabitha and I were together, Marilyn didn't..."

His face turned hot, and he cleared his throat. "Anyway, you'd be doing me a huge favour by posing as my girlfriend. What do you say?"

"I'm not sure, Jace. It's weird to pretend when I..." She stared at the marks on his chest before taking a deep breath. "Yes, I'll do it."

"Thank you. I appreciate this." He hesitated and made a sudden decision. If they left Friday night, he would have an excuse to spend the night with Bria. Maybe she'd want to sleep with him again. "It's an overnight trip. We'll leave Friday after work and return to the city by Saturday evening."

Before she could reply, the door opened, and Lincoln poked his head in. "Hey, I'm going for a drink. Do you want to come with – holy shit, man, what the fuck happened to you?"

Jace grabbed for his shirt as Bria, blushing furiously, skittered past Lincoln and out the door.

"Christ, you look like you've been put through a meat grinder," Lincoln said.

"Shut up, Lincoln." Jace buttoned his shirt.

"Are those bite marks?" Lincoln grinned at him. "Nice! What little hellcat did you pick up at the bar this weekend? And is it serious? Because if it isn't, give me her number. I'd love to get into the pants of the woman who -"

Jace growled at him, his eyes glowing bright green. Lincoln held up his hands. "Easy, buddy. What's gotten into you?"

"Nothing. Just be quiet."

Lincoln's eyes widened, and he studied the open door before turning back to Jace. "Motherfuck. Bria did that, didn't she?"

"No."

"Bullshit. After you kicked me out of the office on Friday, you helped her with her heat."

"Keep your voice down." Jace shut his office door.

"Don't try to deny it, my friend," Lincoln said. "You don't normally stand half-naked in your office with the admin staff."

Jace scrubbed his hand across his face as Lincoln said, "Hell, I had no idea Bria had that in her. She's so tiny and sweet. Maybe I can convince her to give me a chance for her next heat. I'd love to feel those claws of hers sinking into my _"

He grunted with pain when Jace slammed him against the wall. "Keep away from Bria. Do you hear me? If you go anywhere near her, I'll tear you apart."

"Holy shit." Lincoln's voice was soft. "You're falling for Bria."

"No, I'm not." Jace let him go and returned to his desk. He sat down and scowled at Lincoln when the lion shifter sat in the other chair. "I'm busy, Lincoln."

"Are you and Bria dating?"

"No, I just helped her with her heat. I don't want to be in a relationship anymore. You know that."

Lincoln leaned forward. "I know you keep saying that, but I haven't quite figured out if it's because you don't want to be in one or your parents don't want you to be in one."

Jace growled at him, but Lincoln continued anyway. "You can't live your life for your folks. I know what happened with Jonah was awful, but who's to say it wouldn't have happened even if Davra hadn't left him. Jonah needed therapy and medication and -"

"Are you forgetting what happened when Tabitha and I broke up? Depression runs in our family. My aunt killed herself when she was only thirty-eight, and then Jonah, and then I..."

"You were nowhere near that point," Lincoln said. "Don't let your parents convince you that you were. You were hurting, you got help, end of story. You're letting your parents' fear dictate your life, buddy."

"You weren't in my head," Jace said. "How I felt, the things I thought about when Tabitha and I ended it, it was awful and -"

"And it doesn't mean you were going to off yourself like your brother did."

Jace winced. Apparently, Lincoln couldn't contain his usual bluntness any longer.

"Look," Lincoln tugged at the crease in his pants, "your mom and your dad are terrified that you're going to get into a relationship, break up, and then kill yourself just like your brother did. I understand why they're afraid, but that fear is smothering you and stopping you from living your life."

"It isn't."

"It is." Lincoln continued relentlessly. "Maybe you didn't help alleviate their fears when you went a little squirrely after that bitch Tabitha broke your heart. But what you and your parents are both conveniently forgetting is that you didn't spiral down until you thought suicide was the only option. You recognized what was happening and got some help."

"My parents met Bria."

"You're shitting me."

"I'm not." Jace grabbed his tie from the desk and traced his finger along the pattern. "They dropped by my house on Sunday afternoon. Bria's heat was finished, but she was making us something to eat in the kitchen. They walked right in and saw her."

"What happened?"

"Nothing. My mom was a little horrified by how my chest and back looked. Bria was incredibly embarrassed and left immediately. Mom and Dad stayed, and we ate brunch."

"What did they think of her?"

"They didn't think anything of her. They just confirmed right away that it wasn't serious, and I wasn't dating her, and that was it." He wondered if Lincoln could hear the bitterness in his voice. "Anyway, I'm more than willing to help Bria with each of her heats, but she wants a relationship too. I told her I don't do relationships, and she said she didn't want to sleep with me just because of her heat. I wouldn't have helped her with this heat if it hadn't come early. She only fucked me because she was desperate."

"You sure about that?" Lincoln leaned back in his chair and tucked his hands behind his head. "She turned me down flat, and she was in agony from her heat. I could see it and smell it. Besides, the way you reacted when I talked about fucking Bria -"

The growl tore out of his throat immediately, and Lincoln laughed. "Yeah, thanks for making my point. You want a relationship with Bria, and she wants a relationship with you. Go for it, you idiot."

"You didn't see the look on my parents' faces when they thought I might be dating her."

Lincoln sighed and stood up. "You're not your brother Jace. Don't let them convince you that you are."

He left the office. Jace turned in his chair and stared out the window. Fuck, what was he doing? Why the hell did he invite Bria to Ash's engagement party? He had lost his fucking mind.

No, you want to spend time with Bria. You like her.

His tiger growled in agreement. *Give me my mate.*

He sighed and turned back to his computer. He invited Bria because he wanted to use her to keep Marilyn off his goddamn back. He would never have thought of it if his father hadn't mentioned it.

CHAPTER 10

"**K**at, this would be much easier if you were here." Bria stared at Kat's face on the screen of her cell phone.

"I know, but I'm stuck at work, and if you want my opinion on a dress, this is our best option. Show me the yellow one."

Bria turned the phone and showed her the yellow dress. "It's pretty, but am I looking for pretty, or am I looking for knock-your-socks-off hot?"

"Okay, let me see the blue one again." Kat's voice was tinny and low.

Bria pulled the blue one from the rack and held it next to the yellow one. "Which one do you think?"

"Definitely the blue one."

Jace's low voice speaking into her ear almost made her shriek in surprise. She whipped around, still holding her phone out before her, and stared up at the gorgeous tiger shifter. "What are you doing here?"

"It's a mall where people shop. I shop."

Kat's laugh drifted from the phone, and Jace grinned at the screen. "Hello, Kat. It's nice to see you again."

"Nice to see you too, Jace."

Bria turned the phone so the screen was facing her. "Uh, Kat was helping me pick out a dress for this weekend. Right, Kat?"

"That's right. But I have to go. Bye."

"Kat! No, wait…"

The jaguar shifter's face disappeared from the screen, and Bria gave Jace a weak smile. "Uh, she had to go."

"I heard. So, which dress are you going with?"

"I'm not sure. I wanted a second opinion when I was wearing them. I guess I'll wait until tomorrow night to see if Kat can go to the mall."

"No need," Jace said. "I can give you a second opinion. Go and try them on."

"Oh no, that's okay. You're probably busy and…"

Jace scooped up both dresses and carried them to the dressing room at the back of the store. She followed him and watched as he gave the dresses to the attendant.

"Come with me." The attendant was a wolf shifter, and she gave Jace a clear look of appreciation.

Her tiger snarled in jealousy. Bria soothed it as she followed the attendant to one of the rooms. The attendant hurried away, no doubt to flirt with Jace, and Bria grimaced at herself in the mirror. She stripped off her shirt and skirt and tugged the yellow dress over her head. It was pretty, and the colour looked good on her, but she wasn't fond of how it flared around her hips.

She opened the door and stepped out. To her surprise, Jace was sitting in one of the chairs in the waiting area, and the attendant was gone.

He looked her up and down. "This one is cute."

She made a face. "Yeah, it's a no then."

"What's wrong with cute?"

"Nothing's wrong with cute if you're a little kid."

He laughed, and she grinned at him. "I'll try on the blue one."

She returned to the dressing room and took off the yellow dress. She studied the blue one briefly before shrugging out of her bra She had a strapless one at home that she could wear with the dress, but she was perky enough to go without to see what the dress looked like.

The dress was gorgeous, she mused. It was strapless with a sweetheart neckline and a ruched bodice. The skirt flowed down her hips to just above her knees. She pulled the zipper up as far as she could before opening the door and poking her head out.

"Is the attendant around?"

"Nope. What do you need?"

"Uh, my zipper done up."

He stood, and she hesitated before walking to him. She turned, and he zipped up the dress before stroking a finger across her bare upper back. Goosebumps rose on her skin, and her tiger purred before she could stop it. Jace's rumbling purr, in return, made her flush with pleasure.

Before she could do something really stupid like push him into the dressing room and have sex with him, she stepped away and turned to face him. "What do you think?"

He didn't reply, and disappointment flickered through her. "That bad?"

"That good." His voice was a low growl that made her pussy dampen and then clench uselessly around nothing. "You look incredibly sexy, little tiger."

"Thank you," she whispered.

His gaze lingered on her breasts, and she could feel her nipples tightening against the material of the dress. He traced the ruching across the abdomen with his hand, and she could barely contain her moan. When he finally lifted his gaze to her face, and she saw the lust in it, her tiger made a soft and embarrassingly eager mating trill to Jace's tiger.

"Oh God, I'm sorry." She wanted to kill her stupid tiger and her stupid mating call.

Stop it! she snapped inwardly at her tiger. *You're embarrassing me.*

Her tiger hissed at her but retreated. She gave Jace another look of apology. "Sorry."

"It's fine," he said. "You have to get this one for the party."

She smoothed her hand down the skirt. "Yeah? You like this one better than the yellow one?"

He nodded as he studied her mouth. "Much better. There is one problem, though." He stepped closer to her, and she licked her lips when he rubbed her collarbone with his thumb.

"Wh-what?"

"If you wear this dress to the party, I'll have to mark you to keep the other shifters from trying to take you from me."

She stared up at him. His eyes were turning from hazel to jade, and when his tiger called to hers, she purred in reply without even thinking about it. Cat shifters could mark and sometimes did – although they weren't nearly as over-the-top about marking as wolf shifters were – but they usually only marked their mates. It was a testimony to how drunk Jace was the night he kept marking her at the club.

"Maybe I should mark you right now."

His voice was low.

Hypnotic.

"Lift your head, little tiger."

She wanted him to mark her so much.

She wanted to know that she smelled like him.

She wanted any shifter who went near her to smell Jace and know she was his.

She was lifting her head when common sense returned. His mark would last a day or two, and the other shifters at the office would smell it.

He was already bending his head, and she put a hand on his broad chest. "Jace, wait."

He growled at her, and she shook her head. "No, you can't mark me. The others at the office…"

"A kiss then," he said. "Kiss me, little tiger."

"I shouldn't," she whispered as he dipped his head down.

"You should."

She stared at Jace's mouth. "Maybe just once."

He growled his approval. "That's my good girl."

"How are we doing here back here? Need any help or – oh!"

Bria's tiger growled, and her fangs popped out. She clapped her hand over her mouth before she could bare them at the attendant standing behind them.

Jace stepped back, and the attendant took a deep breath before flushing. Bria joined her in turning red. No doubt the wolf shifter could smell Jace's arousal. Hell, she would smell Bria's too.

The attendant gave her a look that practically screamed silent judgment. "Have you decided on a dress?"

"Uh, yes. I'll take this one."

"Perfect." She stared pointedly at Jace.

"Bria, I'll wait for you out there. Okay?"

"Sure, okay."

He left, and the attendant gave her a frosty smile. "Need help with the zipper?"

"Yes, thank you."

SHE HALF-EXPECTED JACE TO BE GONE WHEN SHE CAME OUT OF the dressing room, but he was standing by the till. They stood in awkward silence as the woman behind the counter folded the dress and placed it in a bag.

"That'll be $125.73," the woman said.

Before Bria could grab her wallet from her purse, Jace handed the woman his card.

"Hey, no, you're not buying the dress."

The woman paused, and Jace made a go on motion to her. "I am, Bria."

"I have money," she said defensively.

"I know you do. But the only reason you're buying this dress is because of me. I want to pay for it. You're doing me a favour, remember?"

"No, I'm going as a way to say sorry for scratching the crap out of you during my -"

She shut her mouth with a snap and stared at the sales clerk. She was human, and she studied Bria with curiosity. Jace was grinning, and Bria scowled at him as he turned back to the sales clerk. "Put it on my card, please."

She rang it through, and he took the bag when she handed it to him. He walked out of the store, and Bria followed him. When she tried to take the bag, he pulled it away. "I'll carry it for you."

Dammit, why did he have to be such a gentleman? She sighed and walked beside him as they wandered through the mall. "Thank you for buying the dress."

"You're welcome," he said. "Where to next?"

"I'm done."

"I have to go to the bookstore." Still holding the bag, he turned left, and she had no choice but to follow him to the bookstore. He went straight to the food section and started browsing through the cookbooks.

"Are you looking for anything in particular?" she asked.

"It's my mom's birthday next month. I bought her a spiralizer, and now I'm just looking for a cookbook with recipes."

"Are you always this organized?"

"Nope. Just ask Rosalie."

She laughed, and he grinned at her. "Is Rosalie saying bad things about me?"

"No, just the opposite. She likes working for you a lot."

"She's the best assistant I've ever had. It'll be a damn shame when she becomes an agent."

"You know she wants to do that?" Bria gave him a surprised look.

"I suspected, and now you've confirmed it." He gave her a wicked grin, and she poked him in his flat abdomen.

"You tricked me. Here I was thinking you were a sweet guy.

"I'm very sweet.' He stepped toward her, and she backed up until her ass hit the bookshelf behind her. "I think you know exactly how sweet I can be."

She licked her lips, her tiger purring so loudly she could barely hear anything else. "Jace, I..."

His chest brushed against her breasts, and she tried not to moan. He studied her mouth as he reached beside her head and pulled out a book. "Just what I'm looking for."

He stepped away and she swallowed her disappointment as he leafed through the book. "It's perfect. Ready to go?"

"Yes."

They walked toward the tills, and Bria said, "How are your back and chest?"

"Almost completely healed."

"Really?" She gave him a skeptical look. It had only been two days since she'd given him the salve. She suspected he was lying to her.

"Yes. I keep telling you that you don't need to feel bad about scratching me. It's not that big of a...Rosalie, hey. How are you?"

They were walking through the self-help section and nearly ran straight into the curvy brunette. Rosalie stared wide-eyed at them before clamping the books she held to her chest. She covered them with her arms and gave them a nervous smile.

"Uh, hey, guys. I'm good. What are you doing here?"

"I ran into Bria while she was shopping for a dress. I'm buying a cookbook for my mom's birthday," Jace said. "What books are you buying?"

"Um..." Rosalie stared at Bria. The human had a *holy shit help me* look on her face, and Bria tugged on Jace's arm.

"Hey, do you mind if we get going? I have a thing tonight."

"Sure," Jace said. "See you later, Rosie."

"Bye, Jace."

Jace stepped past her, and Rosalie mouthed 'thank you' to Bria. Bria smiled at her and squeezed her arm before following Jace to the till. He paid for the book, and they walked toward the outside entrance of the bookstore.

"Where are you parked?" Jace asked.

"Not far from here."

"I'll walk you to your car."

They walked silently to her car, and she smiled at him when he put the bag in her backseat. "Thanks, Jace."

"You're welcome."

There was an awkward silence. Jace rubbed at the scruff on his jaw. "I guess I'll see you tomorrow at the office."

"Yes."

"Right. Okay, bye."

"Bye."

He turned to go, and her tiger whined like a housecat. "Jace, wait."

"What's wrong?" He studied her closely.

"Nothing. I – is your back really healed?"

He shrugged. "Mostly. My chest is completely healed – that salve you gave me is amazing – but I couldn't put it on my back, so it's taking longer to heal."

She bit her lip. "Um, your house is on my way home. Do you want me to stop and put some salve on your back?"

"I thought you had a thing."

She smiled a little. "Sorry, I didn't. But Rosalie obviously didn't want us to see what books she bought."

"Seriously?" Jace gave her a surprised look. "Why not?"

"I don't know, but it's why I lied. She wanted us to leave."

"Oh. Well then, yes, I'd like it if you stopped by." He backed away quickly as if afraid she would change her mind. "I'll see you in about fifteen minutes then?"

"Yeah, okay." She climbed into her car and gave Jace a brief wave before starting the car and driving toward the exit.

Her tiger purred and trilled excitedly. What the hell was she doing? Going to Jace's house was a very bad idea, but one she couldn't resist.

ROSALIE PEEKED AROUND THE CORNER OF THE BOOKSHELF. Jace and Bria were paying at the register, and she loosened her grip on her books. God, if they had seen what she was buying...

She took a deep breath. They didn't see them – it was

fine. They were leaving the bookstore, and she heaved another sigh of relief. She decided it was stupid to feel so self-conscious as she hurried toward the cashier. Even if they had seen her books, what was the big deal? She was an adult woman buying books about sex. She studied the books in her arms. There was nothing to be embarrassed about or –

"Crap!" She ran head-first into a warm, hard, oddly familiar wall of flesh. The books flew from her arms and landed on the floor as she staggered back. She stared up at the rough features of Hudson. The polar bear shifter scowled at her, and she gave him a nervous smile.

"I'm sorry."

He grunted in reply, and she watched in slow-motion horror as he bent and reached for her books.

"No, don't - "

It was too late. Hudson had picked up both books and was studying the covers. The one in his ham-sized right hand was bright blue. The woman on the front cover had the striking beauty of a supermodel. A lion, its mouth open in a roar, sat beside her. In yellow font, the title, "A Human's Guide to Sex with a Lion Shifter," was scrawled across the top of the book.

The book in his left hand was black with white lettering. Hudson studied the photo of the handcuffs embossed on the cover, and she wanted to die when he read the title in his low voice. "So You Want to be Kinky. Fifty-Two Ways to Spice up Your Sex Life."

"They're, um, a gag gift for a friend." Her cheeks were so hot she waited for them to catch fire.

"Right," he said.

"I'm sorry for smashing into you again."

"You do that a lot. Maybe you should watch where you're going."

"Uh, yes, I will, um, start doing that." Oh God, she needed to leave, but he still held her books. "Can I have the books back now?"

He studied the books again before studying her. "Lion shifters are nothing but trouble. You should stay away from them."

"I told you – they're books for a friend." Her voice was too high and too thin. Why the fuck didn't she just order the damn books online?

"You're not a very good liar, human." He held the books out, and she snatched them to her chest.

Without another word, he turned and left. She could feel the floor shaking as he walked, and she watched as others in the bookstore turned to stare at him. Her heart thudding in her chest, Rosalie hurried to the checkout.

"Mom, I'm fine. Stop worrying. I had a few errands to run, that's all. No, I'm not feeling sick. Why? My voice is not rusty sounding. No, my throat isn't sore. Mom, I have to go, okay? I'll call you later. I love you, too. Bye, yes, no, I know… okay, bye."

Rosalie sighed and shoved her cell phone into her pocket before pushing through the exit doors. After her humiliating encounter with the polar bear shifter, she went to the food court and consoled herself with sushi before grabbing a coffee from Starbucks. She sipped the hot liquid as she walked across the parking lot. She would go home, get into her pajamas, and maybe do a little reading. She was stupidly excited to read her new books and maybe get ideas on how to seduce Lincoln and…

Shit. She slowed to a stop and stared at the man bent over

the truck's engine. Maybe it wasn't him. Maybe it was some other giant-sized man who just happened to be a damn polar bear.

She sighed again before walking toward Hudson. "Hey there. Car trouble?"

He glanced briefly at her before bending over the engine of his truck again. "Yeah."

His big hands poked and prodded at the engine. When it came to what was under the hood of a car, she knew how to add windshield washer fluid, and that was the extent of her knowledge. Hudson seemed to know what he was doing, but the truck looked about a thousand years old. She wasn't surprised when he returned to the driver's seat and nothing happened when he turned the key.

She expected him to curse, maybe slam his hands on the steering wheel in frustration. Instead, he slid out from behind the wheel, shut the door, and closed the hood with a loud bang.

"Are you going to call a tow truck?" She asked.

"Nah. I know the part I need. I'll pick it up tomorrow and come back and fix it."

"Oh. How will you get home tonight?"

"Walk." He walked away without saying goodbye, and she bit her bottom lip.

"Hey, wait. I can give you a ride home."

He turned and stared at her. "Won't fit in your car."

"I drive a truck."

He looked her up and down. She could see the surprise on his face. "What?"

"A little human like you drives a truck?"

"I'm not little." She wanted to giggle at the absurdity of the conversation. Had she ever once in her life been called little? No. Definitely not.

He trudged back until he stood in front of her. "You look little to me."

She craned her head up to stare at him. He made a good point. Compared to Hudson, she was little. Of course, a damn moving van would look small next to him, so she shouldn't be too flattered.

"Um, my truck isn't parked far from here."

"I can walk."

"I'd like to repay you for helping me at the bar the other night. Let me give you a ride home, okay?"

He shrugged. "Okay."

She shifted her bag of books to her other hand and blushed a little when Hudson stared at the bag. "Ready?"

He nodded and followed her to her truck. He pushed the seat back as far as it would go and climbed into the passenger side. She threw the bag of books in the back and put her coffee in the cupholder between them. She slid behind the wheel and started the truck.

"Um, I'm Rosalie, by the way. You're Hudson, right?" she asked as she buckled her seat belt.

He nodded and slouched a little so the top of his head didn't hit the ceiling. "Yeah."

"What's your address?"

He recited the address, and she jerked in surprise. "That's in Standen Park?"

"Yeah."

"I'm in Standen Court, right next to Standen Park. We're neighbours."

He grunted in reply, and she cleared her throat before driving out of the parking lot. After a few minutes, she said, "So, thanks again for helping me at the bar."

"You're welcome."

"Do you like working there?"

"It's a good place to work."

"That's good." He hadn't asked, but she said, "I work at a real estate agency. I'm a personal assistant, but I'm considering becoming an agent."

He didn't reply, and she stopped at a red light. The silence in the car felt thick and uncomfortable. She studied him out of the corner of her eye. He was wearing jeans with dark brown work boots and a t-shirt. This one fit him way better than his work shirt, but it still stretched across his broad shoulders and clung to his upper arms. He wasn't wearing a jacket despite the cool air.

"Aren't you cold?"

He turned to study her. "I'm a polar bear."

"Oh, right. That was a stupid thing to say. You probably never get cold, huh?"

Another shrug before he stared out the window. She studied the back of his thick neck as the light turned green. She drove forward and cleared her throat again.

"Can I ask you a personal question?" She decided his low grunt meant yes. "Where do you buy your clothes? Pretty sure you can't just walk into a Macy's and buy a pair of jeans."

"Order them online."

"Oh. Like a specialty store for, uh, large shifters?"

"Yeah."

"That must be annoying. Not being able to buy clothes from a store here in the city."

"There are shifter clothing stores here." He scowled at her. "Do you know anything about shifters?"

"Not a lot."

"That guy you were with at the bar was a tiger shifter."

"Yes, but he's my boss. We don't, like, hang out regularly or anything. The new receptionist, Bria, is a tiger shifter, and we've sort of become friends. Are you, uh, friends with any humans?"

"No."

"Oh. Because you don't like humans or…"

"I don't know any humans. Can I ask you a personal question?"

She nodded. "Oh, uh, yes, of course."

"Why do you wanna fuck a lion shifter?"

Her face turned bright red, and she groaned inwardly when she had to stop for another red light. "That's really personal."

"You asked me a personal question."

"There's a big difference between asking someone where they buy their clothes and asking someone about their sex life."

He just shrugged, and she stared out the windshield. She wouldn't tell the polar bear shifter why she wanted to sleep with Lincoln. It was none of his business.

"I don't want to just fuck a lion shifter," she blurted out. "I want to date a lion shifter named Lincoln."

"Why?"

"What do you mean, why? Why does anyone want to date someone? He's handsome and smart and funny. I like him."

He looked her up and down. "You're not his type."

"You don't even know him. Besides, lion shifters like all sorts of women. Even chubby ones," she said defensively.

"Not talking about your looks. And I do know him. He comes to the bar all the time. Goes home with a different shifter every time."

She had an immediate urge to defend Lincoln. "That doesn't make him a bad guy."

"You're too sweet for a lion shifter."

"You don't know that I'm sweet."

"Anyone who needs to buy a book on how to have kinky sex is too sweet for a lion shifter."

"Oh my God! I am not discussing my sex life with you. Besides, there's nothing wrong with expanding your knowledge on certain subjects. Reading is never a bad thing."

He laughed, and a weird trickle of heat went through her belly. He had a nice laugh. An amazing laugh, actually, and her irritation and embarrassment disappeared almost immediately.

"You should stay away from him," he said.

"I'll take your suggestion under advisement." She pulled into the Standen Park complex, and he pointed toward a townhouse.

"It's that one on the end."

She stopped in front of his house, and he reached for the door. "Thanks for the ride."

"You're welcome."

He slid out of the truck. Before he could slam the door shut, she said, "I leave for work around eight. I can stop and pick you up if you want a ride to a car parts store or something."

He hesitated, and she smiled tentatively at him. "I really don't mind."

"Yeah, okay," he grunted. "Thanks."

"You're welcome. See you at eight."

"Bye." He shut the door and walked into his house without looking back.

CHAPTER 11

"Would you like a drink? I have wine or beer."

Bria set her purse on the table as Jace opened the fridge. "A beer is good."

He pulled two bottles out and opened them before handing one to her. "Cheers."

"Cheers." She clinked her bottle against his before swallowing the cold liquid. She was nervous and tense and wanted to drain the bottle quickly. Maybe it would make her stop feeling so anxious. Instead, she took a second, smaller sip. She had to drive home, and if she drank it too quickly, she'd be too tipsy to drive.

You could spend the night.

She shut that thought down real damn quick. "So, um, if you get the salve, I'll put it on your back."

"Sure." He left and returned a few minutes later. "Here you go."

She took the jar of salve as he pulled his shirt over his head and dropped it next to her purse. She took another swallow of beer. His chest was healed, and she itched to trace her fingers over all that smooth, hard flesh.

"Turn around." God, even she could hear the need in her voice.

This was such a bad fucking idea.

He turned, and she studied the healing slashes on his back with relief and guilt. He inhaled before looking over his shoulder. "I told you they were better. Stop feeling so guilty, Bria."

"Right." She unscrewed the lid and scooped out some salve.

Be professional, Bria.

Professional. Yep, she could be professional. No problem.

Ignoring her tiger's excited chirps and meows, she rubbed salve into each slash on his back. He didn't say anything, but she could smell his need for her coming off of him in slow waves. It sent her tiger into a frenzy of excitement, and she could barely think past its loud purring.

Shut up, you idiot!

Her tiger growled at her as she stepped away. "All done."

"Thank you." He turned and grabbed his beer, taking a long drink. She stared at his throat, at how his Adam's apple worked as he swallowed and took another step back. She sipped at her beer as he set his bottle on the table and stared silently at her. God, why wasn't he putting his shirt back on?

"Um, okay, well, I guess I should go."

"You're not finished your drink."

She stared at the bottle in her hand. "Oh, uh, right."

She studied the cabinets, the fridge, the apples in the fruit bowl – anything but his broad naked chest. "Do you think you could put your shirt back on now?"

He grinned at her and crossed his arms over his chest. "You don't like the view?"

She scowled at him and pulled self-consciously at her

shirt. "Do you always walk around half-naked in your kitchen?"

He laughed. "I can't help it if I'm comfortable in my skin. Besides, I work out a lot to look this good. Might as well show it off, right?"

"You've been hanging out with Lincoln too much. You're becoming as arrogant as him."

"Impossible."

"Yeah, you're probably right." She cocked her head at him. "It's weird that you two are friends. You're very different."

He just shrugged. "Lincoln is a good guy. Don't let the arrogance and raging sex addiction fool you."

She smiled a little. "Yeah, I know. He was surprisingly sweet that night at the club."

Jace winced. "I feel like I need to apologize again for that night."

"You don't. Really. It was no big deal."

"I hope I didn't say anything too embarrassing."

"You really can't remember?" She took another small sip of beer.

"No, not really. I don't drink that often, so I'm a bit of a lightweight when it comes to alcohol."

"You don't like the taste of alcohol?"

"No, it's just that drinking isn't great for shifters with de_"

He stopped abruptly, and she gave him a curious look. "Shifters with what?"

"Never mind. Hey, do you want to see something in my basement?"

She raised her eyebrows at him. "In your basement?"

"That came out sounding creepier than I meant. I promise it's nothing kinky."

"That's a shame."

He laughed and held out his hand. "Come on. You'll love it, I promise."

"THIS IS IT?"

"What do you mean, this is it." Jace gave her an indignant look. "It's incredible."

"It's a pool table."

He ran his hand lovingly over the edge of it. "It's not just a pool table. It's a fully restored 1946 Brunswick Anniversary Pocket Billiard Table. These are really hard to find."

"So, you like pool, huh?" Bria touched the green cloth that covered the table.

"I love it. I just got this table a month ago." Jace took a cloth from the cabinet and wiped at the wood on the pool table. "Do you like playing pool?"

"I don't know how," Bria admitted.

Jace's mouth dropped open. "You're kidding me."

"Nope. Never learned."

"That changes right now."

She laughed as he crossed the room and grabbed two pool cues hanging on the wall. "Are you serious?"

"Dead serious." He already had the chalk out and was swiping the top of the cues. "Here, hold these."

She held the long wooden sticks as he racked the balls. "I'll break since you've never played before."

"I don't even know how to hold the stick properly."

"I'll show you." He took the longer of the cues from her. She watched as he bent over the table and took the shot. Three of the balls went in, and she gave him an admiring look.

"That was pretty good."

He just grinned at her. "Your turn. Come here, and I'll show you what to do."

"I THINK WE NEED TO ADMIT THAT I'M NOT MEANT TO BE A pool player." Bria straightened and stared at how the white ball slowly rolled across the table. It didn't hit any other balls and she rolled her eyes.

Jace took a swig of beer. "You just need to practice."

"It's been an hour, and I haven't hit a single ball."

"It's because you're still not holding the cue properly. Here, let me help you."

He moved behind her and pushed on her upper back. "Bend over and put the cue in position."

She bent over the table. "Okay, how's this? It doesn't feel right. It feels..."

Oh shit. Jace had bent over her, and his hard, naked chest pressing against her back immediately turned her on. His big hand covered hers and manipulated it into the proper position on the stick.

"How's that feel?" he asked.

"Good." Her voice was breathless, and she couldn't help rubbing her ass against his growing erection.

"Behave, Bria."

"Me? I'm pretty sure that's not a pool stick poking me in the ass."

His laughter made her flush all over. Or maybe it was how his hands suddenly tugged up her skirt. He bunched it around her waist, and she spread her legs wide when he ran his hand over her ass. She purred, and he rumbled an answering purr before squeezing her ass. "Take the shot, Bria."

She aimed the cue and hit the ball, jerking wildly when Jace's hand slipped between her thighs and cupped her pussy through her panties. The white ball careened to the right, bounced off the side of the table and sunk into the end pocket.

"Dammit."

"Try again." Jace reached with his other hand and fished the ball out of the pocket.

He set it in front of her, his hand rubbing and stroking her clit through her panties. She moaned and rocked her pelvis against his hand. "Jace."

"Try again, little tiger."

She pouted at him, and he pressed a quick kiss against her mouth. "Go ahead."

She reached to set the ball where she wanted it. Her hands were shaking, and she purred again when she heard the sound of Jace's zipper. His cock brushed against the back of her thighs, and she moaned when he stopped touching her.

"Jace, please."

His long, delightfully talented fingers were tugging her panties down her legs. She stepped out of them and spread her legs even wider as he nestled his big body between them. Her hand clenched around the cue, and she trilled in excitement.

"You're not taking the shot, sweetheart. It's like you don't even want to learn how to play pool." Jace's hands slipped under her shirt, and he unhooked the front clasp of her bra and cupped her breasts.

"I don't." She dropped the cue on the table.

He laughed and tugged on her nipples. "What do you want?"

"You know what I want."

"Say it, little tiger."

"I want you to fuck me."

"I want to fuck you too."

"Then fuck me!" She pushed back against him, and he moved one hand to her shoulder as the other reached between them.

He guided his cock into her pussy, and she purred with pleasure when he sunk in deep. Her walls stretched around him, and he cupped her hip with his other hand and waited until she made a mewling sound of need.

"Bria?"

"What?" She gave him a disgruntled look over her shoulder when he didn't move.

"Don't put gouges in my pool table with your claws."

She gaped at him and then burst into giggles. He groaned when it made her tighten around him, and he made two hard thrusts before regaining control. "Jesus, stop laughing. You're going to make me come."

"Are you really still thinking about your damn pool table?"

He grinned at her. "It'll cost a fortune to fix it."

"I won't scratch it."

"Do you promise?"

"Oh my God, yes. I promise. Fuck me!"

He drove into her with a hard thrust that made her stomach dig into the side of the pool table. She pushed back, meeting each of his strokes with an embarrassing amount of enthusiasm.

"Your little pussy is so tight," he muttered as he drove in and out. "I love how wet you are for me."

She moaned in reply, and he reached between her legs. He rubbed at her clit with sure, smooth strokes. She gripped the pool table and was careful not to let her claws out. He held her shoulder with his other hand and pounded into her.

"I'm so close," she gasped. Jace stroked her clit faster. His other hand threaded through her hair, and he pulled her head back as he fucked her hard.

"Don't hold back, baby. Come on my cock."

She cried out, and her entire body shuddered as she climaxed. Behind her, Jace made a low growl before shoving her forward until her upper body was plastered on the pool table. He growled again and thrust in and out until he came with a low howl. He shuddered above her, his big hands holding her tightly against the pool table as he rocked back and forth until he softened inside of her.

"Okay?" He breathed into her ear before pressing a kiss against her throat.

"Really good." She purred to him, and he purred back before easing out of her.

She straightened, and he wrapped his arm around her waist and pressed another kiss against her neck. "Thank you for not scratching my pool table."

She laughed and leaned against his hard warmth. "You're welcome."

They stood silently for a few moments. She waited for Jace to invite her to stay the night, and as the minutes ticked by, she began to feel stupid. Why would he invite her to stay? They weren't dating. Besides, she could try to deny it all she wanted, but she had invited herself to his house tonight for this exact thing. He'd given her what she wanted, and now she needed to leave.

"It's getting late. I should go." She tugged at his arm.

He let her go, and she pulled on her panties and fixed her clothing before patting self-consciously at her hair. "Um, thanks for the drink and teaching me how to play pool."

"Thanks for putting the salve on my back."

"You're welcome." She waited a beat, and when he still didn't invite her to stay, she headed for the stairs. He followed her up the stairs and into the kitchen, silently watching as she grabbed her purse.

"Okay, well, I'll see you at the office tomorrow."

"Yes."

Oh God, could this be any more awkward? She hurried to the front door and slipped on her shoes.

"Bria?" He caught her arm and pulled her into his embrace. "Thank you. I enjoyed tonight."

"I did, too." She smiled at him and tried not to read too much into it when he bent his head and kissed her softly.

"See you tomorrow."

"Bye, Jace." She stepped out of his embrace, opened the door, and slipped out into the cool night air.

"Hey, I keep meaning to ask why you didn't drive your car today." Rosalie wandered into reception and leaned against the desk.

"It needed an oil change, so I left it at the shop for the day and had my friend Kat drop me off at work."

"Oh. Any exciting plans for tonight?"

"No, not really." Bria ignored the surge of guilt she felt at lying to Rosalie. She liked the sweet human a lot and was beginning to think of her as a friend. She didn't lie to friends.

Do you think telling Rosalie you're going with Jace to his cousin's engagement party is a good idea?

Nope, she didn't. "How about you? What are you doing tonight?"

"Oh," Rosalie traced her finger along the top of Bria's desk, "not much. Just going to the movies with Lincoln."

Bria's eyes widened, and she sat forward. "You have a date with Lincoln?"

"No. Yes. I mean, I'm not sure." Rosalie was trying to act casual, but she was almost vibrating with excitement. "He didn't say it was a date when he asked me this morning if I wanted to go to the movies, but he's picking me up at my house and driving me to the theatre."

"That sounds like a date to me."

"Do you think so? Because I thought so too, but then..."

"I think it's a date." Bria wished she could be happier for Rosalie, but she had a bad feeling that Lincoln would break her heart.

Rosalie pulled on a lock of her curly hair. "I was thinking of wearing that blue dress. Do you know which one I mean?"

Bria nodded. "It looks really good on you."

"Thanks. I've worn it a couple of times to the office, but Lincoln hasn't seen me in it. I think it's dressy but not too dressy, you know. Like it says, I want to look good, but I'm not desperate about it."

"I think it's perfect for a movie date," Bria said. "Hey, Rosalie?"

"Yeah?"

"Just be careful around Lincoln, okay? He's a nice guy, but lion shifters are players."

"Not all of them. You said that yourself. Your lion shifter wasn't a player."

"No, he wasn't, but -"

"Bria?" Betty walked into reception. "Would you mind scanning and emailing a document for me? I hate to ask, but I'm already running late for Jay's band recital."

"I don't mind." Bria took the document from the raccoon shifter.

"Thank you. I've put the email address on the stickie on the front. If you could cc me on the email, that would be great. Bye, ladies, have a great weekend."

Betty waved as she ran out the door. Rosalie glanced at her watch, and Bria said, "Why don't you leave a little early?"

"I left early last Friday."

Bria laughed. "I don't mind. I promise. Go home and get ready for your date."

"Are you sure? Jace and Sam are still here. If you have any questions, Sam can help you."

"It'll be fine. Go. Have fun tonight, okay?"

"Thanks, Bria." Rosalie smiled happily at her. "Have a good weekend. I'll talk to you on Monday."

JACE CLOSED DOWN HIS LAPTOP AND CHECKED HIS WATCH before shutting the lights off and locking his office door. Sam had left five minutes ago, and he was alone in the office with Bria. He carried his coffee mug to the kitchen and put it in the dishwasher before leaning against the counter and closing his eyes.

He was feeling jittery and anxious, and not even his therapy appointment with Dr. Martin this afternoon had helped. Of course, he hadn't been truthful with her about what was wrong. She'd known something was upsetting him, but he had skirted around the truth. He should have been open with her. He should have told her that his tiger wanted Bria as its mate, and his human side wanted her too, and it was freaking him the fuck out.

It had taken all his willpower Wednesday night not to ask

Bria to spend the night. He'd been shocked and uneasy by his desire to have her sleep in his bed. He would have asked her to stay if she had lingered even a minute longer.

He rubbed at his forehead. If his parents knew how he was feeling, they would be the ones freaking out.

So why exactly did you invite Bria to Ash's engagement party?

"Jace? What's wrong?" Bria's scent drifted to him, and her soft voice made his tiger purr happily.

He opened his eyes and smiled at her as she entered the kitchen. "Nothing's wrong."

"Are you sure?"

He knew she could smell his confusion and his anxiety, and he did what Dr. Martin kept telling him not to do. He pushed it down deep and masked it with a false cheerfulness.

"I am. Are you ready to go?"

"Yes. I left my car at home today so that if one of the agents came into the office tomorrow, it wouldn't still be in the parking lot. Do you think you can drop me off at home tomorrow night?"

"Of course." They walked to reception, and he watched as Bria fished out an overnight bag under her desk.

"Here, I'll take that." He took it from her and slung it over his shoulder. Bria set the alarm, and they left the office. He put her bag in the trunk beside his, and they climbed into his car.

"Are you hungry?" He started the car and drove out of the parking lot.

"Not starving. Why?"

"I was thinking we'd go out to eat after we checked in at the hotel, but it's a two-hour drive to Langden."

"That's fine, I can wait."

He turned left and headed toward the freeway. "I also, uh, booked us together in the same room. It's the only hotel in

Langden, and my family is driving up tonight and will be staying there, too. No doubt we'll run into some of them in the hotel. It would look odd if they saw us going into different rooms. But if you're uncomfortable with sharing a room…"

"It's not a problem," she said. "I assumed we'd be sharing a room. We are dating, after all."

He wondered if he should tell her he'd booked a room with only one bed. He could have booked a room with two doubles. He'd just deliberately chosen a room with one queen bed.

"Jace?" Bria was giving him a nervous look. "I'm sorry, I didn't mean to make this awkward with the dating comment. I know we're not dating. I was making a stupid joke."

"You didn't," he said. "Really. I'm just a bit distracted. The house showing didn't go well today, and the clients are frustrated."

"It's only the fourth house you've shown them, right?"

"Yeah, but they're impatient to find a place. Anyway, let's talk about something not work-related."

"Okay. Tell me about your cousin and the rest of your family. It'll be easier to sell the idea that we're dating if I know a bit about your family."

"Sure. But before we start, you have to promise you won't judge me based on what I tell you about my slightly crazy family." He grinned at her as she laughed.

"I promise not to judge. Now, you've got two hours to give me a crash course in the Shepherd family. Start talking."

―――――

ROSALIE SMOOTHED HER DRESS DOWN AND FLUFFED HER HAIR A

bit. The woman standing at the sink next to her smiled. "Love your hair."

"Thank you. That's a great lip colour."

"Isn't it?" The woman shook drops of water from her hands. "It's called Voluptuous Violet, which, between you and me, is the stupidest name ever, but I love the colour." She grabbed some paper towels and dried her hands. "Have a great night."

"You too." Rosalie checked her teeth for lipstick before leaving the bathroom. She could see Lincoln ordering at the snack counter, and she made her way through the crowded theatre lobby.

Stupidly, she still wasn't entirely sure if they were on a date. Lincoln was wearing jeans with a dress shirt, so she didn't feel overdressed, but it wasn't like he was holding her hand or anything. He told her she looked beautiful when he picked her up, and they chatted about his plans for the rest of the weekend on the drive to the theatre. She paid for her ticket, but he offered to buy her a drink at the snack bar.

Her steps slowed. Was Lincoln flirting with the woman behind the snack counter? She took a deep breath. Probably. Lincoln was a flirt. If she was going to have a relationship with him, she needed to remember that and not act so jealous. She'd read the lion shifter sex book from front to back, and it had an entire chapter devoted specifically to the lion shifter's flirtatious nature.

"Hello, human."

She stared up at the polar bear shifter who had appeared before her. He held a giant tub of popcorn in one hand and a bottle of water in the other. "Hudson, hi. What are you doing here?"

"Watching a movie." She decided his usual look of irritation was maybe just a touch less irritated. "What else do people do here?"

"I didn't think you liked crowds very much."

"I don't. But I like movies."

"Me too." She cleared her throat. "Are you here with someone?"

"No."

"Oh. I'm here with, um, Lincoln."

He didn't reply, and she cleared her throat again. What movie are you -"

"Oh my God! Hudson, you're here, too. Like, what are the odds of us both having a Friday night off and being at the same theatre?"

The polar bear scowled fiercely at the high-pitched voice before grunting, "Hey."

Rosalie's stomach sunk to her feet. Lincoln had come up behind them carrying a bag of popcorn and two bottles of water. The waitress from Bud's Bar was hanging off his free arm. Lincoln grinned at Rosalie. "Look who I ran into Rosalie. You remember Tori, right? She works at Bud's."

"I do. Hi, Tori."

"Hi." The rabbit shifter wiggled her nose at her. "You're the tallest female human I've ever met. I'm jealous. I hate being so tiny and short."

"Being tall does have its advantages." Rosalie ignored her urge to punch the tiny shifter in her tiny face.

"Are you here on a date with Hudson?" Tori asked brightly.

A look of alarm passed over Hudson's face. "No." He turned and trudged away.

"I'm here with Lincoln," Rosalie said. "If you'll excuse us, we should probably get our seats before - "

"Actually," Lincoln said with a cheerful smile, "I invited

Tori to sit with us. She's seeing the same movie as us and is all alone."

"My mom's watching the kids for me tonight because she knows how much I want to see the new Star Wars. But then, like, my friend Lori totally bailed on me. But I still really wanted to see the movie, so I said to myself – Tori, you are a strong, independent woman, and you can totally go to the movies by yourself. But then I ran into Lincoln, and he was, like, totally sit with us. Isn't he just the sweetest?" Tori said.

"The sweetest." Rosalie took the bottle of water from Lincoln. "Thank you."

"All right, lovely ladies. Let's watch a movie."

Tori giggled and hooked her arm around Lincoln's arm. "Yes, let's."

Feeling sick to her stomach, Rosalie followed them to the theatre.

"It's super busy," Tori said as she stared at the crowd sitting in the small theatre.

"Nice call, Captain Obvious," Rosalie muttered.

"What was that, hon?" Tori smiled at her over her shoulder.

"Nothing," Rosalie said sweetly.

"I don't even think there are three seats together." Lincoln was scanning the theatre.

"Oh look, Hudson's watching this movie too!" Tori waved frantically at the giant polar bear shifter.

He was sitting in the end seat of the very top row on the right side. Only two seats were in the row, and the one beside him was empty. Rosalie wasn't surprised. Forgetting that he looked rather terrifying with his rough features and perma-scowl, his big body filled the seat, and he'd had to flip up the armrest between the seats. She couldn't imagine a stranger wanting to see the movie badly enough to try to sit next to him.

She followed Lincoln and Tori up the steps as Lincoln continued to scan the seats. "There are two seats in this row. I think we're going to have to split up. It looks like it's just these two and the one by the polar bear left."

"Why don't you and I take those two? Rosalie can sit with Hudson." Lincoln winked at Tori before turning and smiling at Rosalie. "You don't mind sitting with the big guy, do you, Rosie-girl?"

"You and I were going to watch the movie together," Rosalie said.

"I know, but there aren't three seats together."

"Tori can sit with Hudson," she said.

"Oh, he, like, totally hates me," Tori said. "I don't even know why, but he probably won't let me sit with him."

"Who could ever hate you, darlin'?" Lincoln pressed a kiss against the top of Tori's head.

"What do you say, Rosie-girl?" Lincoln smiled at her. "You okay sitting with the bear?"

She sighed in defeat. "Yeah, sure."

She headed up the stairs toward Hudson.

He stared at her when she stood next to him. "What?"

"Can I sit with you?"

He scowled. "I thought you were sitting with the lion shifter."

"There aren't enough seats together."

"So, he dumped you on your date for the idiot rabbit?"

"We're not on a date." She could feel the tears wanting to break free of her lashes. "This is the only seat left. Can I sit with you or not?"

He hesitated, and she turned away and started back down the steps. "Forget it."

His big hand curled around her wrist and held her still. He stood and jerked his head at the seat beside him. "Sit down, human."

She was torn between what was more humiliating. Sitting next to Hudson when he so clearly didn't want her to sit with him or have to leave the theatre and wait in the lobby for Lincoln to finish watching the movie with that damn rabbit shifter.

"Sit down, human," Hudson repeated.

The people on the other side of the aisle were staring at them. She moved past Hudson and sat in the seat next to his.

"I need to keep the arm up," he said.

"Okay."

He eased his big body down beside her. The length of him pressed up against her and it clearly made him uncomfortable. He shifted and futilely tried to put some space between them. She wanted to laugh from a combination of embarrassment and anger. Hudson probably wished that Tori was sitting with him. She was annoying as hell and never seemed to shut up, but at least she was tiny and wouldn't take up much room in her seat.

"Sorry," Hudson said.

She glanced up at the big shifter. "For what?"

"I'm in your space." His look of embarrassment eased her own a little.

"It's fine. I don't mind."

He studied her. "You sure?"

She nodded. "Yes. Besides, these hips take up my fair share of the seat anyway."

His gaze dropped to her pelvis, and she blushed a little as he stretched his legs out into the aisle. She realized that a large portion of the people in the theatre were staring at him. He seemed to be doing a good job of ignoring the stares, but she had a moment of pity for him. What must it be like to always have people staring at you? To always feel out of place and too big for the world around you. No wonder polar bear shifters kept to themselves.

"You want some popcorn?" He held the tub of popcorn in her direction.

"Sure, thanks." She loved popcorn but hadn't ordered it. She didn't want to have a greasy face or popcorn stuck in her teeth around Lincoln. She took a handful and tossed it into her mouth. God, what an idiot she was.

———

"DID YOU ENJOY THE MOVIE?" ROSALIE SMILED TENTATIVELY AT Hudson as they walked out of the theatre. Lincoln and Tori were waiting for them near the exit. She tried to ignore how the lion shifter pressed his body against Tori's.

"Yeah, you?"

"I did. I thought it was better than – oh!"

A man was backing up, and he slammed into her and knocked her into Hudson. Without looking at her, the man said, "Watch where you're going, idiot."

Still pressed against Hudson, she felt the vibration of his growl before she heard it. The man froze and turned slowly as Hudson's arm slid around her waist. He stared up at the shifter, and Rosalie swallowed her sudden urge to giggle when his face paled.

"Apologize to the lady." Hudson's voice was low and angry.

"I'm sorry, ma'am," the man said immediately. "I wasn't watching where I was going."

"It's fine," Rosalie said.

Weirdly, the man reached out to pat her on the shoulder.

She didn't know if he was drunk or if Hudson made him so nervous he was acting crazy. Hudson growled again, this one louder and angrier, and the man's hand froze above her shoulder.

Hudson's arm tightened around her waist. "Don't touch her."

"S-sorry," the man said. "I'm, uh, so sorry."

He turned and pushed his way through the crowd of people who were watching the three of them. Rosalie patted Hudson's arm. "Thanks."

He didn't reply, and she glanced up at him, the smile dying on her face. "Hudson? What's wrong?"

"Are you hurt, human?" His dark brown eyes were nearly black, and he looked supremely pissed off.

"What? No, I'm not hurt." Rosalie patted his arm again, feeling more than a little self-conscious as the people around them continued to stare. "Uh, you can let go now."

He made another little growl, and his arm tightened almost painfully across her ribs. She squeaked out a protest, and he abruptly released her. "Sorry.

"That's okay." She reached out and squeezed his forearm. "Thank you."

He scowled at her and pulled his arm away. "I told you I don't like to be touched." He walked toward the exit, the people around them parting silently to make way for him, and after a moment, she followed him.

To her surprise, he stopped in front of Lincoln and Tori. Lincoln grinned at him. "Hey, big guy. You enjoy the movie?"

"Yeah."

"Good, good. Rosalie, how about you?"

She nodded and watched as Tori put her arm around Lincoln's waist.

"Tori and I were thinking of going to Trinity's. What do you say, Rosalie?" Lincoln said.

"No, thanks." The nightclub was not her scene, and Lincoln knew that.

"C'mon, Rosie-girl, it'll be fun. The night is still young."

"I'm really tired. I want to call it a night."

Tori squeezed Lincoln's waist. "Let's go, hon."

"Can I meet you there? Rosalie and I drove together. I need to give her a ride home first."

Tori pouted prettily. "Seriously? I have to be home by, like, midnight."

"It won't take long," Lincoln said. "I'll meet you there in -"

"Don't worry about it," Rosalie said. "I can find my own way home." The thought of Lincoln driving her home before he hung out with the rabbit shifter, who he would undoubtedly have sex with, made her nauseous.

Lincoln gave her a look of delight. "Thanks, Rosie-girl. I owe you one."

"Sure. Have fun."

"We totally will," Tori said.

Lincoln pressed a kiss against Rosalie's cheek. "See you at the office on Monday."

"You bet. Bye."

Lincoln and Tori walked out of the movie theatre. She waited a few seconds before nodding to Hudson, standing silently beside her. 'Bye, Hudson. Have a good weekend."

She pushed through the doors and walked down the sidewalk a few feet before pulling her phone from her purse. Before she could call for an Uber, Hudson stood beside her again.

"I'll give you a ride home."

"I can call an Uber."

He grunted in annoyance. "I said I'll give you a ride home."

"Fine," she said.

"Let's go." His voice was impatient.

"I'm going." She scowled and followed him to his truck. He unlocked the doors, and she yanked the passenger door open and climbed in as he slid behind the wheel. He drove out of the parking lot, and when they stopped at the red light, she said, "Go ahead and say it."

"Say what?"

"I told you so."

He didn't reply, and she glared at him. "It's not an 'I told you so' situation anyway. We weren't on a date. We're just friends."

"But he's the lion shifter you want to fuck."

She blushed. "I didn't say that."

"You didn't have to. I can smell it on you."

She buried her face in her hands. "I have got to stop hanging out with shifters."

"That guy's a typical lion shifter. Full of nothing but bullshit."

"Oh? You hang out with a lot of lion shifters, do you?"

"No," he admitted.

"You don't know anything about Lincoln, so it's not fair of you to judge him."

"I know it's a shitty thing to dump your date for another woman."

"It wasn't a date!" She took a deep breath. "Look, can we just not talk about Lincoln right now?"

He didn't reply, and she stared out the window, trying not to cry and wishing she was just home already. When he pulled into her complex, she directed him to her townhouse. He stopped in front of it, and she unbuckled her seatbelt.

"Thank you for the ride home."

"You want to hang out sometime?"

She paused in opening the door and gave Hudson a look of surprise. "What?"

"You want to hang out?" He cleared his throat. "Just as friends. I'm not looking for a girlfriend."

"You don't even like me."

"You're all right for a human." He shrugged. "I like going to the movies. You like going to the movies and didn't eat much of my popcorn."

"Which are the requirements for being your friend?"

"Give me your cell number. The next time I go to the movies, I'll text you. If you want to go, great. If not...whatever. I just thought you might like having a friend who doesn't ditch you when you go to the movies."

He pulled his cell phone out and gave her an expectant look. She hesitated and then recited her number. There was no harm in giving him her number. She went to a lot of movies by herself. Pathetically enough, she didn't have a lot of friends. Her mother required a lot of attention, and most of Rosalie's evenings and weekends were spent with her. Her mother hated going to the theatre, though. It would be nice to have someone to go with to the movies.

"Okay, bye." The impatience was back in Hudson's voice.

She realized she was still sitting in Hudson's truck, and he gave her a clear *get the hell out of my truck* look. She opened the door and jumped to the ground. "Bye, Hudson."

She shut the door and walked to her townhouse. He waited until she was inside before driving away. She watched his tail lights fade before crouching and picking up the grey tabby weaving around her feet.

"Hey, Mr. Pibbles. My night sucked. How was yours?"

CHAPTER 12

"Why don't you sit and relax while I check us in."

"Sure." Bria smiled at Jace and wandered over to the seating area in the lobby. She studied the art on the wall as Jace spoke to the front desk clerk. The hotel was nice, considering that Langden was a small town with less than five thousand people. It had seven floors with a pool and a small gym on the main floor. She glanced at Jace before staring into the fireplace.

The two-hour ride to the hotel was pleasant enough. Jace spent most of it telling her about his family. She told him they didn't sound that much crazier than hers. He laughed and told her to wait until she met his Aunt Frieda in person. After that, they spoke about their favourite TV shows, hobbies, restaurants they enjoyed in the city – all very pleasant, safe things. Things that friends talked about.

"Jace."

The low purr and the scent of lion made Bria's hackles rise. Her tiger growled, and she soothed it absently. She turned to see a large blonde woman drape around Jace and hug him tightly.

He patted her back awkwardly before stepping away. "Hello, Marilyn. It's good to see you again."

"It's so good to see you." The lion shifter's voice was pure sex. "You look so good."

"Thanks." Jace took another step back. "You look, uh, very well."

"What floor are you on?" Marilyn asked. "I'm on the third. Maybe we could have dinner tonight and a nightcap?"

Bria ignored her tiger's jealous hiss. The lion shifter was stunning. She was almost six feet tall with long blonde hair to her waist and bright green eyes. Her body was all smooth skin and sleek curves, and Bria ran a hand over her own non-existent hips a bit self-consciously.

She took a deep breath. She was here for a reason, and it was showtime. She joined them and smiled at Jace. "Honey? Did you get the room key?"

Jace immediately put his arm around her waist and drew her into his embrace. "Almost. I'd like you to meet an old friend. Bria, this is Marilyn. Marilyn, this is my girlfriend, Bria."

Marilyn's pupils narrowed to slits for a brief moment before she blinked, and they returned to normal. "Girlfriend? I heard you've been single since you and Tabitha split up."

"You heard wrong."

Marilyn sniffed at Bria. "You're small for a tiger. Do you have a genetic deformity?"

"Marilyn," Jace scowled at her, "that's rude."

"It's fine." Bria smiled at Marilyn as the front desk clerk handed two keycards to Jace. "It was nice to meet you, Marilyn."

She turned to Jace. "Let's go to the room. We should have a," she trailed her fingers over his flat abdomen and gave him a sexy smile, "nap before dinner. Don't you?"

"Yes," Jace said.

Bria turned back to Marilyn. "Jace and I love napping. We nap a lot."

Before the lion shifter could reply, Bria tugged Jace toward the elevator. "Bye, Marilyn. We'll see you at the party tomorrow."

She pushed the elevator button. The doors opened, and she pulled Jace into it and dropped her bag on the floor. "What floor?"

"Five."

She pushed the button, and the doors slid shut. Jace stared at her, and she started to giggle. "The napping part was too much, wasn't it? I knew it was too much, but I couldn't resist."

He laughed and shook his head. "No, it was funny. Thanks for your help."

She curtsied dramatically. "Anytime. I might be tiny, but I'm excellent at scaring away overzealous lion shifters."

"You really are," he said so solemnly that she giggled again.

The doors opened, and he grabbed both bags. They walked to the room, and he opened the door and ushered her inside. She studied the bed before smiling at him. "This is nice."

"They only had rooms with one bed still available," he said. He flushed and dropped the bags on a padded bench next to the dresser before crossing the room to the minuscule loveseat tucked into the corner. "I can, uh, sleep on this."

She set her purse on the bed and joined him at the loveseat. "Hey, Jace?"

"Yeah?"

She took his hands and squeezed them. "This is feeling awkward, and it doesn't have to be. I'm here to play the part of your adoring girlfriend. To keep things simple, why don't we keep the pretend girlfriend thing going even when we're alone? We'll return to being just friends once you drop me off at home tomorrow night. It's easiest this way. Do you agree?"

"Yes. If you're sure that you're okay with it."

"I am. Oh, and don't worry, I won't start thinking it's real and go all *Fatal Attraction* on you later," she said teasingly.

"Excellent news, little tiger." He gave her a flirty grin and put his arms around her waist. "So, if we're pretending to be dating even when we're alone, does that mean I can get you naked and...nap with you?"

"Why, Mr. Shepherd, what kind of girl do you think I am? I require a nice meal before I'll nap with a man."

He pressed a kiss against her mouth. "In that case, let's get out of here and find someplace to eat immediately."

"How's your steak?"

"So good." Bria stabbed a piece of meat with her fork and tossed it into her mouth. "This place is amazing."

"Yeah, I've been here a few times when I visit Ashley and her family. An alligator shifter and his sons own it. He started the restaurant about twenty-five years ago."

"Cool." Bria ate another piece of steak before sipping at her wine. "So, did you grow up here?"

"No, I grew up in the city. My dad and mom moved to the city about three years after they were mated. My grandparents and my aunt have lived here their entire lives, though, and I spent a lot of summers here with Ashley and Scott."

"Scott is Ashley's older brother. He's married to Penny, and they have four children?"

He nodded. "That's right. A set of twins and two singles."

"That's a lot of kids for a tiger shifter."

"Penny is a cheetah shifter and loves kids." Jace ate the last of his steak and sat back in his chair.

"Ashley's marrying a bull shifter? Is that right?" Bria paused with a piece of steak on her fork.

Jace leaned forward, grabbed her hand and ate the steak from her fork before grinning at her. "Yep. His name is Reggie."

She pulled her plate a little closer to her when he eyed it. "Back off, buddy. This is mine."

He laughed and sat back in his seat again. "Are you nervous about meeting my family tomorrow?"

"Nope. I make a really good first impression. Well, usually. Not so much with your parents this time, but I'll win them over tomorrow." She grinned at him and ate another bite of steak. "Are you nervous?"

He shrugged. "Sometimes my family can be a bit much."

"No more than mine, I'm sure."

"You haven't met Aunt Frieda yet."

"You keep talking about your Aunt Frieda. I have to admit I'm really curious to meet her now." Bria sipped at her wine again. "I feel like I'm going to get along with her."

Jace laughed. "Tabitha hated her. Said she was a nosy old busybody who couldn't keep her mouth shut about anything. She made me swear never to leave her alone with Aunt Frieda or anyone else in my family. One time... fuck, what am I doing?"

He gave her an apologetic look. "Sorry. That was fucking stupid of me."

"It's fine." She hesitated and then decided to go for it. "Will you tell me why you and Tabitha broke up?"

"She wanted kids."

He didn't look her in the eye, and he fidgeted in his chair. Bria decided he wasn't lying to her, but there was more to the breakup than what he told her.

"You don't want any?" she asked.

He shook his head. "No, I don't. When we first started dating, Tabitha said she didn't want kids either. A couple of years later, she admitted that she'd lied and thought she could get me to change my mind. I loved her very much but couldn't bring myself to agree to have kids. Not when…"

"Not when what?"

He tapped his finger nervously against the leg of the table. "Not when I wouldn't be a very good dad."

"Why do you think you wouldn't be a good dad?"

"I just know I wouldn't. I like kids, but I've never had the urge to be a dad, you know? Tabitha broke up with me when it became clear that I would never change my mind."

"I'm sorry."

"Thanks." He studied the tablecloth before glancing at her. "Do you want kids?"

"I could go either way. I don't have a burning desire to be a mom, and if I never had a kid, I wouldn't be devastated or think my life was a waste or anything. But if I meet someone who does want kids, I'd be willing to pop one or two out."

He smiled a little, and she laughed. "I know that sounds like I wouldn't be a very good mom, but I would be. I like kids."

She pushed away her plate, and Jace smiled at her. "Do you want dessert?"

"What I want," she drank the rest of her wine in one swallow before smiling sweetly at him, "is to go back to our hotel room and fuck your brains out."

Jace grinned and immediately waved down the server. "Could we get the bill, please?"

Bria stuffed her toothbrush into her toiletry bag and studied herself in the mirror. She smoothed her hair and tugged at the hem of her short, silk nightgown. It was pretty and looked good on her, but it wasn't her sexiest nightgown. While packing for the trip, she'd decided she didn't want to look like she was trying too hard. At the time, she wasn't even certain that she'd be sleeping with Jace on the trip.

You probably shouldn't be. You know this is only going to make things harder, right? Pretending to be his girlfriend, even when you're alone, is a stupid thing to do. He doesn't want you for anything other than sex, and he's never going –

"Shut up," she muttered to her reflection. "Just shut up."

Indulging in a little make-believe fantasy that she and Jace were dating didn't hurt anyone. She knew it wasn't real, and he knew it wasn't real. It would be fine.

She smoothed her hair again and walked out of the bedroom. Jace stood by the bed, wearing just his boxer briefs. If she'd been wearing panties, they'd be soaked.

He stared at her, his gaze dropping to her small breasts. Her nipples beaded into hard points, poking noticeably against the silk fabric, and the scent of Jace's lust washed over her.

"I like your nightgown."

"What? This old thing?" She grinned at him.

He reached out and tugged her into his arms. She rubbed his warm back as he cupped her face. "Bria, are you sure about this?"

"Yes. Why? Have you changed your mind about having sex with me?"

"Hell, no."

"Good, because I was thinking earlier about how many times you've gone down on me."

He growled, and his big hand slipped under her nightgown to grip her bare ass. He nuzzled her throat. "You want my tongue in your sweet pussy again, baby?"

She shuddered with pleasure and pressed her pelvis against his erection. "Actually, I was thinking it was time to return the favour."

He growled again, a low sound of need, and her tiger purred to him. He purred back, and she pressed a kiss against his bare chest. "Do you want that, Jace? Do you want my mouth on your cock?"

"Yes. Fuck, yes."

"Good." She tugged at the waistband of his briefs. "Take these off and lie on your back."

He did as she asked. His tiger purred happily when she stripped off her nightgown and straddled him. He held her hips and twisted his pelvis. She slapped his chest lightly when the head of his dick pushed against her entrance.

"Behave."

He grinned wickedly at her. "Hey, if you're gonna put your tight pussy right above my dick, I'm gonna fuck it."

She laughed and scooted down until she was straddling his thick thighs. She wrapped her hand around his cock and stroked up and down. "I like your cock."

"It likes you too." He groaned, his hips rising with the rhythm of her hand.

She leaned over him, and he moaned in disappointment when she pressed a kiss against his flat abdomen. She licked his v-line and purred when his hands delved into her hair. He tried to push her toward his cock, and she raised her head and grinned at him.

"Patience, handsome."

"Please, little tiger."

She rubbed his cock a little harder and licked around his belly button. Normally, she hated being reminded of her small size. The way Jace said it, though, made her hotter than fire.

She studied his perfect body as she stroked his cock with one hand and traced her fingers over his chest with the other. Now that she wasn't in her heat, she could focus on something other than her need to come. She rubbed her fingers over one flat nipple. When he moaned and jerked beneath her, she grinned and bent over him.

Her wet tongue ghosted over his nipple. He groaned, his hands fisting in her hair, and she licked his nipple again.

"Fuck!" The word exploded from his mouth.

She kissed across his chest to his other nipple and gave it the same treatment.

"Mother of hell, Bria! Please!"

"What's wrong, honey?" She licked his nipple again before nibbling at his collarbone. "You don't like this?"

"Please, baby. I want more." His voice was a low and tortured moan. "I need your mouth on my dick."

She kissed him slowly, their tongues sliding against each other. She nipped at his bottom lip. He slid his hands to her ass and squeezed it hard before grinding his dick against her.

"Behave, honey."

"If you don't give me your mouth or your pussy, I'm going to lose my fucking mind." He growled.

She smiled and rubbed her tits against his chest. "So impatient. Am I going to have to tie you to the bed?"

"Bria." He gave her a warning look that she ignored. When he cupped her breasts and pulled roughly on her nipples, she bit him on the shoulder. It wasn't a hard bite, but he cursed and ground against her again.

"You really do like the biting, don't you?" she teased.

"Bria!"

She kissed her way down his firm body, her lips tasting and teasing his hard, warm skin. He dropped his hands to the bed, holding the sheet in tight fists when her mouth hovered over his cock. She licked away the precome that had beaded out of the tip. He groaned and pleaded under his breath.

Taking pity on him, she took him into her mouth. She sucked on just the head, teasing the ridge with the tip of her tongue before licking along the underside of his thick shaft. She cupped his balls, playing gently with them as she bobbed her head up and down his cock.

He was making a moaning/purring noise, and hell, had a sound ever turned her on more? She didn't think so. She took as much of him into her wet mouth as she could and purred.

He cried out at the vibration against his cock, and his hips jerked up. Bria held the base of his cock and sucked hard and fast, pulling him in and out of her mouth in a quick rhythm as his purring turned insanely loud. His cock was swelling in her mouth, turning fatter and harder with every suck. She sat up, and he growled and bared his fangs at her.

She scooted forward and guided his cock into her pussy. His growl of satisfaction sent shivers up and down her spine.

"Fuck me hard, little tiger."

She had wanted to go slow, wanted to tease and torment, but his hot words demanded obedience. She braced her hands on his chest and rode him hard. He met every thrust, his hands curling around her to cup her ass and push her harder and faster.

She reached down and rubbed her clit. It sent fresh pleasure coursing through her, and she had to fight not to dig her nails into Jace's chest. She wouldn't scratch and maim him like she did during her heat. She would keep control this time.

Her tiger trilled a mating call to him. Before she could apologize, he returned the call. She bounced faster, using his chest as leverage as she rubbed furiously at her clit.

"Little tiger, I can't..."

She watched in fascination as his eyes flashed jade and his pupils narrowed to slits. A roar of pure pleasure escaped from his throat as his entire body stiffened, and he arched beneath her. Warm wetness flooded her pussy, and it triggered her orgasm. She rubbed at her clit as her climax washed over her, keeping her gaze on Jace as the last of his climax shuddered through him.

She leaned forward and rested her cheek on his hard chest. His deep purr blocked out everything, and she closed her eyes as he caressed her back with his rough hands.

"I'm sorry," he finally said.

She raised her head. "Sorry for what?"

"I came before you did."

She laughed. "Actually, it was mostly at the same time."

"You had to make yourself come." He smoothed her hair back from her face.

"So?"

"I like being the one to make you come. It should be me. You shouldn't have to do all the work."

She climbed off him and pulled the sheets up before snuggling into his warmth. He held her close, his fingers tracing circles on her hip. She rested her hand on his flat abdomen. "You made me come about a thousand times last weekend, and you're upset because I did it myself this time?"

"It should always be me." The stubbornness in his voice was adorable. "I'm your mate, and it's my responsibility to…"

His hand had frozen against her hip, and she could smell the regret wafting from him in thick waves. "I didn't mean that." He winced and patted her hip. "I'm sorry. I shouldn't have -"

Her sudden surge of happiness died quickly. Determined not to make things awkward because of his slip of the tongue, she said, "Oh my God, you are the worst at pillow talk."

She sat up a little and grinned at him. "Look, I get that I am incredible in bed, and you're not the first tiger to start spouting off mate talk after I give them a blow job, but try to be a little cooler about it, would you?"

His look of relief somehow made her feel worse. He squeezed her hip as she rested her head on his chest again. "You didn't bite or scratch."

"I have better control when I'm not in my heat."

"You know you can still bite and scratch me, right? I told you I don't mind."

"I know."

"Why didn't you then?"

She extended a claw and made a light scratch mark across his abdomen. "There. Is that better?"

He laughed and slapped her butt. "Smartass."

"You're the one who's obsessed with being bitten and scratched."

He rolled her onto her back and threw one heavy thigh over hers before bending his head and sucking on her nipple. "I like being marked by you, little tiger."

She moaned as his fingers toyed with her other nipple. Mother of God, she was getting turned on again. "Jace, it's getting late."

"Not that late." He licked her throat. "I think we need to try this again. Make sure that it's done properly, and I'm the one who makes you come. What do you think?"

She cupped his face and placed a lingering kiss on his mouth. "I think that's a very good idea, Mr. Shepherd."

CHAPTER 13

"Jace! I'm so glad you could make it." A tall, slender tiger shifter with long dark hair and green eyes threw her arms around Jace and hugged him hard.

"Me too, Ash. Congrats on the engagement."

"Thanks! I don't know if you know, but Marilyn is here." The tiger shifter rolled her eyes. "I didn't want to invite her, but you know how Mom is. Anyway, just wanted to warn you. You know she'll try to get into your pants like always."

Jace stepped away from his cousin and put his arm around Bria's waist. "Mom warned me she was coming. Ash, this is my girlfriend Bria. Bria, this is my cousin Ashley."

"It's so nice to meet you." Bria held her hand out, and Ashley shook it with an excited trill.

"Oh my God! Jace, you didn't tell me you had a girlfriend! Aren't you just the most gorgeous little thing ever! I love your dress. That blue matches your eyes perfectly. Where did you buy it? It's so awesome to meet you! How did you and Jace meet?"

"The Shifters Love dating app," Jace said.

Bria hid her small grin as Jace squeezed her hip.

"Oh my God! That's how Reggie and I met! Reggie! Babe, come here."

The bull shifter, who was only about 5'10 but wide and powerful looking, walked across the lawn toward them. He walked like a typical bull shifter, his head down and his muscular arms swinging with every stride. His head was shaved, and he had multiple facial piercings. Bria studied the small golden ring in his nasal septum as he drew closer.

He stopped beside Ashley, and she threw her arm around his waist. "Babe, you remember my cousin Jace. This is his girlfriend, Bria."

"Hey, good to see you again." Reggie shook Jace's hand and then Bria's. He had a hard grip, but he smiled good-naturedly at her. "Hi, I'm Reggie. Good to meet you."

He pressed a kiss against Ash's cheek. "My aunt wants you to come and meet my cousin. The one who flew in from Maryland."

"Sure." Ashley pointed to the long table on the stone patio. A giant punchbowl and platters of food covered it. "Help yourself to the food before it's all gone, okay? Dad poured like an entire bottle of vodka in the punch when Mom wasn't looking, so you might want to go easy on it."

Jace laughed. "Thanks for the warning."

Bria waited until they were out of earshot. "The dating app?"

Jace grinned at her. "What? I thought it was a brilliant last-minute save. We never talked about our 'how we met' story."

"Hey, I'm impressed by your quick thinking," Bria said.

"I'm more than just a pretty face, you know. I'm smart, funny, and I have a really big -"

"Jace?"

Bria pasted a smile on her face. She recognized the voice

behind them and her nervous system went on high alert. Her tiger made a low whine of anxiety, and she soothed her absently as she and Jace turned. She smiled confidently at Jace's parents.

"Hey, Mom. Hey, Dad." Jace shook his father's hand and kissed his mother's cheek.

"Hi, honey." Jace's mom patted his shoulder. "We missed you at breakfast this morning at Franco's. Almost the whole family was there."

"Sorry. We slept in."

She supposed if sleeping in meant Jace had pinned her against the shower wall and fucked her until she was begging him to let her come, then yeah, she guessed they had slept in.

There was an awkward silence, and then Jace said, "You remember Bria."

"We do," Jace's dad said. "Nice to see you again, Bria."

"Nice to see you too, Mr. Shepherd." She held out her hand, and he studied it briefly before shaking it.

Bria held out her hand to Jace's mom. The tiger shifter seemed even more reluctant than her husband to touch her hand, but she finally gave it a quick, brief shake. Bria smiled at her. "That's a very pretty dress, Mrs. Shepherd."

"Thank you." Jace's mom turned to him. "Jace, can we speak to you privately for a moment?"

"Actually, Bria and I are starving and are headed to the buffet table. We'll talk later." Jace steered her away from his parents.

Bria took a quick look behind her. Jace's father gave her a worried look, but his mother looked almost frozen with fear. They turned abruptly and walked away.

"Well, that was horrifyingly awful," Bria said.

"It was fine." Jace grabbed two paper plates and handed one to her.

"It wasn't. I know I didn't make a good first impression with your parents, but, Jace," she tugged on his arm until he looked at her, "your mom looked terrified to see me."

"She wasn't." Jace wouldn't look her in the eye. "Oh good, my Aunt Raylene made her famous potato salad. You have to try some."

She knew a subject change when she heard one. Sighing inwardly, she followed Jace down the buffet table. "Raylene is Ashley's mom?"

"Yes. This is her and my Uncle Stan's house."

"Raylene is your mom's sister or your dad's?"

"My dad's. Here, try some of the pork." He put a couple of pieces on her plate, and she added some potato salad and tossed salad. Jace piled his plate high with various cuts of meat.

There were small round tables set up across the lawn, and Jace pointed to an empty one. "We'll sit over there, okay?"

"Sure." She followed him to the table. As they sat down, she realized Jace's mother was standing by the patio doors and staring at them. Bria smiled at her, and the woman's face paled before she turned and walked into the house.

Her stomach churning, Bria poked at the salad on her plate. She had no idea why Jace's parents acted so strange around her, but it freaked her out.

"WHO ARE YOU AGAIN?" THE OLDER WOMAN SAT DOWN WITH A heavy thump next to Bria.

Bria smiled at her. "I'm Bria. I'm Jace's girlfriend."

It was almost three hours later. She had met a bunch of Jace's family, including the tiger shifter who just sat beside her and some childhood friends. All of them were warm and welcoming, which made Jace's parents' reaction that much more puzzling. Of course, she mused, she had sliced and diced their son until his chest looked like mincemeat. Maybe that was just something they would never get over. Not that it mattered anyway. This was make-believe. By this evening, her pretend relationship with Jace would be finished.

"Oh, right. That explains why that lion shifter is giving you such frosty looks."

Bria glanced across the yard at Marilyn. The lion shifter looked away immediately, and the older woman laughed. "She's been wanting to bone my nephew since they were teenagers. Did you know that?"

"Jace mentioned it to me."

"Between you and me, it makes me laugh to watch her be so pissed off. Usually, what Marilyn wants, Marilyn gets. Her parents have been spoiling her since she was a kitten. Jace is the first thing she's wanted that she can't have."

The woman stroked her surprisingly thick mustache before tugging at her sideburns. "Did we meet earlier?"

"We did. You're Aunt Frieda, right?"

"Yeah. Jace's dad is my baby brother. What did you say your name was?"

"Bria."

"You're a little bit of a thing for a tiger. Still, you're pretty enough. Jace could do worse."

Bria laughed. "Thank you, I think."

"It's a compliment." Frieda leaned forward and peered at Jace standing by the buffet table, talking to Reggie and a few other shifters. "His last girlfriend was a real piece of work. He ever talk about Tabitha?"

"A little," Bria said.

"She broke his heart. You ain't gonna break his heart, are ya?"

"No, ma'am."

"Good, good. Jace's mama can't stand to lose another of her boys." Frieda sat back in her chair. "You know about Jonah?"

"Yes."

"Real shame when he killed himself like that."

Bria clenched her hands together in a tight fist. "Do you know why Jonah committed suicide?"

Frieda squinted at her. "Jace didn't tell you?"

"He said that his brother had died but -"

"Jonah hung himself in his bedroom after his mate up and left him. Terrible time for that family. Not all that surprising, though."

"What do you mean?" Bria's heart bobbed around in her churning stomach acid.

"Depression runs on Velma's side of the family. Her sister killed herself when she was – oh, I don't know – thirty-seven or thirty-eight. Then Jonah killed himself, and then not six months later, that stupid idiot Tabitha broke Jace's heart, and he got real depressed, just like his big brother. We was all afraid that he was going to kill himself too."

"Oh God," Bria said. "What – what happened?"

"None of us know." Frieda shrugged. "Velma and Bobby are real close-mouthed about it. Most of us think they got Jace into some kind of therapy program and then pumped him full of drugs to keep him happy. He's seemed fine since, but he ain't had a girlfriend since Tabitha, and it's been over two years now."

She poked Bria on the arm. "You need to be real careful with him, and real sweet to him. He's a good man but fragile. Velma and Bobby have worked hard to keep their baby boy safe and happy, and you can't be messing that up. You hear me?"

"Yes, ma'am." Bria was barely listening to the old tiger shifter. She was studying Jace. She hadn't known him very long, but he didn't seem fragile to her. He seemed confident and strong. He grinned at something Reggie said to him, and she felt a surge of affection bordering dangerously close to love.

Shit, she wasn't falling in love with Jace. She couldn't be.

"Jace obviously ain't my kid," Aunt Frieda was still talking, "and I know how worried Velma and Bobby are about him, but I wouldn't have been putting him on no drugs. He just needs to stop worrying so much and appreciate the good things in life. Not let his mommy and daddy pump him full of drugs."

"I don't think they can just pump him full of drugs," Bria said. "Jace is a grown man, and they can't make him take medication against his will."

Frieda made a snort of displeasure. "Either way, he don't need no drugs. Between you and me, I think this depression thing is a load of hogwash. A person just needs to choose to be happy and quit this depression foolishness.

"It's not a choice. It's a chemical imbalance in the brain." Bria continued to stare at Jace. His parents had tugged him away from Reggie and the other shifters and were talking animatedly to him. "

"That's just something doctors say so they can charge you for drugs and make a bigger paycheque. Kids nowadays are being drugged for everything. Why, back in my day, if you were sad, you just pulled up your pants and got over it. Life can't be sunshine and roses all the time."

"Excuse me." Bria stood and smiled faintly at Frieda before starting toward Jace and his parents. Jace looked both tired and upset, and she couldn't ignore her tiger's need to soothe him any longer.

"You said that Bria didn't mean anything to you." His mom held his father's hand in a tight grip. "That's what you said, Jace. You said she meant nothing to you."

"No, I never said that. Dad said that."

"You promised you weren't dating her." His mother clutched at his forearm with her free hand. "Honey, you can't date her. Okay?"

"I'm not." He hated seeing his mother so upset. "Bria's here to keep Marilyn off my back." He glanced at his dad. "It was your idea, remember?"

"So, you're just using Bria then, right?" his dad said.

Jace winced. "I'm not using her. She agreed to help me because we're friends."

"Just friends." his mother said anxiously.

"Yes."

"You look pretty happy with her. You guys have been attached at the hip, and she seems to know a lot about you."

"We're pretending." He was suddenly exhausted and sick to his stomach. "Mom, stop worrying, okay? Bria is a friend."

Both his parents continued to give him worried looks. It had been a mistake to bring Bria here. What the hell was he thinking? His tiger made a low call of distress, and a dark cloud settled over him. He should never have –

"Jace?"

Bria's soft voice made his tiger purr. His tiger sat up, his distress gone immediately. Bria slipped her arm around his waist and gave him a hesitant smile. "Hi."

"Hi." He put his arm around her shoulders and held her close. He could smell fresh misery pouring off of his mother. He hated upsetting her, but he couldn't stop touching Bria.

She made the darkness retreat.

She made him feel...right.

"Everything okay?" Bria gave him a worried look, and he leaned down and kissed her forehead.

"Yes, but I was telling my folks we're heading out. I know you have that...thing tomorrow morning, so I don't want to keep you too late."

"I appreciate that." Bria immediately played along with his lie. She smiled at his parents. "It was nice to see you again, Mr. and Mrs. Shepherd."

"Nice to see you too," his father replied. His mother didn't say anything.

Bria squeezed his waist. "Should we say goodbye to Ashley and Reggie before we go?"

"Yes. I'll talk to you guys later, okay?" Jace hugged his mother.

"Bye, son." His father patted him roughly on the back as his mother clung to him.

"Jace," she whispered, "I love you. You know that, right?"

"I do," he said. "Don't worry. Everything's fine."

JACE PARKED HIS CAR IN FRONT OF BRIA'S APARTMENT building. They had spent most of the ride home in silence. He hated the awkwardness between them. Desperate to spend more time with her, he'd tried to convince her to go for dinner once they were back in the city, but she'd politely turned him down. She gave him a startled look when he shut the car off.

"I'll carry your bag up for you," he said.

"You don't have to do that."

"I want to." He got out of the car before she could keep

arguing. He wanted to see Bria's apartment and feel close to her for a little longer.

They walked into her building and took the elevator to the tenth floor. She was pale and fidgety, but she tried to smile at him as she opened the door to her apartment. "It's a bit messy."

"That's okay." He followed her down the hallway, checking out the small living room as they passed it, and set her bag on the kitchen floor. Her place was small, but he liked how she had decorated it and told her that.

"Thanks." She took off her jacket and draped it over a chair. She was still wearing the blue dress he had bought, and he studied the way it clung to her perfect breasts. God, he wanted her. He wanted to take her to her bedroom, peel off that dress, and make love to her until she was moaning his name.

Instead, he said, "I guess I should go."

When she didn't reply, he gave her a faint smile. "Thank you again for your help. I really appreciated it. I'll see you on Monday at the office."

"Jace, wait."

He turned around, his tiger purring and heart thud-thud-thudding in his chest. "Yeah?"

"I know we said just until this evening, but do you want to spend the night?"

He took a few steps toward her and pulled her into his arms. "Yes."

"Are you sure? No pressure or commitment. Don't feel like you have to -"

He cut her off with a hard, deep kiss. She pressed her tiny body against him, and he cupped one firm breast before pulling his mouth away. "Stop talking and show me where your bedroom is, little tiger."

She laughed and clutched at his shoulders when he picked her up. "Down the hallway, last door on the right."

He carried her to her bedroom, and she groaned when he walked into the room. "Oh man, I really should have tidied up."

Her bed was unmade, a pile of laundry was on the chair, and shoes were scattered along the floor.

"It's not that messy."

"I should have made the bed," she said as he stood beside it and set her on her feet.

"It's no big deal, little tiger." He caressed the exposed skin on her back above her dress before pulling the zipper down. He eased the dress down her body, and she stepped out of it. He draped it across her vanity before studying her slender body.

"You're beautiful."

"Thank you." She helped him out of his suit jacket, tie, and shirt. She was wearing a strapless bra, and he traced the curve of her breast above the satin cup.

"I love your breasts."

She made a face. "They're small."

"They're perfect." He unclipped her bra and tossed it behind him. He pulled her into his arms and pressed his erection against her flat stomach before squeezing her ass. "You also have a perfect ass."

She grinned. "You flatter me, sir."

"It's the truth." He cupped her breast and rolled her nipple between his fingers. She arched her back and moaned. God, he loved how responsive she was to his touch. He could make love to her every night for twenty years and never tire of her.

He pushed her panties down her legs, and she stepped out of them before reaching for his belt. She helped him remove the rest of his clothes and then led him to her bed. She relaxed on her back, and he curled on his side and tugged on her until she turned to face him. He kissed her repeatedly, taking his time in tasting her as he explored her upper body with his fingertips.

He wanted to take it slow, wanted to tease and seduce until she was desperate for him. When she reached for his cock, he pulled her hand away and kissed the palm of it. "Not yet, baby."

"I want you."

"I want you too." He kissed her again before pushing her onto her back. He leaned over her and began a slow and deliberate exploration with his mouth and tongue. He kissed his way down her body, spending long moments on her breasts and teasing her nipples into hard peaks. When she was moaning and pleading, he continued down her body. He traced each rib with his tongue, circled her belly button, and nibbled on her hips.

He licked her inner thighs, smiling when she clutched at his hair and tried to push his face toward her wet pussy.

"Patience."

"No," she moaned. "No, I can't wait."

"You can." He licked her inner thighs again and gently blew until goosebumps rose on her skin. He kissed his way to her inner knee and nuzzled it. He laughed when she jerked and pulled her leg away.

"Tickles," she muttered.

"Sorry, baby." He kissed the top of her knee and licked his way up her upper thigh. When his mouth finally hovered over her pussy, she was moaning and wiggling and arching her hips.

He licked away her sweet cream and sucked on her clit. It swelled in his mouth, and he probed at her opening with one finger. She arched and took him into her. He wanted to be inside of her when she came, and he ignored her hiss of anger when he sat up and pulled his finger free.

"Jace!" She growled at him, and he nudged her thighs.

"Open for me, little tiger."

She spread her legs wide, and he settled between them, rubbing his dick over her sensitive clit until she was panting and moaning and close to coming. She growled again and sank her claws into his back when he stopped.

He relished in the pain as he guided his dick to her snug entrance and pushed inside. Her hot wetness surrounded him like a glove, and he sank in to the hilt. He called to his mate, and she answered with an eager little trill. He rested on his forearms above her, his hard chest pressing against her breasts, and kissed her.

She returned his kiss, and he made his mating call again. Her answering trill filled him with pure happiness, and he brushed his mouth against hers.

"Look at me, Bria."

Her eyelids fluttered open, and she gave him a hazy smile. "You feel so good, honey."

"So do you, baby. Don't look away. Okay?"

"Okay," she moaned.

Her blue eyes had turned a golden yellow, and her pupils were dark slits. She purred and trilled as he pushed in and out of her with slow, deliberate strokes. "You like that, baby?"

"Yes. Please don't stop."

"I won't. Don't look away."

She stared into his eyes as he slid in and out of her. She licked her lips and made a little pleading noise. "Harder, honey."

"Like this?" He moved a little faster, letting his pubic bone rub against her clit with every downward stroke. "Is this what you need, baby?"

"Yes." She stared up at him as she met each of his strokes. "Feels good."

"So good," he whispered. He moved a little faster. He studied the lovely golden colour of Bria's eyes as he pushed deeper and harder.

"Oh, oh God." Bria's eyes drifted shut, and he made a little growl.

"Look at me."

She blinked and stared up at him. "I'm so close, I – I..."

Her eyes flared with golden light, and she arched into him, her tiny body shuddering and shaking beneath his as she came around his cock. Her pussy tightened around his hard flesh, he drove deep, and his climax rippled through him. It was hard, intense, and the best orgasm of his life. He stared intently at her as he came and came again, his seed pushing deep inside of her. She clutched at his arms and didn't look away until both their bodies had stopped shaking, and he rested his forehead against hers.

"Holy shit," he whispered.

"Yeah." She laughed shakily. "That was, um ..."

"Intense." He rolled off of her, and she immediately curled on her side with her back to him. He spooned her and kissed the back of her shoulder. "What's wrong?"

"Nothing," she said.

He slid his arm around her and cupped her breast. "Are you sure?"

"Yes. Are you spending the night?"

"I'd like that."

"Me too."

He cupped her face and tried to turn her head. She resisted, and he tugged harder. "Look at me, Bria."

She sighed and stared at him. He could see the tears on

her cheeks, and he purred to her. "Why are you crying, baby?"

"I'm not," she said. "It was just intense, and I don't know... I'm fine, though. Really."

"Are you sure?"

"Yes."

"I can leave if you want."

She shook her head immediately and wrapped her tiny hand around his forearm. "I don't want that. Stay the night with me."

"Okay." He pulled her even closer and nuzzled her hair. She relaxed against him, and he stared at the ceiling, listening to her soft breathing and feeling the steady beat of her heart beneath his hand.

CHAPTER 14

Bria opened the fridge and grabbed the container of leftovers. She popped a piece of cold roast beef into her mouth and took out a bottle of water. She tightened the belt on her robe and ran her fingers through her wet hair before eating another piece of roast beef.

There was a knock on her apartment door. She glanced down the hallway toward her bedroom before checking the peephole and opening the door.

"Hi, honey." Kat kissed her cheek and pushed past her. "Why are you in your robe? It's three in the afternoon. Are you sick?"

"No, I'm not sick."

"Stripes, how's it going?" Ronin grinned at her as he followed Kat inside.

"Hi, Ronin. Uh, what are you guys doing here?"

Kat and Ronin walked to the kitchen, and she glanced at her bedroom again before joining them. Ronin was holding the container of roast beef, and he raised his eyebrows at her as his hand hovered over the meat.

"Go ahead."

"Thanks." As Kat removed her jacket, he popped a hunk of meat into his mouth.

"What, uh, what are you guys doing here?" Bria repeated

"Bowling." Ronin ate another piece of meat.

"What?"

"We're going bowling with Willow and Mal and Maggie and Porter," Kat said. "Come with us."

"Oh, thanks, but I don't -"

"I'm not taking no for an answer," Kat said. "Mal and Porter's brother Heath will be there too, so it's not like it will be all couples and you."

"They're trying to set you up with Heath," Ronin said.

Kat hissed at him, and he laughed. "What?"

"That was going to be a..."

"Happy surprise?" Ronin leaned down and kissed Kat's forehead. "Sorry, Kitten."

"Thanks for the invitation, but I really can't," Bria said.

Kat took her hands. "Honey, you can. Heath is a nice guy, and I think you'll like him. Just give him a chance and -"

"Bria?" Jace strolled into the kitchen with just a towel wrapped around his waist. "I was thinking that after my shower, maybe we could go out for a bite to eat. I'm starving and..."

"Jace?" Kat dropped Bria's hands.

"Hi, Kat. It's good to see you again."

"Uh, you too."

There was silence, and then Ronin stepped forward and held out his hand. "Ronin Smith, I'm Kat's mate."

Jace shook his hand. "Jace Shepherd. Nice to meet you."

"Likewise."

Bria tried not to blush. Kat was staring at her, and it was too quiet in the kitchen. Why the hell did she even answer the door?

"Well, I didn't realize you had company," Jace said, "so I'll get dressed and... Bria, I'll see you tomorrow, okay?"

"Okay," she said.

"How do you feel about bowling?" Ronin asked before Jace could leave the kitchen.

Jace stared blankly at him. "I'm sorry?"

"Bowling. You know...big balls, loud music, gross shoes...bowling."

"Uh, it's okay. I guess."

"You any good at it?"

Jace glanced at Bria. "Not bad."

"He's on my team," Ronin said to Kat.

"I thought I was on your team," Kat said.

"No offense, but I've seen you bowl before, and you suck at it, Kitten."

"I'm not that bad," Kat protested.

"You're not that good."

Kat hissed at him again, and Ronin laughed. "What do you say, Jace? You in for a fun afternoon of bowling? I got my own disinfectant spray for the shoes. I'll let you borrow it."

Jace studied Bria. "Sure, if Bria's okay with it."

"I am," Bria said. "I'd like it if you joined us."

"Okay. Give me ten minutes to shower, and I'll be ready."

He left the kitchen, and Ronin fanned his face with his hand before whistling. "Nice work, Stripes. He's not a bad looking man. Am I right?"

Kat took Bria's hands again. "Why is Jace here?"

"I told you I was going to his cousin's engagement party this weekend."

"I know. I also know the party was over yesterday."

Bria blushed but didn't say anything.

"It's Sunday afternoon. Why is he still here?" Kat asked.

"Pretty sure they were banging," Ronin said cheerfully.

"Ronin!"

"What? Am I wrong?" he asked Bria.

She shook her head, and a grin spread across his face. He held up his fist, and she bumped it.

"He's your boss," Kat said.

"You're my boss," Ronin said.

"Not helping, bird!"

"What? I'm being very helpful. Why can I bang my boss, but Bria can't bang hers? That doesn't seem fair."

"It's more complicated than that," Kat said. "Bria, I don't want you getting hurt."

"I know. Everything's fine." She glanced at Ronin. "Can we talk about this later, Kit Kat?"

"Yes. But we *will* talk about it later," Kat said.

"I know. I'm going to get dressed. Be right back."

She hurried into her bedroom. Jace was standing by the bed, and she smiled nervously at him before opening her closet. He touched her back, and she turned to face him.

"Are you sure you want me to go?" he asked.

"Yes," she said.

He searched her face. "I don't have to if it makes you uncomfortable."

"It doesn't. Really. In fact, you'd be doing me a favour. They're trying to set me up with a guy, but I'm not really interested. If you're there..."

His eyes flashed bright green for a second, and she could smell his jealousy.

It doesn't mean anything, she told herself.

"Do you want me to pretend to be your boyfriend?" he asked with a small smile.

Her cheeks turned pink. "Yeah, I guess I do. If you don't mind?"

He leaned down and kissed her. "I don't mind at all, little tiger."

"I HAD A LOT OF FUN THIS AFTERNOON. THANKS FOR LETTING me tag along." Jace pulled into the parking lot of her building and put the car in park.

"I'm glad you came." Bria fidgeted with her seat belt. She wanted to ask Jace to come upstairs, wanted to ask him to spend the night with her again, but that was crazy. Spending the weekend with him and pretending he was her boyfriend had been amazing. Too amazing. For someone who didn't want a relationship, he was really good at it.

She'd had so much fun with him while bowling. They'd all gone for dinner together afterwards. Jace was funny and smart and got along well with everyone. He and Ronin had hit it off, and they'd even planned for Ronin to drop by and play pool. Jace had played the part of her adoring boyfriend to perfection, and she'd soaked in his affection.

"I like your friends."

"They like you too." Bria unclicked her seat belt. It was time to go before she started to think this pretend game of boyfriend/girlfriend with Jace was real. "Thanks for the ride home. I'll see you tomorrow."

"Bria," he caught her hand as she opened the car door, "invite me to spend the night."

"What?" She had to have misheard him.

He rubbed his thumb over the pulse point in her wrist. His eyes glowed in the dim light. "Invite me to spend the night, little tiger."

"Jace, would you like to spend the night with me?" She whispered.

"Very much." He shut the car off, and they walked silently to her apartment.

When she locked the door behind them, he picked her up and carried her toward the bedroom. She giggled and kissed his throat. "You know, I can walk to the bedroom."

"This makes me look strong and manly."

Her giggles turned to laughter. "Oh yes, very manly. I can hardly control my need for you when you carry me around like a sack of potatoes."

He growled at her and dropped her on the bed before stripping off his shirt. "Be nice, or you'll get a spanking."

"Promises, promises, Mr. Shepherd," she purred.

His eyes widened, and he grinned at her. "You may just be the perfect woman."

"You're just figuring that out now?" She rubbed her foot across the bulge in his jeans. "Why don't you show me how naughty you can be?"

His purring filled the room, and she moaned happily when he dropped down onto her and cupped her breast. "Whatever you want, little tiger."

"ROSALIE, WILL YOU TELL ME WHAT'S WRONG?" BRIA TOUCHED the pretty human's arm.

It was Monday, and she was surprised that Rosalie was sitting with her in the kitchen for lunch. She had avoided not just Bria all morning but everyone else as well.

"There's nothing wrong." Rosalie poked at the sandwich, sitting half-eaten in front of her.

"There is, honey. I can smell how sad you are."

"Of course you can," she sighed. "Can't I just be sad for no particular reason?"

"Yes, but I think there's a reason. Did something happen on your date with Lincoln? You never told me how it -"

"It wasn't a date." Rosalie wrapped up her sandwich and tossed it in the trash. "I was wrong. It was just a friend thing."

"I'm sorry."

She shrugged. "Not your fault, I'm an idiot."

"You aren't. I thought it was a date, too."

"Well, it wasn't. He ran into that rabbit waitress from Bud's and sat with her during the movie, and then went to Trinity's with her after the movie."

"He what? You had to sit alone at the movie he invited you to?" Bria could have cheerfully punched Lincoln in his stupid face.

"The theatre was full, and there weren't three seats together."

"Still, to make you sit by yourself when -"

"I didn't sit by myself. I, uh, sat with Hudson."

"Hudson? *Hudson?* Polar bear shifter Hudson from Bud's?"

Rosalie brushed the bread crumbs off the table. "Yeah. He was at the movies too. We, uh, we keep running into each other at the most random places. Anyway, I sat with him, and he gave me a ride home when Lincoln decided to go out to the club."

"Hudson gave you a ride home?"

"What?"

Bria shrugged. "Well, I don't know the guy, but he seems kind of... not nice. Plus, if he's a typical polar bear shifter, he doesn't want to be around other shifters or humans if he doesn't have to be."

"He's nice," Rosalie said defensively. "Well, maybe not nice, but he's not, like, mean or anything. We're friends."

"Seriously?"

"Kind of. I think. He said we could maybe go to the movies together sometimes."

"Does he want to be more than friends?"

Rosalie laughed bitterly. "God, no. He made that perfectly clear. Friends only. Story of my life, you know?"

Bria patted her arm. "Lincoln is an ass, Rosalie. He's not even a good friend."

"He is," Rosalie snapped. "He's just...flirty and... oh, never mind. I don't want to talk about it."

Bria sat quietly, and after only a few seconds, Rosalie said, "I'm sorry. I didn't mean to yell at you."

"You didn't. I'm sorry I was being so nosy."

"You weren't. How did your date go?"

"I didn't have one." Bria gave her a confused look.

Rosalie checked the door to the kitchen before lowering her voice. "Remember this morning when the phones were ringing off the hook, and I took a couple of calls?"

"Yeah."

"One of those calls was Jace's cousin, Ashley."

Bria's sandwich tasted like sawdust in her mouth. She swallowed it down painfully. "Oh yeah?"

"Yes. She's a sweetheart. The last time she visited Jace, he got bogged down with a client and Ash and I hung out for an evening. She still texts me and emails me from time to time."

"That's, uh, nice," Bria said.

"Anyway, she wanted to talk to Jace, but he was out of the office. We ended up chatting, and she mentioned how much she adored Jace's date at her engagement party this weekend. Said she was the tiniest tiger shifter ever, but super sweet. Said it was obvious how much she and Jace were into each other."

Bria took a drink of water. Rosalie leaned closer and

grinned at her. "She asked me if I had gotten the chance to meet Bria - Jace's new girlfriend."

Bria paled and set her water bottle on the table. "I can explain."

"You don't have to," Rosalie said. "It's no big deal if you and Jace are dating. Jace told me himself that he was attracted to you."

"We aren't dating," Bria said. "I was doing him a favour and posing as his girlfriend."

"Why?"

"It's a long story. Will you do me a favour and keep this to yourself? I don't want people thinking I'm banging the boss or something."

Rosalie studied her for a moment. "*Are* you banging the boss?"

"No, of course not."

"Are you always this bad at lying?"

Bria pressed her lips together and stared at the table. Rosalie touched her hand. "I'm not going to say anything to anyone. I promise."

"Thanks. I appreciate it."

They sat in silence before Bria gathered up her lunch bag "I'm going for a walk and get some fresh air. You want to come with me?"

"Sure. Just let me change out of these heels first," Rosalie said.

Bria returned to reception and slipped out of her heels and into her running shoes. Her cell buzzed, and she fished it out of her pocket. Her mouth dropped open as she read the text from Jace.

Hi. Hope your day is going well. Do you want to have dinner at my place tonight?

What the hell was happening? She read the message

again. Her tiger was purring and trilling at the prospect of having sex with her mate again.

Knock it off, she snapped at her tiger. *He said dinner, not sex. Besides, you just slept with him this morning.*

Jace had woken her early. They'd made love and cuddled for a bit before he left for his place to shower and change. He'd been out of the office all morning, and from the looks of his calendar, he would be out this afternoon, too.

She couldn't go to his place tonight.

She shouldn't go to his place tonight.

Her tiger whined pitifully at her. Fuck it, she decided. She would go to Jace's house for dinner and ask him what the hell was going on. Either they were going to start dating, or they weren't, but she wouldn't play the "maybe we are, maybe we aren't" game anymore.

Sure. What time? Can I bring something?

She put on her coat and buttoned it. Her cell phone buzzed again.

Seven. A bottle of wine. Leave your panties at home.

Heat trickled through her, and she shoved her cell phone into her pocket with a guilty smile when Rosalie walked into reception. "Ready?"

"Yes." She followed Rosalie out of the office.

"Hi, you look nice." Jace kissed her on the cheek and hung up her coat before taking the bottle of wine from her.

"Thanks." Bria followed him into the kitchen. "It smells delicious in here."

"I'm an excellent cook. Just one of my many talents." Jace opened the bottle of wine and poured her a glass.

"Yes, many." She took a sip of wine and squeaked in

surprise when Jace put his arm around her and squeezed her ass through her jeans.

"No panties. That's my good girl." He gave her a smug smile.

"You don't know I'm not wearing panties." She poked him in the chest.

He nuzzled her throat and rubbed her ass. "I can't feel any panty lines."

"Maybe I'm wearing a thong."

"Are you?"

She hesitated. "No."

He purred, and she purred back. He rubbed his nose against hers before kissing her until she was moaning and clutching at his arms. "Why don't we go to your bedroom?"

"Food first, then fucking." He nipped her bottom lip.

"How about fucking, then food, then more fucking?"

He laughed. "Tempting, but the sauce will burn, and then I'll have to order pizza, and I've had pizza way too many times this month already."

She pouted at him. "Fine. What can I do to help?"

"Can you chop up some peppers for the sauce?"

"Yep."

"Thanks." He kissed her again and then set her up at the island with a chopping board, knife and two yellow peppers.

"How was your day?" He was browning the meat, and he raised his voice to be heard over the sizzle.

"Good. Busy. How did the showings go?"

"The first two in the morning were total busts, but the three in the afternoon were good. They all put offers in."

"Were they accepted?" she asked.

"Two were. One is in negotiations. I might have to duck out to take a few phone calls during dinner. Sorry in advance."

"It's fine." She sliced open the first pepper and cleaned out the seeds before chopping it into long strips. "Are you in the office tomorrow?"

"Yes. I've got some paperwork to finish and a meeting with Betty."

She sliced up the second half of the pepper before starting on the next one. She should be talking to Jace about why he suddenly acted like they were in a relationship, but she didn't want to. She wanted to keep pretending this was all real. She wanted to act like she and Jace were a couple, and he was falling in love with her, just like she was in love with him.

She studied the back of his dark head, feeling another surge of affection that felt too much like love. Maybe he was changing his mind. The way he was acting certainly suggested he was. She knew she was grinning, but she couldn't hide it. Jace was starting to fall for her.

"What are you making over there?" she asked.

Jace kneaded a ball of dough. "Pasta."

"You're making your own pasta?" She stopped slicing the pepper.

"Yep."

"Holy crap."

"Told you I had many talents."

"I am sincerely impressed."

"Yeah?" He wiggled his eyebrows at her. "Remember this moment later because, secretly, this is only the second time I've made pasta, and it didn't turn out so well the first time."

She laughed. "Fantastic. Looking forward to trying it."

"I'm sure it'll be -"

The doorbell rang, and Jace glanced at his hands. "Would you mind getting that? I ordered some new balls for the pool table, which are supposed to be delivered today."

"Sure." She set the knife down and headed to the front

door. She opened it and stared in surprise at the woman standing on Jace's doorstep. "Mrs. Shepherd. Hi."

"What are you doing here?" His mother gave her a worried look.

"Jace invited me for dinner."

"Why?"

She didn't know what to say to that, so she took a step back. "Um, come on in. Jace is in the kitchen."

Jace's mom swept past her, and Bria followed her into the kitchen. Before she could say anything, Jace said, "Well, what do you think of my new balls? If you're a very good girl, I'll show them to you later. Maybe even let you play with them."

"Jace!" Bria said. "Your mom is here."

Jace swung around and stared at his mother. "Mom? What are you doing here?"

"We need to talk. Alone." His mother stared pointedly at Bria.

"It's not a good time," Jace said. "I'll call you tomorrow and -"

"No." His mother was starting to sound a little hysterical. "We need to talk right now, Jace."

Jace shook his head. "I'll call you tomorrow and -"

Jace's mom gave Bria a wild-eyed look. "Please leave. This is a family matter that I need to speak to Jace about."

"Of course." Bria grabbed her purse from under the island.

"Bria, no. You don't have to -"

"It's fine." She gave Jace a faint smile. "We'll talk later."

"Bria -"

"Bye, Jace. Bye, Mrs. Shepherd." She hurried out of the kitchen, shoved her feet into her shoes and snagged her coat. She could hear Jace coming down the hallway, and she quickly ran out of the house and shut the door. She climbed into her car and drove away as Jace stepped onto the front stoop.

Her heart was thudding, and she drove only a few minutes before pulling onto a side street and parking. The fear and anger radiating from Jace's mom made her hands shake and her stomach queasy. His mom feared and hated her, and Bria could do nothing about it. She'd never win her over. Bria would never convince her that she wouldn't hurt Jace... she'd been stupid to think she could have a relationship with him. Even if she could persuade Jace to date her, there was no swaying his parents. They would drive a wedge between them. She knew it without a doubt.

You don't know that. Jace is a good guy. If he wants to be with you, do you really think he'll let his parents tell him he can't?

Jace *was* a good guy, and he loved his parents. Why would he choose her over them? He wouldn't. He shouldn't. She buried her face in her hands and tried to hold back the hot tears. God, what a fucked-up mess this was.

JACE SLAMMED THE FRONT DOOR SHUT AND STALKED BACK TO the kitchen. His tiger was growling, and he glared at his mother. "What are you doing?"

"What am I doing? What are *you* doing?" Velma asked.

"Having dinner with a friend until you rudely interrupted."

"She's more than a friend. Stop trying to pretend she isn't."

"Fine," he said. "She's more than a friend, Mom. I like her. I like her a lot, and I want to date her."

Velma paced back and forth. "Honey, you can't. You know you can't."

"Yes, I can. Bria's not going to hurt me. She's great, and if you would give her a chance, you'd see that -"

Velma hissed at him. "Tabitha was great too, remember? Until she left because she decided you were too weak and fragile."

His cheeks reddened. "I'm not weak or fragile."

"I know you're not. But does this Bria know that you suffer from depression? Does she know you take medication for it and go to weekly therapy?"

"No, but I'll tell her. She won't care. She's not like Tabitha."

"Honey," Velma cupped his face, "you don't know that. How well do you know her?"

"I know her well enough."

"You don't. You like her, I know. I can see it, I can smell it, and, honey I wish I could be happy for you. I really do. But this is a mistake. You're not ready to be in a relationship again."

"I am." He gave her a stubborn look. "I'm fine, Mom. I'm in a good place."

"Are you? Do you remember what it was like when Tabitha left? Because I do. You were a mess. You didn't leave your house, you didn't shower or eat. Your father and I were terrified you would do what your brother did and -"

"I'm not Jonah!" he snarled.

His mom flinched back, and guilt coursed through him. "I'm sorry. I didn't mean to yell."

"We know you're not your brother, but you suffer from the same disease. You were suicidal when Tabitha left."

"Mom, I -"

"It almost killed your father when you got sick. Do you know that?"

"What? What are you talking about?" he asked.

She leaned against the counter, tears starting to drip down her face. "Jonah's death was very difficult on him. When you got sick, the stress was too much, and he had a heart attack."

Jace staggered backward. The meat was starting to burn, and he watched numbly as his mother shut off the burner and moved the pan to a different one. "Dad had a heart attack?"

"Yes."

"Why didn't you tell me?"

"Because you weren't doing well yourself. You were still struggling, and your dad didn't want to worry you," she said.

"I can't believe you didn't tell me," he said.

"We wanted to protect you." Velma squeezed his arm. "What happens if this Bria breaks up with you? What if you spiral down again? Your father wouldn't survive another heart attack."

Guilt suffocated him. His father had almost died because of him, and he'd had no fucking idea.

"Mom, I didn't know. I…"

"We can't lose you too, honey. I know you like Bria, but you need more time. Give it another year or so, and you'll be ready then. You'll find a nice girl and be happy with her. I know you will. Please. Promise me you won't see Bria again."

He stared at his mother as guilt and sorrow, and his growing love for Bria warred within him.

She cupped his face again. "We love you. Please don't tear this family apart."

"I won't," he rasped. "I won't, Mom. I'll tell Bria we can't be together."

She started to cry and pressed a kiss against his cheek. "I'm sorry, Jace. I am, but you're doing the right thing. I love you, honey."

"I love you too."

She hugged him hard, and he returned her hug as he stared out the kitchen window. The thought of not being with Bria, of never touching her soft skin or hearing her mating call, brought the familiar black cloud descending over him.

She would never be his, and he'd have to watch as she found a new mate and built a life with someone else. More blackness crowded into him, and he swallowed hard. He needed to talk to Bria, and she would hate him when he was done.

CHAPTER 15

He showed up just before nine. Bria let him into her apartment and wrapped her arms around her torso instead of his. He looked tired and sad, and she wanted desperately to comfort him, but he was stiff and uncomfortable, and he wouldn't look her in the eye.

She had spent the last few hours hoping he would choose her. Such a selfish, terrible thing to do, but she couldn't help it.

He hadn't chosen her.

She'd known when she opened the door and saw him standing there with his drawn face and hunched shoulders. He was a ghost of his usual self, and she felt pure hatred for his mother for a moment. What had she said to him?

"I'm sorry to come by without calling." He shoved his hands into his coat pockets.

"It's okay. Come in."

He followed her into the living room and sat on the couch. She perched nervously beside him as he studied his hands. "I'm sorry my mom interrupted us like that."

"You don't have to apologize," she said. "I understand."

There was a bitter undertone to his laugh. "You don't. But you're about to."

"Jace, I -"

"I need to tell you something, Bria. Okay? Will you listen and hear me out?"

"Yes." She folded her hands together so she wouldn't try to hold his.

"Depression runs in my family. My aunt committed suicide when she was in her thirties, and you know that my brother Jonah killed himself. He had severe depression. My mom suspected he did, and she tried to get him help, but he refused. It was bad in his teens but got a little better after he graduated high school. He met his mate, Davra, and they moved in together. The depression seemed to be gone. Or maybe he had just hidden it well. I don't know. Anyway, it came back, and he was struggling. Davra couldn't deal with it. She left him, and a month later, he hung himself in his bedroom."

"I'm so sorry." She had to touch him. She had to.

He took her hand when she curled it around his and held it tightly. "I was diagnosed with depression, too. I'm not as stubborn as Jonah, though. I was willing to try medication, and it helped. After Jonah died, it got pretty bad, so I started seeing a therapist. Her name is Dr. Martin. She's nice. She's good at what she does."

She squeezed his hand, and he studied her momentarily before staring at the floor again. "Tabitha tried to be support-ive, but I knew it bothered her. Jonah had been dead for almost a year, and I was still doing therapy. She thought I was weak because I needed medication and therapy. Tabitha used the no kids thing as her reason for leaving, but it wasn't just that. She hated that I couldn't force myself to be happy.

Couldn't beat the depression. Honestly, I wasn't surprised when she left me."

He paused. "My depression got worse, and I had suicidal thoughts a couple of weeks after she moved out. I made the mistake of telling my parents. I shouldn't have, I don't know why I did, but they freaked out. Mom wanted to put me in the hospital, but I was an adult, and she couldn't force me to go. But I did get help."

He gave her another fleeting glance. "I told Dr. Martin what was happening. She worked with my doctor to adjust my medications, and she made me do therapy sessions three times a week instead of just once. It helped. I started to feel more like myself. But my parents were so worried. They were sure I was going to kill myself like Jonah. I felt guilty about what I was putting them through, you know?"

Bria squeezed his hand. "Kids always worry their parents, honey."

"I know but… I decided the best thing to do is avoid relationships for a while. I told my mom and dad, and," he paused, "they were so happy and *relieved*. I couldn't blame them for it. They had already lost one son because of a relationship gone bad and almost lost their other one. Seeing how relieved they were made me realize I was making the right decision. I joined the Heat Me Up site and haven't let myself get attached to anyone."

He fell silent, and she shifted closer to him on the couch. She rested her head on his shoulder, and he stiffened a little before kissing the top of her head. "Only then I met you. And you're sweet and funny and so damn beautiful. I told myself that I didn't want anything more than sex, but I was wrong. You wanted a relationship with me, and I was starting to want that, too."

She brushed her hand through his thick hair. "I know, honey."

"My parents don't want me to date you. They don't think I'm ready to be in a relationship again."

"What do you believe?"

"It doesn't matter." He stared at their entwined hands.

"It does matter. You can't live your life doing what your parents want you to do. You're an adult and -"

"My dad had a heart attack."

"What? Today?"

"No, after I got sick. I had no idea. Mom told me tonight that Jonah's death and the stress of me being sick was too much for him, and he had a heart attack. They kept it from me because I was still struggling."

His voice was full of harsh fear. "I almost killed my father, Bria."

"Honey, no. Look at me." She cupped his face. "You didn't. Your mother should never have told you that, or at the very least, worded it differently. It isn't your fault that your father had a heart attack."

"It is," he said. "I want to be with you, but I can't. If we break up, and I can't handle it…"

"Who says we'll break up?"

"Who says we won't," he countered. "Life isn't full of guarantees."

She didn't reply, and he squeezed her hand again. "I can't take the risk, Bria. I like you a lot, but I can't risk my dad dying because of me."

She wanted to tell him he was being dramatic, wanted to shake him and force him to see how his mother's fear was influencing him. Instead, because she didn't want to hurt him more than he already was, she sat quietly and waited for him to break her heart.

He let go of her hand and shifted further away from her. "I'm sorry. I can't be with you anymore, Bria. Not even to help you with your heat. I know you hate me now and -"

She cupped his face again and made him look at her. "I don't hate you."

"You should. I've led you on the last few days and -"

"You haven't. I don't hate you, Jace. I hurt for you and wish things were different, but I understand."

"Do you?" He gave her a searching look.

"I'm trying to understand." She rubbed his cheek with her thumb. She wanted to kiss him but let him go and stood up. "Thanks for stopping by and explaining. I appreciate it."

He stood. "I - you're not going to quit, are you? This doesn't have to affect our working relationship."

"I think I have to quit."

"I wish you wouldn't. I already feel like a piece of shit and -"

"You shouldn't." She made herself smile at him. "But I like you a lot, and seeing you every day will be difficult. Especially when my heat is coming up."

She forced another smile. "Could you imagine how embarrassing it would be for everyone if I tried to hump you in the boardroom during a staff meeting?"

"I can work from home. I can stay in my office when I do need to come in and -"

"No," she said. "That's not a workable solution. This is your business and your livelihood. I'll find another job."

"Promise me you won't quit until you find a new one," he said. "It's bad enough you're losing your job because of me. I don't want you homeless and starving either."

"Yeah, okay."

"Do you promise?"

"I promise I'll try to stay until I find something else." She patted him on the arm. "You should go."

She walked him to the door. He opened it and then turned abruptly. He pulled her into his arms and kissed her with a desperate sort of need.

He tasted like sorrow and regret and love all mixed in together. Bria returned his kiss, trying not to cry and failing.

He cupped her face and kissed her again. "I'm sorry."

He walked out of her apartment without looking back.

"GOOD AFTERNOON, SHEPHERD REAL ESTATE. BRIA SPEAKING."

"Yes, may I speak with Jace Shepherd, please."

Bria shifted the phone to her other hand. "He's not in today. Can I take a message for him?"

The woman on the other line hesitated. "Yes. Could you have him call Valerie Martin, please? He missed our appointment this morning, and I'd like to reschedule."

"Are you Dr. Martin?" Bria blurted.

There was a long, drawn-out silence before the woman said. "Yes."

"Jace has the flu."

"Ah." The relief in the woman's voice was palpable. "That's why he hasn't returned my calls. Thank you. Just have Jace call me to reschedule when he's back in the office."

"I will." Bria hung up the phone. Adrenaline spiked through her veins, and her hands were ice cold.

It was Friday afternoon. Jace hadn't been in the office once this week. He'd texted Rosalie Tuesday afternoon that he had the flu and wasn't coming to the office. Bria tried to tell herself all week that he really did have the flu and nothing else. But her unease had grown stronger with each passing day. Now, it had turned to straight panic.

Don't panic. If he has the flu, then it's possible he wouldn't answer his phone and forget his appointment.

Her inner voice was right, but her tiger was yowling and whining for her to go to their mate.

She stood and hurried to Rosalie's desk. "Rosalie, you're texting and talking to Jace, right?"

Rosalie saved the document she was working on. "Yes."

"Have you talked to him today?"

"No, not today. Why? What's wrong?"

"Nothing." Bria lowered her voice. "Jace lives alone, and I was worried about him."

"It is a little weird for him to be sick this long. I didn't think shifters got the flu or colds like humans."

"We can get sick, but it usually only lasts a day or two, and then we heal ourselves. But sometimes, it can take longer if it's a really bad illness."

"Oh. Well, I'm sure he's okay. His mom is probably checking on him."

"Probably." Bria chewed at her bottom lip. "But you haven't talked to him at all today?"

"No. Unless he texted me, and I missed it." Rosalie grabbed her cell phone and scrolled across the screen. "He texted me Wednesday afternoon."

"Wednesday?" Bria could hear the panic in her voice. "It's Friday, Rosalie."

"I know, but if he's sick -"

"Can you listen for phones for a minute?"

"Sure. What's wrong?"

"Nothing." Her panic eating away at her, Bria nearly ran down the hall to Lincoln's office. The lion shifter was just ending a phone call, and he gave her a surprised look when she walked in and closed his office door.

"Have you talked to Jace today?"

"No. He has the flu," Lincoln replied. "Why?"

"Have you talked to him at all since Tuesday?" Her voice had an unpleasant shrill to it. "Did he sound like he had the flu?"

"I haven't talked to him, just texted." Lincoln gave her a careful look. "What's going on, Bria?"

"When did you text him?"

"I don't know."

"Look!"

He grabbed his phone. "Uh, Tuesday afternoon."

"Shit."

"What's wrong?" Lincoln sniffed the air. "Why are you panicking over Jace having the flu?"

"I don't think he has the flu. Since when has a shifter had the flu for four days, Lincoln?" The shrillness was growing right along with her fear.

"What are you talking about?" He came around the desk and touched her shoulder. "You're shaking like a leaf. Sit down and tell me what the hell is going on."

Fifteen minutes later, she followed Lincoln to Rosalie's desk.

"Rosalie?" Lincoln's voice held no trace of its usual flirtiness.

"Lincoln? What's wrong?" She stood up immediately and gave him an anxious look.

"Can you watch the front desk? Bria and I need to run an errand."

"Um, sure. Is everything okay?" Rosalie studied Bria's pale face.

"Yes, we won't be long. Thanks, Rosalie," Lincoln said. "Bria, let's go."

She followed him to his car and buckled her seat belt as Lincoln drove out of the parking lot.

"He's probably fine," Lincoln said.

"Yes."

"I mean, we're probably just overreacting. Jace knows when things are getting bad, and he needs help. He wouldn't do anything stupid."

"He missed his appointment with Dr. Martin," she reminded him.

"He's fine," Lincoln repeated as he sped up. "We'll go to his house, and he'll be fine."

He almost sounded like he believed it.

JACE SNEEZED REPEATEDLY BEFORE RUBBING HIS ACHING temples. He was weak and shaky but feeling a little better than before. He pushed the electric tea kettle button and dropped a teabag into the mug.

After leaving Bria's place, he'd gone home, poured himself a drink and sat in the dark kitchen until almost two in the morning. The look on Bria's face, the look on his mother's face. haunted him. The depression was closing in on him, threatening to fill him up until he couldn't breathe or think. The urge to let it was overwhelmingly strong, but he'd fought it back.

As miserable as he was right now, he didn't want to go back to how he was after Tabitha left him. But, holy shit, this was so much worse. He loved Bria and wanted to spend the rest of his life with her. Knowing he couldn't made him want to let the darkness swallow him whole.

He'd finally gone to bed but tossed and turned until the early morning light crept into his bedroom. He didn't want to get out of bed. He got out anyway.

He chalked up his growing headache and the ache in his bones to his sleepless night and met his clients at the showing. By the time he was finished, he was pale and sweaty and had a fever.

He'd returned home, texted Rosalie, and spent the rest of the afternoon and evening alternating between vomiting in the bathroom and shaking and shivering in his bed. His natural healing ability was working overtime, but the flu was bad. He'd woken up Thursday morning with the ache and fever gone but with a cold to take its place.

He sneezed again and eyed the cupboard. He hadn't eaten anything since Monday. Maybe it was time to try some toast. Honestly, he wasn't even sure what day it was. He reached for his phone and frowned. What the hell had he done with it? He knew he'd texted Rosalie at some point, but when was that?

He shut off the teakettle and poured water into the mug before returning to his bedroom. His phone wasn't on either nightstand or the floor beside the bed. He picked up his pillow and pulled back the covers before reaching for Bria's pillow.

Not Bria's pillow, his inner voice said immediately. *She's not yours. Never was and never will be. Get used to it. You're going to be alone forever, buddy.*

His tiger whined softly at the mere thought of Bria. It had been more or less quiet for the last few days. He rarely got sick, and his tiger had no capacity to deal with the flu and cold symptoms he was battling. It had retreated like a sulky teenager refusing to leave its room.

Stop it, he scolded it. *She's not our mate.*

His tiger growled, and he ignored it before lifting the other pillow. His cell phone was under it, so he grabbed it and returned to the kitchen. He sipped cautiously at his tea. If it didn't make him feel sick, he'd try some dry toast next.

He pushed the button on his phone. Holy shit, it was Friday. He groaned when he saw the missed calls and text messages from his mother. Her messages were growing increasingly urgent in tone. He vaguely remembered putting his phone to silent at some point. The dinging of it was too loud for his aching head.

"Shit," he muttered. There was a missed call and a text message from Dr. Martin. He had missed his appointment with her this morning.

He would text his mother and then give Dr. Martin's office a quick call. He should also text Rosalie to let her know he was fine. She'd tell Bria, who would probably be worried about him

No, she won't. You broke her heart. She doesn't give a shit about you anymore.

"Jace?"

He jumped and nearly fell off the chair. His growl of surprise turned into a coughing fit. He coughed and coughed as a big hand rubbed his back. When the coughing eased, and he could breathe again, he said, "Dad? You scared the hell out of me."

"Sorry, son." His dad sat down in the chair next to him. "I should have knocked."

"What are you doing here?"

"You look like shit." His dad put his big, callused hand on his forehead.

"I'm fine. Just had the flu and now a cold."

"You sure that's all it was?" His father gave him that cautious look he remembered so well after Tabitha left him.

"Yes. I'm fine, Dad. Why are you here?"

He wasn't. He was far from fine, and as soon as he felt better, he felt confident that the darkness would be waiting for him. He could feel it now, creeping around the edges, lurking and waiting for the chance to consume him.

"Your mother was worried about you. You haven't been returning her calls."

"My phone was on silent, and I've been sleeping most of the last few days." He forced a smile at his father. "Don't look at me like that. I'm doing okay."

"Have you eaten anything?"

He shook his head. His father stood and moved to the counter. "I'll make you some toast."

"Thanks."

"Your mother's been real upset the last few days. I finally sat her down and made her tell me what was wrong."

"I didn't mean to upset her."

His father popped the bread into the toaster before turning to face him. "Do you love Bria?"

Jace paused with the mug of tea halfway to his mouth. "What?"

"Do you love her? Be honest with me, kid."

"Like you and Mom were honest with me about your heart attack?"

The toast popped up, and his father put it on a plate and joined him at the table. "We shouldn't have kept that from you. I'm sorry we did. Do you love her?"

Jace stared at the toast. "Yes."

His father reached out and squeezed his hand for a moment. "Look at me, son. What happened to me wasn't your fault."

"It was."

"No, it wasn't. I'm sorry that your mother made it sound

like it was. I understand why she did it – she's terrified we'll lose you like we lost Jonah – but it wasn't right of her to do that to you. My heart attack had nothing to do with you."

"You were stressed because of what I was putting you through," Jace said. "Mom told me that -"

"Your mom is afraid, and sometimes when a person is afraid like that, they'll do and say anything to keep the people they love safe. When you brought Bria to your cousin's engagement party, we could see what it was. We could smell your love for her. It scared your mother badly. I knew that it scared her, but I never thought she would tell you that what happened to me was your fault. It wasn't. I had a heart attack – a mild one – because of several reasons."

"Why didn't you tell me? It was a real shitty thing to keep it from me."

"Yeah, it was, and I'm sorry we did. But I was completely healed from it within a week, and you were going through a rough time. I didn't want to make it worse, nor did your mother."

"How is your health now?"

"Really good. No problems, and like I said, healed completely. I'm worried about you."

"You don't need to be."

"So you and Bria are still together then?"

"No."

His father sighed. "If you love her, you should be with her."

"I can't. If it doesn't work out -"

"If it doesn't work out, we'll deal with it."

"Mom doesn't want me to be with anyone right now. She thinks I'm not ready, and the idea of me dating Bria terrifies her."

"Yes," his father admitted, "it does. But that's her issue, not yours. I know you love your mother, but you can't live your life for her or me. You have to do what makes you happy. It isn't right that we tried to bend you to our will and tried to make you be alone because we figured it was the best way to keep you safe. I'm sorry we did that to you. I hope you can forgive us and start living your life."

Jace didn't reply. His father leaned forward and took his hand again. "Your mother will be upset, but I'll help her get through it, I promise. I told her I would encourage you to date Bria."

"What did she say?"

"She cried, then she growled and tried to bite me." His father grinned. "Then she apologized for trying to bite me and made me a sandwich."

Jace smiled, and his father squeezed his hands. "She'll be okay, son. I promise you. It'll take her a while to get used to the idea, and maybe we won't be having you and Bria over for dinner anytime soon, but she'll accept it sooner than you think. She's a good mother who only wants what's best for you. She's just afraid."

"She doesn't have to be. I'm good. Being with Bria makes me even better."

"Then be with her."

"I think it's too late," Jace said. "I broke her heart. She said she understood and didn't hate me, but I've been hot and cold with her the entire time she's known me. Why would she believe me now?"

"You gotta try, kid." His father stood before bending and giving him a rough kiss on the forehead. "I love you."

"I love you too."

"I know. Now go out there and get your girl back. But can I give you some advice?"

"Sure."

"Shower first."

———

Lincoln pounded on Jace's front door a third time before yanking his keys out of his pocket. He searched through them as Bria said, "Hurry, Lincoln."

"I'm hurrying," he growled. He found the right one and shoved it into the lock. He pushed the door open and immediately called Jace's name.

There was no reply and he ran to the kitchen. "Jace, buddy, you in here? Shit."

He stuck his head back into the hallway. "He's not in here."

Bria ran up the stairs. Lincoln was right behind her, and she hurried down the hall to Jace's bedroom. "Jace! Jace, are you in here? Oh my God!"

Lincoln made a grunt of surprise behind her. "What the hell?"

Jace walked out of the bathroom, completely naked and drying his hair with a towel. "Bria? Lincoln? What are you doing here?"

"Holy shit, put some clothes on, man," Lincoln said. "You think I wanna see your dick?"

Jace stared blankly at his body before bunching the towel in front of his crotch. "You're the one who barged into my house while I was showering."

"Because we thought you were gonna do something stupid," Lincoln said. "Why the fuck aren't you answering your goddamn phone?"

"Because I've been sick, and it was on silent." Jace dropped his gaze to Bria. "Um, hi. I was just about to come and see you."

"You were?" Bria cupped her elbows and took a hesitant step toward him. She studied him carefully. His nose was swollen and red, and he had dark circles under his eyes. He sounded completely stuffed up, and as she watched, he suddenly tucked his face into the crook of his elbow and sneezed explosively.

"Gross." Lincoln backed out of the room. "I'm out. I'll ask Rosalie to cover phones for the rest of the day. You two lovebirds kiss and make up."

"Thank you, Lincoln." Bria didn't look away from Jace.

"Anytime." He left the room, and they heard the front door slam shut a few minutes later.

"I'm sorry," Bria said. "I shouldn't have asked Lincoln to bring me over, but I was worried about you and -"

"I love you."

She stepped back, hugging her torso as she stared wide-eyed at Jace. "What?"

"I love you. I'm sorry that I hurt you. I love you, and I want to be with you."

"Do you have a fever? Are you delirious?" Bria stared up at him when he crossed the room and stopped in front of her.

She wanted to throw her arms around him. Instead, she reached up and pressed her hand against his forehead. He smiled at her. "I'm not delirious. I'm an idiot, but a completely clear-headed idiot."

"Jace, I..."

"I have to touch you," he said in a low voice. "Please, let me touch you."

She nodded, and he dropped his towel, threw his arms around her waist and picked her up. He buried his face in her neck and kissed her throat repeatedly as she hugged him and rubbed his back.

"I love you," he said again.

"I love you too."

He leaned back so he could see her face. "You love me?"

She smiled a little. "You know I do. You can smell it."

"Maybe, but I like hearing it too."

She kissed him on the mouth and growled when he pulled his head back. He grinned at her. "I have a cold. I don't want to give you my germs."

She purred to him, and he purred back before carrying her to the bed. "Lie down with me for a bit."

They crawled into bed, and she rested her head on his chest. He was purring and calling to her and she blinked back the tears. She was very happy and also very confused.

"Jace?"

"Yeah?"

She sat up and stared at him before resting her hand on his chest. "Why the sudden change? Sunday, you said you could never be with me."

"My dad came to see me today. He told me that what my mom said wasn't true. He told me I should be with you if I loved you."

He sat up and took her hand. "Honestly, even if Dad hadn't come by to talk to me, I wouldn't have been able to stay away from you. I kept telling myself that I would and *could*, but deep down, I knew that once I saw you again…"

He squeezed her hand. "I was an idiot to think I could ignore my feelings for you.

She rubbed her hand across his warm skin. "Dr. Martin called the office today. When I realized you had missed your appointment with her, I might have freaked out a little. I told Lincoln what had happened with us, and that's when he drove me over here. Even though I knew you didn't want to be with me, I couldn't stay away. I needed to make sure you were okay."

"I love that you did," he said. "I love that you wanted to be there for me even when I broke your heart. It won't be easy being with me. But I promise always to be honest about how I'm feeling."

She cupped his face and kissed him again. "We all have our issues, right? I'm far from perfect."

"I don't know, you seem pretty perfect to me. Other than your truly terrible pool playing skills."

She laughed and poked him in his flat stomach. "I make up for it with my truly amazing sex skills."

He purred loudly and nuzzled her neck. "You certainly do, little tiger. Speaking of which, why don't we get you naked and see where it leads."

She purred back and reached for the buttons on her shirt. "That, Mr. Shepherd, is an excellent idea."

Keep reading for an excerpt from Elizabeth Kelly's next novel in the Shifters Series
"Rosalie Undone"

ROSALIE UNDONE

(THE SHIFTERS SERIES BOOK SIX)

"You okay, buddy?" Judd leaned against the bar.

"Fine." Hudson twisted off the cap to a beer bottle and handed it to the deer shifter. She gave him a nervous smile of thanks and handed him some cash before disappearing into the crowd.

"You sure?"

"Why wouldn't I be?"

"Because a lion shifter is hitting on your woman."

"She's not my woman." He kept his gaze on the bar. He'd rip the lion shifter apart if he even looked at Rosalie and saw him touching her. He was holding on to his self-control by the thinnest of threads.

His hand clenched around the bar rag when he caught a whiff of the lion's scent. He looked up just in time to see the asshole walk down the hallway toward the bathroom. He chanced a glance at Rosalie. She was sitting by herself at the table and staring at him. She gave him a nervous smile and a little wave.

He gave her a short nod, and the smile on her face disappeared. When she mouthed, "What's wrong?" he immediately looked away.

"I can kick the lion shifter out," Judd said. "Make up some excuse and give him the boot so you don't have to watch him keep touching her."

Fresh new anger rushed through Hudson. He glared at Judd. "He's touching her?"

"Uh," Judd shook his head quickly, "probably not. I mean, I don't know. I didn't get a good look at them and -"

Hudson threw the rag into the sink. "Porter? Can I take a five-minute break?"

Porter nodded from the other end of the bar. "Yeah, take your full fifteen."

"Thanks."

"Hudson, don't do anything stupid. Okay?" Judd grabbed his arm.

"Let go of me," Hudson said.

"Just don't do something dumb to that lion shifter," Judd said.

"I just want to talk to him," Hudson said in a low voice. His fangs dropped, and he bared them at Judd. "Let go of me. I won't ask again."

"Well, shit." Judd released him.

Hudson stepped out from behind the bar and headed down the hallway. The lion shifter was coming out of the bathroom. Surprisingly, the hallway was empty, and Hudson stopped in the middle of it, blocking the lion's path.

The lion cocked his head and looked him up and down. "Excuse me, please."

"Stay away from the human."

The shifter's gaze turned cool, and he gave him an insolent look. "Does she belong to you, polar bear? Because I can't smell even a whiff of your scent on her. Besides, since when do polar bears fuck humans?"

Hudson growled at him, and the lion shifter made a low hiss in return.

"Do not touch her again, lion shifter, or I'll tear you apart."

"She came on to me," the shifter said. "If she's your woman, you'd best get a handle on her before she decides fucking a lion shifter is more fun than fucking a polar bear with anger issues."

Hudson snarled and grabbed the lion shifter by the throat. He slammed him up against the wall and glared at the impudent little prick. "Don't look at her, don't touch her, don't even get within a foot of her, or I'll -"

"Hudson? Hudson, what are you doing? Let him go!" Rosalie hurried forward and grabbed his arm. She yanked on it, her eyes wide and frightened looking. "Hudson, stop."

He released the lion and stepped back, breathing harshly as the lion shifter coughed and then dragged in a breath of air.

"Koren? Are you okay?" When Rosalie tried to get close to the lion, Hudson growled and wrapped his arm around her waist. He pulled her up against his body as she made a startled noise and stared up at him. "Hudson, what is wrong with you?"

"Don't touch him."

"I…what?"

Koren straightened his shirt and pushed away from the wall. He rubbed at his throat before giving Rosalie a thin smile. He walked away, and when Rosalie tried to follow him back into the bar, Hudson tightened his grip on her waist.

"Koren, wait!" Rosalie called. She yanked on Hudson's arm before glaring up at him. "Hey, let go of me."

He released her but grabbed her hand before she could follow the lion shifter. "Rosalie, come with me."

"What? Where?"

He held her hand tightly as two female raccoon shifters, giggling and swaying drunkenly, wandered into the hallway.

"Oh wow, you're totally the biggest dude I've ever seen. I think I wanna climb you like a tree," the one on the left slurred out and then hiccupped.

Completely ignoring the drunk raccoon shifters, Hudson tugged Rosalie into Porter's office and slammed the door shut.

Porter's office was small. Rosalie backed up until her butt hit the edge of his desk. She glared at Hudson when he slammed the door shut and gave her an angry look.

"What's your problem, Hudson?"

"My problem? You're out there trying to pick up a goddamn lion shifter, and you want to know what my problem is?"

"Koren is nice and -"

"You don't know anything about him, Rosalie."

"Do you?"

"No, but that's not the point. He could be dangerous."

"Or he could be a perfectly normal guy who wants to sleep with me."

Hudson's face turned red, and he growled deep in his chest. "You're going to sleep with him?"

"Yes, probably. I think. I mean, if you didn't scare him off, then yeah, yeah, I'm going to sleep with him."

His scowl was so deep she could practically climb into it. "No, you're not. You are not taking that lion shifter home."

Her mouth dropped open. "I'm an adult, and you don't get to tell me what to do. If I want to sleep with a lion shifter, I will, and you can't stop me."

He growled again, and she glared at him. "Growl all you want. I'm not afraid of you."

"I thought you were in love with that idiot Lincoln," he said. "I thought you wanted to fuck him."

Now it was her turn to go red. "Stop being crude."

"It's the truth, isn't it?"

"Yes, but you don't have to be so, so -"

"If you're in love with the stupid lion, then why are you going to fuck a different stupid lion?"

Her temper flared. "For practice, okay? Lincoln likes kink, and I have two weeks to learn and practice some sex stuff before I ask him out."

"Two weeks to practice," he repeated.

"Yes." She tugged at the top of her dress. "I don't have much experience, and I need to change that if I'm going to seduce Lincoln so..."

"How many shifters are you planning on sleeping with?"

"Not that it's any of your business, but as many as it takes to learn to do what Lincoln wants in bed," she said, "and before you start slut shaming me, there's nothing wrong with a woman having multiple sex partners if that's what she -"

"No."

"No, what? Why are you growing a beard?" Her eyes widened as the shoulder seams of his t-shirt ripped. "Are you shifting? Stop shifting!"

He took a deep breath, and she watched in fascination as his body slowly returned to normal size and the beard faded from his jaw.

"You're not sleeping with other shifters," Hudson said.

"Uh, yeah, I am," she said.

"No."

"Stop saying no! I need to learn how to be kinky and -"

"I'll teach you."

"If I even want to have a chance at winning over Lincoln, I have to stop being so shy in bed and start... what did you say?" She stared at the giant bear shifter.

"I'll teach you how to be kinky in bed."

She gaped at him and then burst into laughter. "Good one, Hudson. Seriously, that was funny. But, if you don't mind, I need to see if Koren -"

"I'm not joking, Rosalie." Hudson stepped toward her.

Her laughter died out. "You are. Of course you are."

"I'm not."

"But you're not attracted to me. You hate it when I touch you. You won't even be able to..."

He stepped even closer. Even with her heels making her six feet, she still had to stare up at him as he rested his big hands on the desk on either side of her. "Won't even be able to what?"

"Get it up." Her voice came out in a high squeak that didn't sound remotely like her usual voice.

"Are you saying I'm impotent?"

"What? No, no, I'm not saying that." She couldn't seem to look away from his gaze. "I'm saying you're not attracted to me, so you're not going to..."

Her voice ended in another of those weird little squeaks when he traced one thick finger over her collarbone.

"H-Hudson, what are you doing?"

He bent his head and sniffed her neck. "A shifter would have to be blind or stupid not to be attracted to you, little human. Do you think I'm stupid?"

"No, but... you don't like to be touched by me," she whispered.

He gave a lock of her hair a gentle tug before bending his head again. Hudson licked her collarbone this time, and every muscle deep in her lower belly clenched. She was suddenly finding it hard to breathe, and her nipples were hard points against the fabric of her bra.

Oh God, was she getting wet?

She was getting wet.

For Hudson.

Desperate to regain control, she lied through her teeth. "I'm not attracted to you."

He laughed, that warm, deep laugh that she heard so rarely. It had the same effect it always did. Butterflies swarmed to life in her stomach, and goosebumps rose on her arms.

"There you go, trying to lie again, little human."

"I'm not lying. I'm not -"

His lips pressed against hers as one heavy arm curled around her waist. He drew her up against him, and she grabbed his arms, sinking her fingers into his hard flesh. Dear God, was he – was that his erection pressing against her belly?

He sucked on her bottom lip before pressing soft kisses against her mouth. He teased and coaxed, licking the seam of her lips with the tip of his tongue as his big hand rubbed her lower back through her shirt. He was being so damn gentle. Until now, she would never have believed this type of gentleness could exist in Hudson.

"Open your mouth, sweet Rosie." His low voice saying her nickname sent fresh arousal through her. She opened her mouth immediately.

He growled his approval and licked her upper lip before sucking on it. He traced her bottom lip with his tongue before kissing his way to her ear. He sucked on her earlobe, and her heart banged against her ribcage. She was growing increasingly distracted by the low pleading for a kiss. Who the hell was sounding so desperate? So needy?

"Shh, little Rosie." Hudson's breath tickled her ear. "I'll give you what you need."

Holy shit. She was the one pleading.

Another low moan slipped out. "Hudson, please kiss me."

He nipped her bottom lip, and she moaned happily when he slipped his tongue into her mouth. He angled his mouth over hers, his hand threading through her hair and cupping the back of her skull to hold her steady as he tasted her. She rubbed her tongue against his, slid her arms around his waist, and shoved her hands up the back of his shirt. His skin was deliciously hot against her fingertips. She pressed herself up against that hard length digging into her belly.

He kissed her repeatedly. Kissed her until she was weak and trembling and fuzzy-headed. There was a gentleness in each brush of his mouth against hers, but she could sense the hunger beneath it, like he was holding back, maybe. Like he was afraid that he would hurt her or scare her.

"I want more," she breathed against his mouth. She reached for his big hand, where it rested against her hip, and tried to tug it to her breast. "More, Hudson."

She was frantic for his touch. She wanted to see what was under that gentleness. She wanted to make him lose control.

"Not here, Rosie."

"Yes!" If she hadn't been so damn horny, she might have been embarrassed by the whine in her voice. "Hudson!"

He kissed her again, but she couldn't pry his hand away from her hip no matter how hard she tried. She stood on her tiptoes and rubbed her aching pussy directly against his erection. It brought a low groan from his throat, and excitement rushed through her. His hand tightened on her hip, and she rubbed against him again.

"Please." She licked his mouth, and his low growl sent a wave of lust through her. She licked his mouth again and scratched her nails across his lower back. "Please."

His second growl was louder. Hungrier. He kissed her hard just as the door to Porter's office opened.

"Hudson, are you… shit."

Hudson pulled away from her, and she staggered back against the desk. She stared wide-eyed at Judd standing in the doorway.

"You can't do this in here, man. Porter's a good guy, but he'll fire you for fucking a human in his office," Judd said.

"We weren't, he wasn't…" Rosalie touched her swollen mouth as Hudson made a sound of frustration.

The three of them stood in silence before Rosalie straightened her back. "I have to go."

"Rosalie, don't let the lion shifter touch you," Hudson said.

She turned to him, ready to let loose with a barrage of indignant and well-deserved retorts about how he didn't have the right to tell her who she could or couldn't touch. The look of intensity on his face shut her mouth with a snap. She nodded mutely.

"Promise me," he said.

"I promise," she whispered before pushing past Judd and walking rapidly down the hallway and back into the bar. She needed to find Maggie and get the hell out of the bar before Koren tried to touch her. If Hudson saw Koren touching her, he'd kill him. She was sure of it.

Don't be stupid, Rosalie. Hudson wouldn't kill a guy just for touching you. God, you really think you're all that, don't you?

She almost laughed when she saw Koren. Her fear had

been for nothing. The lion shifter was back standing at the bar, already flirting with another woman.

"Rosalie? What the hell is going on?" Maggie was suddenly standing next to her, and Rosalie grabbed her hand.

"I want to leave. Please, can we leave?"

Maggie studied her face. "Your mouth is swollen. Oh my God, did Koren hurt you? Did he -"

"No, no, nothing like that," Rosalie said. "Something's happened, and I need to talk – can we go somewhere more private?"

"Of course." Maggie squeezed her hand, and Rosalie followed her out of the bar.

ABOUT THE AUTHOR

Elizabeth Kelly was born and raised in Ontario, Canada. She moved west as a teenager and now lives in Alberta with her husband and a menagerie of pets. She firmly believes that a person can survive solely on sushi and coffee, and only her husband's mad cooking skills prevents her from proving that theory.

For more information about Elizabeth, check out her website at

www.elizabethkelly.ca

facebook.com/EKellyBooks
instagram.com/elizabethkelly_author
amazon.com/Elizabeth-Kelly/e/B00EOHZ0MS
bookbub.com/authors/elizabeth-kelly

ALSO BY ELIZABETH KELLY

Tempted Series

Tempted

Twice Tempted

Forever Tempted

Breathless

Tempted Trilogy (Books 1-3)

Red Moon Series

Red Moon

Red Moon Rising

Dark Moon

Alpha Moon

Pale Moon

The Recruit Series

The Recruit (Book One)

The Recruit (Book Two)

The Recruit (Book Three)

The Recruit (Book Four)

The Recruit (Book Five)

The Recruit (Book Six)

The Shifters Series

Willow and the Wolf (Book One)

Ava and the Bear (Book Two)

Place Your Trust in Me (Book Three)

Individual Books

The Necessary Engagement

Amelia's Touch

The Rancher's Daughter

Healing Gabriel

The Contract

A Home for Lily

Saving Charlotte

Shameless

The Fairy Tales Collection

Broken

An Unlikely Seduction

Holiday Romance

The Christmas Wife

The Christmas Rescue

The Christmas Nanny

The Christmas Boss

Sordid Games